I0555530

South of Sahara

_____

Rod Barkley

ATLANTIC PUBLISHING

This is a work of fiction. The characters, incidents and dialogues are products of the author's imagination and are not to be construed as real. Any resemblance to actual events or persons, living or dead, is entirely coincidental.

South of Sahara

Copyright © 2015 by Rod Barkley

Published by
Atlantic Publishing & Media
Los Angeles, California

ISBN: 978-0-9849662-1-9

Printed in the United States of America

10 9 8 7 6

For Vicki

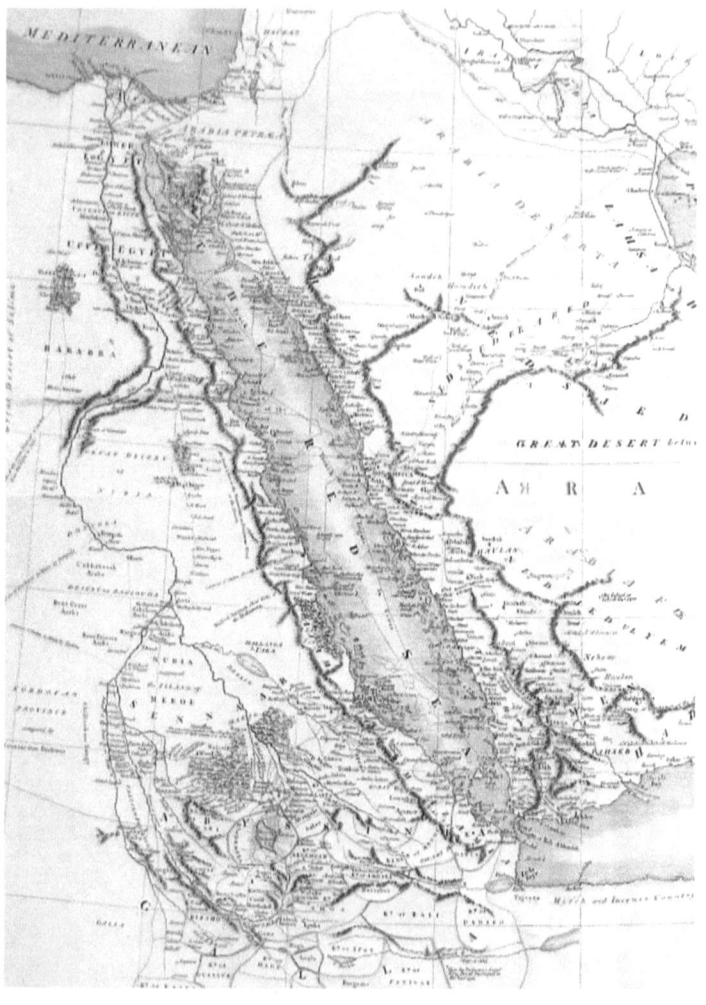

Chapter 1

THE SKIES over the African coast were clear that morning as the camoflaged seaplane turned inland and began its slow descent toward the tiny spot on the map. The pilot looked down through binoculars. Below them, a shimmering blue line of river emerged from the clouds. The surface was calm and none of the tribesman who might normally be fishing could be seen. It was a good sign, he thought. The fewer witnesses the better.

The pilot, an American named Joe McQueen, had flown many times into Africa, but rescue missions in the jungles of Portuguese West held a special kind of risk. Besides malaria and typhoid, the cobras and other predators were some of the biggest in Africa. Yes, he thought, these were worrying, but the real threat was always the same: man.

After the German-lead raids on the Portuguese colonies 20 years earlier, Lisbon had sent troops to reinforce order and the prisons had been emptied out with "settlers" for the new land. In the years of warfare that followed, slavery had been abolished, but the practice of paid serfdom persisted. Now, in 1940, the lands east of Luanda teemed with unrest, and ambushes were commonplace. Many Europeans had vanished on the river without a trace and no sensible pilot would attempt a landing except in an emergency.

As the plane circled lower, some of these facts went through McQueen's mind as he checked again the direction of the wind, set the flaps and began looking for a calm stretch of water. It was a risk, he knew, but he was prepared. The seaplane, a Grumman Goose, was well suited to the job, with deep wing chords that gave more lift and modified Lycoming engines that produced over 2,000 hp of thrust. There were extra large fuel tanks and plenty of firepower. But ultimately it came down to luck, and time. Could they make contact quickly and get out before attracting attention? Were any of the tribes at war? Were any of the missing party still alive?

McQueen's reverie was interrupted. "Watch out for logs, Joe," Eddie shouted over the roar of the engines. McQueen nodded and altered his descent slightly. His copilot was a smallish Irishman with an upturned nose who loved machinery and had a nose for trouble.

With engines shrieking, the plane cleared the trees by ten feet and touched down at 70 knots. Minutes later they were taxiing up to the bank under the shelter of a huge Obaya tree. McQueen cut the engines and looked around. The river was strangely silent. Satisfied they were alone, he gave the order to start unloading their gear. This consisted of various rifles, pistols, and what McQueen called his "serious toys": hand grenades and plastic explosives. They worked quickly and quietly, the routine almost automatic.

As the gear was being unloaded, no one noticed the tall, middle aged man on the opposite bank, invisible in the bush. His face and clothes were mud stained from too many weeks on the river and in front of him was a stack of small crates marked 'medicine'. In reality, these contained funeral masks he had just traded to a party of tribesmen for machine pistols, highly coveted by the locals. The three donkeys had been a last minute bonus.

Like McQueen, the trader, who was a Swiss named Gautier, had stayed alive in this part of Africa for 20 years by being careful. When the first sound of engines had reached him he had gotten out of sight and waited, stunned to see anyone attempting a landing on this part of the river. When the plane didn't crash he became curious and raising the binoculars took a moment to study the pilot who had just made the near impossible landing.

The pilot was a big man, he could see, about 6'2", well muscled and with an athletic gait. He carried a heavy caliber rifle slung over one shoulder and a large knife. He didn't waste time looking at the crocodiles on the far bank or at the big male tiger that had just come down to the water for a cautious drink, but set about cutting down heavy branches.

Suddenly, the man grinned and had to stifle a shout of recognition as it hit him. Of course! It had to be. Joe McQueen, the only man crazy enough to land a plane on this little river on the verge of a tribal war. For a moment he thought of warning his sometime competitor, but then he remembered McQueen on a job usually meant trouble and returned to loading up his crates.

Inside the plane the work continued. Eddie, who had flown in the British Air corps as an 18-year old, took pains to check each piece of gear, especially the radio. Like all Irishmen, he loved to talk, and the radio was his personal obsession. Like McQueen he knew the risks involved, but the pay was good and he knew the adventure would always provide him with endless stories with which to regale his friends back in Lisbon. If he lived.

He had been told to prepare a bivouac for three days on the river while their clients showed up, and he had brought what he thought was reasonable and prudent. This meant a case of beans, six bottles of whisky and enough heavy caliber ammunition to hold off a small army. Eddie was a practical man.

McQueen looked at his watch and at the position of the sun, then hauled the heavy radio antenna out of the Goose and began erecting the 40' mast that would allow them to make contact with the survivors of the mining exploration party that had gone missing six weeks earlier, if they were still alive. The job had come his way through the Ambassador, as so many had recently, and while there was private money behind his fee he knew that Clayton Ellison had another agenda; to look for signs of German incursions that might threaten the copper mines in the north.

But there had been only one message, hand delivered by a native to the company's office in Cape Town, informing them that they had been attacked, that there were three of the party still alive and that they would make for the Lucala, which was the closest river in Portuguese West that had the potential to land a seaplane and take off again. It was a desperate plan, but there was no other.

McQueen thought about all this for a moment, about the elements he might be up against and what he might do in different circumstances, but he had been in such situations many times before and in any case there was no time for rumination. The company had met his price, and he would not rest until he had extracted the men or located their bodies. It was a question of honor. With a slight shrug he got back to work. The tower had to rise above the trees before it would be effective, he reminded himself.

Four hours later, they waited under the shade of the wing in the hot, sticky silence. There had been no response to the first messages, sent in uncoded Morse since nothing better was possible, and they knew they would be spending the night on the river. This posed its own risks, but they were manageable. While Eddie was listening at the radio, McQueen had a look around and knelt down beside him. There was something wrong.

"Pretty quiet," he said, watching a stray hippo coming out of the water 50 yards away. "Hear anything?"

"No, just some broken chatter. Can't make out the language. Sounds like it's far off. You figure they're dead?"

"Maybe. Been a week since anyone saw 'em. When's the next radio check?"

"Three o'clock," said Eddie. McQueen looked at his old Hamilton with the black leather strap: 45 minutes to go.

"You ever seen it like this before, like somethin's scared everything off?" Eddie wondered aloud. "There should be tribesman here this time of day with their women. And birds."

"Might be a big cat," opined McQueen. "I'll work my way down to the high ground behind that bend. Stay on the radio." He looked up at the sun, then noticed the whisky bottle next to Eddie. "And stay off the sauce."

"OK, skipper," said Eddie as he got to his feet and started checking his gear. There was no more talk, and McQueen was soon a shadow under the trees that quickly vanished into the green shade.

McQueen had assumed that the engineers would have a guide with them, and there was an old caravan trail nearby, which they would have to use to get to the river. He picked up the trail after a few minutes and began to move slowly up country. He had gone about a mile when he realized he was being followed by someone about 200 yards behind. There was a shallow ravine in deep shadow and he got into it and waited. He had some dried fruit and a canteen of water, smeared mud on his face and over his clothes to cut down on the glare, and as he ate took his time looking around. A large cobra slid by 30 meters away. It was unusual for them to be out during the day and then he saw the reason. It was following a small pig which had gone astray. Otherwise the jungle was very still and the light only penetrated to the floor in a few places, giving excellent cover to a tracker. The scene felt silent, as if waiting.

He began to hear something odd. It was a man's voice and the voice was faint, panicky, mumbling something. He removed the safety from his Thompson automatic rifle, checked that he had spare magazines in his pack and got silently to his feet. He waited. The man had gone silent.

Had the cobra got him? He carefully removed the silencer/flash suppressor that Wembley had made for him and screwed it into place. This would effectively cut down the range by 50 yards, but there was work to do and he was alone. He put his field binoculars up to his eyes and began to scan the surroundings as his eyes adjusted to the gloom.

Five minutes later the tracker who had been following him and who no doubt was eager to report the arrival of the Goose and its treasures came into view, still a hundred yards out, a smallish man of perhaps 5'4" and very thin. He was armed with a long stave the tribe called a knobkerrie. McQueen looked around, located the pig, still busy eating, and made a decision. He could see the cobra closing in and tossed a rock. It hit the pig which squealed loudly and in its panic ran straight to the giant snake. In the din that followed, McQueen located the tracker, raised his rifle and fired a single burst just as the pig's squeals reached a crescendo. The man dropped to the ground, half of his head blown away by the soft nosed bullets.

But it had not been perfect. Somehow the man had uttered a scream and now it would be a race against time. He moved forward quickly, crouching low, careful to avoid the path and its dangers. 80 yards farther in he saw him.

The man was tied to a stake in a small clearing. He was gagged and there was blood on the ground. The blood came from the other two men, both hanging upside down and covered in ants, which were quickly reducing the carcasses to bone. He estimated they had been hanging for at least three days. Of his attackers there was no sign.

It was a trap, a good one he had to admit, and he had been long enough in the Congo basin to know the signs. The wires would be concealed in the vines which hung down to the ground, the nets carefully hidden under the carpeting of leaves. As he tripped one of the wires the nets would close and if they were big enough he would be taken. He looked up. They would be up in the trees, he reasoned, if they were near at all, and as he scanned the upper branches in the gloom he began to make his plan. There was a giant boab tree next to him and silently he began to climb. In a few moments he was invisible from the ground.

To the man tied to the ground, whose name was Waring, none of this had registered in his half-dreaming state. Death was now preferable to waiting, and he hoped it would come soon. He had witnessed his two companions put to death when they wouldn't cooperate with a ransom note, and now he had been tied to the tree for three days, fed only once a day. His captors, who had started out as porters, spoke perfect English, which made the ordeal all the more horrifying because they were obviously enjoying it. To keep his sanity, he concentrated on sleeping.

But now there was a new sound, very close, that he had not heard before. He opened his eyes and looked slowly from left to right. The snake was about 50 feet away. It was at least 18 feet long. It had missed the pig and was now doubly hungry. The man began to moan softly, involuntarily, knowing his end had arrived, wondering where his captors were and why they allowed it. Was this some new torture, some scheme for forcing him to reveal his secrets? But the death wish now fled as quickly as it had been born. The snake was moving toward him. He called out several times, but the giant snake paid no heed and raised up to look around, then started toward him with surprising speed. He began to scream.

As the great predator gathered itself to strike, its sensory mechanism told it there was something near, but so great was its hunger that it ignored the message a fraction of a second too long. As it turned its head the man glided silently down from the tree, holding onto the taut nylon cord, the 18" heavy machete honed to surgical sharpness in his right hand, and with almost no sound brought the blade up behind the snake's head, neatly severing it at the 8th vertebra. As the body began to contort wildly, he let go the cord and landed a few feet from Waring, then looked up at the branches for any sign of activity. There was none. It might be a lucky day after all, he thought, and allowed himself a grin as he wiped the sweat and the viscera of the snake off his forehead.

Waring, his eyes so wide that the whites showed all around, stared at him, shaking violently. He tried to talk but nothing came out and a thin line of spit ran down his chin. McQueen wasted not a second as he began to untie the man, who reeked of excrement and vomit and helped him to his feet.

"Who are you?" he finally stammered out, panting the words with difficulty.

"Later. Can you walk?"

"I think so."

"When do they usually come?"

"When the sun is going down, but how did you..."

"Later. Hold on to this." McQueen looped a thin rope saddle under the man and looked up with his binoculars. Yes, it was still there, the steel pulley with the nylon line running through it. He estimated the man's weight at 180. It was going to be close.

The spear was absolutely silent when it came, and would have impaled Waring except that he chose that moment to cough violently and bend over. "Hold on!" McQueen shouted as he pulled down violently on the line and Waring shot up into the air 15 feet and then swung forward. When he was beyond the nets, McQueen let go and Waring crashed to the ground, stunned but unhurt. More spears were coming in now but from apparently only one man. He unslung the Thompson, took off the silencer and unleashed a short burst. Three natives broke cover and charged him. The next burst cut the first man in half and blew the top of the other man's cranium into the tree. The third man put his hands up.

"Speak English?" The black man mumbled a few obscenities. McQueen grinned, looking over his trappings. "Long way from Lunda Norte. You should have stayed home." McQueen approached him and quickly handcuffed the man to a tree. He walked over to Waring and helped him up.

"Recognize him?"

"He's the leader."

"Right. That's Zumbo. Been on the run for over a year, raiding the Congo copper mines over the border. You just earned me a bonus, Waring. Help me tie him up."

It was two hours later. At the river, Eddie had heard the gunfire and was watching the trail when three figures approached. McQueen had his arm around Waring, who was limping badly. Behind them, Zumbo followed slowly, his ankles and wrists bound so as to permit only steps of 12". As they approached the Goose, Eddie put away his weapon and began to break camp. McQueen noticed a couple of small crates near the radio, the lid pried off revealing the smallish gold covered funeral masks.

"Where did you get that?" asked McQueen. Eddie smiled.

"Oh, just a local fella, hangin' around. Got him tied up in the bush if you want to talk to him. Said he's a friend of yours." McQueen looked at the crates, figuring the weight, then looked at his passengers.

"Gautier. We can't afford the weight. Get rid of it, and cut him loose."

"But boss...." Eddie knew it was pointless to argue. "How about just one?" McQueen picked up one of the masks, felt the heft.

"Half a crate. That's it. Help me get our friends aboard, and watch yourself with the big one. He bites." Eddie swallowed hard and took the chain holding the shackled native and lead him to the Goose.

"You're lucky to be alive, buster," he said in Swahili, and Zumbo spat on the ground. Eddie began to truss him up.

"Just a minute," said Waring, and walked to the river, stripped off all his clothes and waded in. "For God's sake, have you got any soap?" he asked.

Two days later, the Goose was descending through rain clouds to the small British outpost on the Nile at Wadelai, just north of Lake Victoria. They had seen no signs of

German raiding parties. For McQueen, getting back on British protectorate soil meant a hot bath and some decent food. He was also glad to be getting rid of his passenger, who rode in chains at the back of the plane and never stopped complaining about his treatment.

As the Goose taxied up to the dock two British soldiers and an officer approached, rifles at the ready. McQueen recognized Lt. Howard and grinned. "State your business, McQueen," the officer said.

"Brought you a little present."

"The hell you say. Smuggling diamonds again?"

"Show him, Eddie."

They got the plane tied up and as Howard and his escort stared in disbelief, Eddie, with great fanfare, brought their captive out for the men to see. Howard roared with laughter because Zumba was a wanted man across southern Africa. "Zumba! Where the hell did you get him? Last we heard he was terrorizing British settlers in Yoruba."

"Oh, he's been a busy boy, working with his new German friends," said McQueen.

"Indeed. And you got him to talk about that?"

"I did."

"How?" The suspicion was palpable.

"I was very civilized. Let's say we made a little deal. And you owe me a hundred pounds, Howard, for doing your dirty work."

Howard laughed. "Joe McQueen, civilized? All right, come in and have a drink and we'll talk about it. Didn't realize you were in the bounty hunter business."

"It pays."

"Yes, I was expecting that."

"Hold on now. Half the money's mine, remember that Joe," interjected Eddie as he handed the chain to the soldiers. "I fed him. We got time for a beer?"

"No. Just take care of the goose, Eddie. I want those spark plugs changed. We leave in the morning, first light," McQueen said, and as the soldiers took charge of the now thoroughly dispirited ex-bandit, the two friends walked up the pier toward the small British garrison house talking non-stop.

"All right," Howard said, "how did you do it, and what about these Germans?"

Chapter 2

EIGHT DAYS LATER they were back in Lisbon. The flight across the Congo had been marred by bad weather and delays at a fuel depot, and they had made repairs when the Goose struck a submerged tree while landing at Lagos, but finally after stops in Dakar and the Canary Islands they had limped into a landing at the Tagus River and immediately put the plane into the shop.

That afternoon Eddie came down from his apartment in the Alfama, the old Moorish quarter, to the Almeira Cafe on the Largo Portas do Sol, overlooking the ocean and the ships coming in. Lisbon was a tonic to him, and he was very fond of its twisting streets and little cable cars. He liked to sit in the good sun and nurse a drink, particularly when they had just come back from a tough job, and he was congratulating himself this morning on being alive.

Eddie was also a history buff, with a growing collection of rare books on Greek and Roman literature, and found endless opportunities working for McQueen to visit first hand some of the ancient cities described in his collection.

The fact that this was often done under gunfire did little to diminish the pleasure of walking the ancient streets and corridors of long vanished civilizations, and he had managed to bring back quite a collection of artifacts from their adventures, some of which he sold at exorbitant rates to the tourists.

The Almeira was also a favorite hangout of the German expatriates who were almost an occupying force under the Portuguese dictator Salazar. Although the president was officially neutral, he liked to remind his British friends that the 14th century Treaty of Windsor between Lisbon and London was the oldest treaty still in force in the world, while quietly thwarting the efforts of his consuls to aid the escape of Jews from Europe. And so the city teamed with spies, double agents and countless Portuguese citizens eager to sell a scrap of information to anyone who would pay. In the meantime, the Portuguese grew rich selling Tungsten to the Germans for their tanks and occasionally feeding the Abwehr agents misinformation paid for by the British, employing the talents of self-created Portuguese double agents with fantastic imaginations. All in all, Eddie reflected as he tasted the excellent whisky, it was a good business, frequently entertaining, from which everyone but the Nazis profited.

For Eddie, who cared little for politics and everything about the greater context of history, it was also a good place to keep an eye on the various refugees, expatriate bankers, Russian agents and assorted hucksters who might need freight service in a hurry and thus become a customer. With Lisbon the only free port in Europe for the refugees trying to escape to the new world, there was always someone. And with McQueen known as the best man in the high-risk freight business, and the luckiest, business was good. As chief salesman, he had very little work to do except show up at the Almeira and wait.

Soon the word would go out that Eddie and McQueen were back, had survived another barely plausible exploit - which Eddie never ceased to embellish upon - and the offers would start to drift in. Someone needed resupply for a clandestine refugee camp in a remote corner of the Black Sea. A man wanted by the British MI6 had to be gotten out of a tough spot in Tangier within 24 hours. The French ambassador needed a certain man flown out of German controlled Gdansk under cover of darkness, no questions asked. The more impossible sounding the job, the blacker the background, the higher the price. In truth Eddie enjoyed this part of his life immensely, since the offers often came attached to beautiful women.

But he was looking forward to today for another reason. He had sold the masks they liberated from Gautier for a good price to some British collectors, and he was going to be meeting with a Lisbon real estate broker for lunch to discuss adding to his already considerable portfolio of apartments.

And so on this sunny morning he sat quietly under his favorite umbrella and read a biography of Ptolemy and his adventures in Africa. Next to him in case he should get bored, was a copy of the Lisbon *Diario*, which was carrying stories about the German absorption of Austria and the pained but feckless reactions from the British, while the real estate man showed him pictures of various properties. Eddie asked a few questions, picked out a couple, they agreed on terms and that was that. He was a cash buyer and cash was king. A few more trips, the realtor said, and he could retire a wealthy man.

A few moments after the realtor left, the waiter, Joao, a muscular young man from the Algarve who had once been a boxer and had the scars over his eye to prove it, came over with a weak whisky and water and inclined his head to the left.

"Compliments of the gentleman at the bar," he said, using a distinctive roll of the eyes to indicate the man was no gentleman before moving off. Eddie took his time about putting down the paper and tasting the drink before glancing at the bar. A heavy set middle aged man, well dressed as only the Germans could do in the hot climate of Lisbon in August, smiled at him. Eddie smiled back, nodded and raised the glass of whisky in salute as the man hurried over.

"Good morning. My name is Beck," he said, his voice a cautious whisper. "The concierge at the Palacio said I might find you here. I have a most urgent matter I'd like to discuss with Mr. McQueen," he continued in a heavily accented English as he wiped his brow with the back of his hand.

"Please, have a seat. Will you have a drink?" Eddie asked, sizing the man up and motioning for Joao to bring another. The heavy set man sat down and ran a handkerchief over his face. "However, I should warn you that Mr. McQueen accepts almost no new assignments these days except by referral, what with the world bein' what it is," Eddie said with a sympathetic smile. "You understand."

"Oh, I understand, of course, and believe me when I say that if this were not of the utmost importance I wouldn't trouble you. The truth is, my associates are very eager to prevent a certain man, an Austrian, from leaving Lisbon. We believe he may have contacted you. We are prepared to pay handsomely if you will turn him over to us the next time he contacts you." Beck pulled out his wallet and Eddie could see a thick wad of Reichmarks peeking out of the leather folds. Something about the man made his stomach turn. Perhaps it was the rat-like look to his teeth when he smiled, or maybe it was the knowledge of what they would do to the Austrian if they caught him. In one easy movement Eddie got to his feet.

"OK, get lost," he said, and there was finality in his voice.

"What's the matter? Where are you going"" the German asked.

"Get lost, I said," repeated Eddie as he started for the exit. Beck put a hand on his shoulder and turned him back around.

"Who do you think you are? My money's as good as anyone's. Here," said the fat man. As he reached into his wallet Eddie brought up his right fist and with surgical skill landed it on the German's nose, breaking it cleanly and causing a howl of pain from Beck that startled everyone in the cafe as he fell back in his chair and then on to the ground. Eddie picked up a loose Reichmark, wiped the blood off his fist with it and tossed it back to the man, then started to push his way through the crowd.

As he reached the bar he acknowledged a few congratulatory handshakes and also the purposeful stares of three young French girls who he knew casually. It was going to be a very good day, he thought. He was about to invite the girls over when he noticed the neatly dressed man at the bar. As was their custom, the British liked to keep a low profile in Lisbon, and that meant their agents were adept at blending in. The man at the bar, whom Eddie knew only as Hamilton, was upholding this tradition with his second whisky. Spotting Eddie he inclined his head in a gesture which either meant he had information to share or wanted to buy a drink. As the British were notoriously tight with money, either prospect interested him and Eddie sat down next to him and waited.

Hamilton was the sort of man often described in popular literature as cold and calculating. He looked Eddie up and down carefully, satisfied himself that he wasn't being followed, and motioned for the bartender to pour another drink. There was no need to discuss the particulars since the bartender already knew Eddie's preference.

Thus fortified, Hamilton quietly pushed across the bar a small book of matches. To the casual observer it meant nothing, but when Eddie saw the inside cover and the single word "Archelon" followed by a zero, he stiffened imperceptibly and nodded. The agent Hamilton had been running had disappeared, and his body had been found. Their next job was now off.

"Bloody inconvenient," was all Hamilton had to say, paid the bill and got up. Before he left, he leaned over and, quite close to Eddie's ear, said "By the way, the blonde at the door. You owe me."

As Hamilton left the young woman near the exit shifted slightly and continued her vigil, quietly watching Eddie and waiting for her moment. She might have been a fashion model or a lawyer. Her hair was ash blonde and she was dressed in a wool suit and sunglasses that almost but not quite concealed her perfect figure. He thought he had seen her before. She had the relaxed confidence that comes from an expensive education, and Eddie knew immediately this was business and the thought depressed him. Casually, she removed the sunglasses and looked at him. She was very pretty, with very blue eyes, almost turquoise. He found a napkin and started wrapping his bruised knuckles.

When she was sure no one was watching them, she moved to the bar, not looking at him. "That was quite a show you put on. I would have expected it from your boss, but you did all right. Guess it runs in the family." He took a sip of the whisky and looked at her more carefully. Her ash blonde hair was pulled straight back from her forehead and she never fooled with it or patted it back in place. It was the sort of intelligent beauty that knows a lot more than it speaks, and Eddie found himself wishing he were a few inches taller. "My name is Margaret Underwood. I cabled you, remember?" The voice had a faint English midlands accent. Eddie tried to recall.

The whisky had loosened his tongue, and he leaned over and lowered his voice. "You wouldn't be related to Henry Underwood by any chance?" he finally ventured. "You know, the crazy old man we sprung from prison in Crete for stealing all those artifacts?" he asked, already knowing the answer.

"My father, yes. And it's called exporting, I believe. But look who's talking. Aren't you the man who stole all those German bonds last year in Zurich?"

Eddie looked around, then smiled. "Me and Joe. You're well informed, aren't you, miss?"

"I try to keep one eye open. My father told me about you. And your boss. He said that you were over priced. And the best in the business." She looked around the bar. "I didn't know he meant drinking."

"All depends on how bad you need something, doesn't it? Now, what can I do for you, Miss Underwood?"

"Where can we talk?"

"Right here. "He sat back and waited. She dropped the tough girl act like an old coat as she slumped against the bar. "I left him six weeks ago on the Nile. He was going up country to another dig, near Juba, up one of the tributaries."

"Yeah, sure, I know it. Tough country."

"All I could get out of him was to go get help, someone with a seaplane. He said that if I couldn't find any sensible pilot I could always try this Joe McQueen character in Lisbon, but I'd be taking my life in my hands. Quite an endorsement."

"I've heard it before."

"I'll bet you have. I tried everyone I could find from Cairo to Cyprus to Palermo. You'd have thought I wanted to land in front of the Reichstag! Nobody would even talk about it. So here I am." As she finished he had the impression she was hiding her frustration rather well, and he relented slightly. Unobtrusively, he moved down the bar to a quiet spot where a large banana palm shielded them from most of the cafe.

"That's it's a real fine story you tell Miss, but how do I know any of it's true?" he asked with a sidelong glance.

"Why would I make up something like that? You don't actually think I'm doing this to make a pass at you?" she asked in a voice dripping with scorn. "I'm not that desperate."

Eddie, enjoying it, straightened up. "See, we get a lot of desperate characters in Lisbon these days and it pays to ask questions." He sipped his drink and waited. If she was lying it would now unravel quickly and he could get on with business. Two English agents had entered the bar, men he knew well, and they looked like a few drinks would pry loose something he could talk to Joe about. It was that kind of day.

"Well?" he asked her. She gave him a cold look.

"Never mind. I'll do it myself," she said, and turning on her heel walked out.

•   •   •

The American embassy was located in a quiet street off the Baixa in downtown Lisbon. All the buildings predated the American civil war, some by centuries, when Portugal had been the hub of European expansionism, but none of this history was on the mind of the newly installed Ambassador, Clayton Ellison, as he looked again at the cable, recently decoded, from the State Department. He was in his late 50s, a distinguished looking man who had no small talk and liked people who came to the point. Around the embassy he was building a reputation for abruptness, he knew, but it couldn't be helped. The staff, who idolized him, called him the Boss.

The report in front of him detailed recent Japanese gains in China, German rearmament efforts, including heavy purchases of tungsten from Portugal, and other matters which all spelled one thing to the Ambassador. War was coming. But his country was unprepared and Ellison, a friend of the President's from his earlier service in the Navy department, was becoming a worried man. The weekly reports painted a picture of the Axis powers growing ever stronger as England clung to appeasement and America to its first Neutrality Act, signed in 1935 and already showing signs of strain. There was also the growing fear that Germany might find a way to deal a sudden, overwhelming blow to the democracies in the early stages of the war before the West could fully rearm.

He had expressed his reservations about neutrality to the State Department numerous times, only to be told to keep his head down and avoid war. It surprised him that he had been assigned such a sensitive post as Lisbon, but he meant to use his time well, and thus was born a conspiracy. On his last trip to Washington, his instructions from Cordell Hull, the Secretary of State, had been to avoid anything that would compromise American neutrality, and he was bound to this pledge. He knew that Hull was ambivalent about the act, but such was politics. He also knew several friends in the Navy department who were highly realistic men, quietly making plans to fight a two front war, and what they wanted was information, the kind that was impossible to get.

As word quietly seeped out in the Pentagon that there was someone at State who spoke their language, Ellison found himself being invited to the kind of cocktail parties where the future of the country could be debated without fear of saying the wrong thing. He met several times that September with his friends in the Navy and War departments, and before long a very quiet unit had formed, known only as Group 301, consisting of several flag officers, a few State Department staffers and the assistant CNO, all of whom could see that Ellison was in a position to supply the information that America would need to stay in the game if war came.

After a few very quiet meetings it was all set. The Navy would provide assistance to Ellison in the form of a few trustworthy men and whatever equipment could be redeployed without raising suspicions in Washington. He was given a list of Senators and Congressmen to avoid. He was made privy to the most confidential Navy and Army assessments of the people in the Third Reich and Imperial Japan who were the decision makers, and then he was sworn to secrecy. Through their contacts in the White House, they would be able to protect the Ambassador up to a point; but so long as America remained officially neutral, he would have to operate in the shadows.

"Someone here to see you, Mr. Ambassador," said his secretary Maria.

"I'm not expecting anyone."

"It's Mr. Silva," she said and waited. Antonio Silva was the chief Protocol officer in the Portuguese government and reported directly to President Salazar. He was a difficult man and just now Ellison would have preferred to be left alone, but Silva wielded great influence in Lisbon and it was important to remain in his good graces.

"Ask him to come in, Maria," he said, and put a thick file into his briefcase. Moments later, a short, dapper man in his 60s looked in and smiled. Silva had a deep, almost baritone voice that he used to great advantage, and it now exuded warmth.

"Mr. Ambassador, thanks for letting me interrupt. Something has come up."

"Can we talk in the car? I can drop you at your office."

Ten minutes later, the big Buick Phaeton was gliding through the twisting streets of Lisbon, the most colorful and vibrant city of all Ellison's past assignments. Silva was taking a long time in coming to the point.

"Something to do with American grain imports I hope," Ellison smiled.

"Not quite. It's come to our attention that an American flyer, Joe McQueen, has been, shall we say, causing the German government some embarrassment. I believe you know the man."

"Yes, I do. A good man."

"To be sure. You understand our position, Clayton. We try not to offend anyone."

"While profiting from everyone?"

"Well, we have to keep the lights on. Neutrality is a priceless commodity to us. We can't take any risks offending the Third Reich. I was hoping you could use your influence to restrict him to purely commercial endeavors." Silva smiled broadly and waited. Ellison knew the routine, and replied that he would certainly look into it. Honor had been satisfied, and when he dropped Silva at the government palace, the two men shook hands warmly.

Ellison looked in his briefcase and thought over his options as the car drove him toward the small airport bordering the Tagus River, some 15 miles away. Among the many complications, his new clandestine responsibility had put a strain on his relationship with his wife, who was ardently neutral, and which meant many late nights of work that he could tell her nothing about.

But chiefly he thought about the strange man he had been introduced to a few months prior by Captain Rodgers, his military attaché in the Lisbon office. There had been a lot of talk with his colleagues in Group 301 about what sort of man Ellison needed to carry out his clandestine work, and one name kept bubbling to the top. Joe McQueen was a Navy commander with a reputation as a tough minded, highly principled man who had gotten derailed into a desk job in Baltimore over some impolitic comments he had made about the nonsense of neutrality when at a party in

Washington. He had been a Navy flier, one of the best, and when, after a fist fight with a particularly obnoxious pro-neutrality captain it was obvious he would be sitting out the war counting paperclips, he had resigned his commission, used up his life savings and bought a Grumman Goose, which he had crated and shipped to Lisbon. His idea, Ellison was to learn, was to get back to flying while keeping an eye on potential enemies against the day when the Navy would again need his services. A patriotic man of few words, he was admired and respected by everyone who had ever known him, including the Ambassador.

The opportunity came sooner than he thought. Rodgers and McQueen met shortly after he arrived in Lisbon, and after several meetings in Lisbon and talks that went late into the night, Ellison knew he had found his man.

As the Buick pulled up to the old aerodrome, he made his decision. A small building, the aerodrome hugged the Tagus River just below the point where the ancient Castle of Sao Jorge looked over the river to the sea and where DaGama and so many other Portuguese explorers had sailed off into the unknown. It was now used weekly by Pan Am for the clipper flights to New York and by a few other small carriers who provided cargo runs to Spain and England. The main hanger was large enough to hold four or five planes at a time and there were repair shops and a large room for fabricating aluminum or cloth replacement parts for those occasions when a submerged obstacle punctured a hole in the hull.

Ellison always enjoyed the relaxed and collegial atmosphere at the aerodrome where pilots swapped stories about the assignments they had tried or missed and lied about the girls they knew in Corsica or Naples, which seemed to be populated with extravagant characters even by Lisbon's standards. On most days it was quiet, but today there were two seaplanes, an old Fokker and a DeHavilland in for repairs. It was lunchtime and most of the men munched on traditional Portuguese asordo, which was a kind of bread soup, and drank sweet tea as they worked. They were serious men who respected orders and no one talked.

Joe looked up from the workbench where he was conferring with an old mechanic named Scott over a fuel pump. Standing in the light of the hanger door, silhouetted by the heavy sun outside stood the Ambassador. He was looking over the Goose with no small measure of pride. At his orders it had been outfitted with extended range tanks and armament that made possible some of the more dangerous assignments which came his way. It had been especially difficult to requisition the long range 20mm cannon from the Army and have it mounted in the nose of the Goose, but after a few cables with the State Department

Ellison had finally prevailed and he knew from McQueen's confidential briefings that it had been the margin of victory several times.

Seeing the ambassador, McQueen put down his tools and held out a hand to this austere man with the cool nerves of a gambler. Such meetings always meant the likelihood of action, and that suited McQueen to a tee.

"How have you been, Joe?" asked Ellison warmly. He had a richly resonant, authoritative voice that always seemed to hint at veiled power.

"Just fine, Mr. Ambassador, good to see you," he said with a grin and they shook hands enthusiastically as only men sharing a great secret can do. "Thanks for the present." McQueen gestured toward the new high-speed nose cannon the Navy department had installed a few days earlier. "This mean we're off on another turkey shoot?" Ellison put a hand on his shoulder.

"Could be. Joe, I have a little matter I want to talk to you about. Is there some place we can talk?" he asked.

• • •

It was 20 minutes later in the foreman's small office in the hanger, and the Ambassador was just finishing his story. "Well, that's about all I know. Her name is Margaret Underwood. We've checked out her story and it seems legitimate, but there's a twist. She doesn't know it, but a

German agent has been following her since she returned to Europe. If the Germans are up to anything in Africa we want to know about it. Could be anything, fomenting a revolt against the British, trying to upset their flow of war materiel, you name it. I know it's a longshot, but I'd like to find out a little more."

"Yes, sir, long as you're buying lunch."

"Good man. She's waiting outside. I'll let her tell the story. If you need anything, get in touch with Captain Rodgers."

"Aye aye, sir.

The Ambassador went to the door and motioned for the young woman to come over. Eddie had been waiting to speak to McQueen, keeping his distance, and he now joined them. Margaret looked a little flustered for a moment, seeing Eddie. "Joe, this is Miss Underwood," said the Ambassador. He smiled at both of them and walked off toward his waiting car. McQueen pulled out a chair. "You're Henry's daughter, aren't you?" he asked. This got her attention and he looked her over carefully, then nodded in his slow, deliberate way and held out a hand.

Chapter 3

THE SUN was beginning to set when she had finished her story and sat back in her chair. He had listened carefully and respectfully, had even jotted down a few notes, but otherwise said or did nothing committal. She hadn't noticed the tall thin man who stood 50 yards outside the hanger entrance near an old triplane as if he was admiring it. McQueen caught sight of the man and watched until he left. He knew the man to be a Portuguese agent working at the German embassy.

"So I just need someone to fly me back to Banbuku to help me bring him home. I know your services are expensive but I can pay." There was a long silence, broken only by the sound of a metal grinder briefly at work. She handed him an envelope full of cash.

"If that's not enough..." she began, but he shook his head.

"No, that's plenty. But I know your father, knew him well. Did he tell you that?"

"No, not in so many words, but he mentioned your name a few times. Was there a problem?"

"Not exactly." He hesitated a moment. "The truth is we're too busy right now to take on anything like this, even for the Ambassador. If he's gone missing anywhere in that area, he's probably dead. It's not the kind of place that takes prisoners, if you know what I mean. If you still want to go, I can recommend a couple of good men might be willing to give it a try." She shook her head.

"I've already talked to them. No one else will even consider it. What is the problem with my father? I know he can be difficult at times..."

He could see there was no way out of it. "Difficult? Try impossible. Look, I admire the man very much but he has a knack for finding dry holes and getting into trouble. I lost a good plane a few years ago trying to fly him out of Panama City and I'm not eager to try again. I'm sorry." He started back to work.

"Dry hole?" she asked. She opened her purse and took out a small box. Inside was a small artifact, and even McQueen's limited knowledge of Egyptology told him this was authentic, and immensely old.

"Where did you get this?"

"He gave it to me, in Banbuku." McQueen looked at it, turned it over in his hand.

"Looks like something from the old kingdom."

"He said it was the 6th Dynasty," she replied as he looked it over. It was a jeweled funeral fan, about 7" long, made of gold and inlayed with rubies and topaz.

"He said it was worth five thousand dollars to a collector," she added.

"Probably triple that if it's genuine. Where did you say this came from?" They walked over to the large world map on the wall, marked and dotted with notations and navigation bearings from past trips. She went to the area just northwest of Juba and put her finger on a large plateau.

"Somewhere near here. That's where he was working. He never told me the exact location. He had found some natives who told him about a burial ground, dating back to the 6th Dynasty, something incredible, but he wouldn't talk about it. I know it has something to do with his work at the university and the trouble he had, and I begged him to return with me and come back in the Spring but he's fanatical about this thing, whatever it is." She finished and waited. He gave her back the artifact and went to the door. It was quitting time, and several of the mechanics were walking out. Something caught McQueen's eye and and he watched a moment until one of the men came by.

"Pete, you know who that tall guy is, the one over there? And the bald guy near the tool crib."

"Couple of Germans, why?"

"Skip it." McQueen watched as the tall man and his companion joined up and walked out the door. He thought a moment then turned back to the girl, who was on her feet.

"By the way, he said to say he was sorry about the mess in Dakar," she said.

"He did."

"Yes. He said this would make up for it."

McQueen thought some more. "There's a little cabaret in the Baixa, just off the Commercio plaza, called Dowds. Run by a friend of mine. Meet me there tonight at 11. Come alone."

It being late summer, the night did not come until almost 9 o'clock, and as McQueen walked into the small cabaret the old familiar smell of desperation and despair assailed his senses. It was the smell of deals being made, deals gone bad and the fear that comes with betting your life on a roll of the dice. The bar was an outlier to the main refugee haunts and often got the wealthier clientele who wanted to keep a low profile. But tonight it was packed with immigrants from eastern Europe and the ever-present Portuguese secret police. Like everyone else, they knew that some of the best counterfeiters in the business frequented Dowds and that exit visas to Uruguay and Argentina could be had for a price, providing the buyer was discreet.

At the piano was a young woman McQueen had seen before, Sylvie Montaigne. According to Hamilton she was on the Abwehr payroll, which was a pity because there was no more beautiful woman in Lisbon, a city full of beautiful women. She smiled at McQueen as he walked in. His friend Enrique was behind the bar, dressed as always in his cream colored suit, and seeing McQueen he held up a hand and shouted "Joe!"

Enrique had escaped Italy just ahead of the Nazis because of his religion, and decided to exact revenge on the Germans by opening the cabaret and playing nothing but English songs.

"How's business?" asked McQueen, looking around for the girl.

"Who knows? My bookkeeper is Portuguese, and all he says is we're making money."

"What about her?" asked McQueen, indicating the singer.

"Sylvie? I would say business is brisk." The bartender waved for Enrique and McQueen found a table.

Eddie, now wearing a dark blue suit and tie, slid easily through the crowd and sat down at the table, his eyes questioning their purpose for being here. He leaned closer to McQueen. "You got a call a little while ago from that Langerhoff character. The one we're supposed to be flying out to Bristol. Sounded pretty shook up."

"Yeah, about what?" Eddie was about to answer when a woman's scream, just outside the back door, pierced the din of the bar. McQueen was quick to his feet and with Eddie at his heels hurried to the door.

The woman who had screamed had turned away from the sight of the businessman laying face up, his eyes frozen in death and staring at the sky. The handle of a big switchblade knife protruded from his heart and a puddle of blood was forming under his shoulder blade. McQueen recognized the man. It was Langerhoff. There was a chain around his wrist that had been attached to a briefcase. All that remained was a few links of chain. As the first policeman arrived, the scene began to return to normal. In a few moments the corpse was covered and in the normal routine a truck would arrive in minutes and take it to the morgue. At all events no fuss or notice would be made of the death. Lisbon had a certain reputation for gaiety to uphold and the death of one more refugee meant very little. McQueen took Eddie aside.

"Keep an eye out for the girl. I'll be inside," he said.

"OK, boss. We got trouble?"

"Not yet."

Inside the bar a number of ragged looking Hungarians and Bulgars had briefly suspended their business to make sure the deceased was not one of theirs, than had returned to the usual work of trying to buy information. Elsewhere in the bar the usual sellers were doing a brisk business in forged documents as McQueen stepped back inside and went to his table. He knew that if the girl were being followed, it would be impossible for the man to hide inside the bar now.

Ten minutes later as he was finishing his first drink, she walked in. The body of Langerhoff had been put onto a gurney, and as it moved out a short furtive man in a cheap suit quietly slipped in, hugging the shadows. So, that was the game, he thought. The Germans want her alive, but not until they find out who she knows. But why? The question ate at the edges of his subconscious and would continue to do so, he knew, until he had solved it. McQueen glanced across the room at Eddie, who had seen the whole thing, and nodded. Before she spotted McQueen, Eddie had a word with one of Salazar's agents and the Kulzer, who was rumored to work for Himmler, was quietly led away, protesting in broken Portuguese.

· · ·

Ten minutes later, they sat in the back booth of the ancient cafe with the obligingly darkened lights and waited as the waitress brought two coffees. There were only a couple of old women here, talking in the far corner. The waiter was an old man who took no interest in them and glanced at his watch again, looking forward to closing up.

McQueen watched him without seeming to for a moment, then turned to her.

"Sorry this can't be more romantic, but it pays to take precautions. Did you know you were being followed?"

"It's Lisbon. Isn't everyone?" she smiled.

"It's the same one from earlier. They've probably been on you since you got here. Any idea why?"

"I can't say." She shifted uneasily in her chair.

"I only spotted one of them, so we're going to have to keep this short. Try again to tell me why the Germans might be interested in you. And I want the whole story or it's no deal and I walk."

She was tired from the weeks of running and dead ends and rejection, and she knew it would be a mistake to try and deceive this man McQueen. She glanced at his strong face, at the way his eyes bored into hers, and decided. "All right. It started about six months ago. I was working in Paris when the letter came, with a Cairo postmark. It had been forwarded a couple of times and it was three months old. It was in my father's writing and it was very brief, one page. All it said was that he was sick and that he had found something and he needed me. There was a ticket inside and this."

She held up a small gold coin, and the light reflected on it. There was a face on the coin, worn down and weathered but the gold still showed traces of the Upper Kingdom insignia. Incredibly, it was the likeness of Menes, first Pharaoh of the Old Kingdom and one of the most elusive characters in all Egyptology. McQueen stared at it for a moment. He spotted Eddie and waved him over.

"Ever seen anything like this before?" Eddie looked at the coin.

"Probably a fake," he said, looking it over. "The Egyptians didn't start using coins until Ptolemy, around 500BC."

"That's what I thought, at first," she said. "Then another one came, this time with a note begging me to keep it safe. His letter claimed he's found hundreds of these."

"You know how he is with facts," he said drily. "Where's the second coin?"

"Somewhere safe." McQueen was ready to walk out, but something about the cool inviting way she looked at him made him decide to play along. He settled back and had a sip of the excellent Ethiopian coffee and waited. The lights seemed to grow dimmer as she took a deep breath and closed her eyes, opening up the painful memories. Then finally it began.

"All right. It was July when he found the door."

• • •

From the air, there was only the endless rolling dunes of the Sahara. In the far distance, the thin blue line of the Nile was barely visible, but here there was nothing except a few sandy canyons and the barely discernable traces of an ancient caravan trail that had once linked Cairo to Takuedda in the Sokoto highlands north of Cameroun. The great vulture, its wingspan over 12 feet, began to circle. There was something below and it was moving.

Down in the deep canyon, a native worker looked up and noticed the circling scavengers and cursed again his fortune as he hauled the sand from the dig up the narrow winding path. Like the other men, he had not been paid in over a month and was emaciated by overwork, lack of food and water, and wanted only to collect his pay and escape this cursed place. There were only five of them left now, five out of 37 men who had started out from Khartoum. Perhaps something will strike the Englishman today, he thought as he watched the circling birds and felt the harsh bite of the sand in his mouth. Perhaps the birds would be satisfied with the bodies of the men killed in the sand storm.

Also watching was a small dark man who went by many names but on this expedition was known as Casim, his horribly scarred face obscured by the low hat he wore. He had an odd smile that never varied and kept away from the other men. Seeing the carrion birds he wiped the sweat from his brow as he carried the sand out of the dig and onto the flat, featureless desert. Above him, the hot Egyptian sun pounded down without mercy on the men as they dug their way down the long buried stairway. It would not be long know, he thought.

Casim's business was thievery and occasionally assassination, and he had survived many encounters that would have killed a less prudent man by being cautious and waiting for the right moment. He studied the workers again, measuring, calculating their loyalties. What would they do when the moment came, he wondered? How would he react? But his principal interest was in the Englishman, Underwood, and the .45 caliber pistol that was always on his hip.

He knew the old man had been awake for almost three days now, and that his strength was rapidly ebbing. He also knew that Underwood knew how to use the gun, that he seemed to have a sixth sense about danger and that he was therefore a man to be respected. Inside his shirt, the long, razor sharp blade of the dagger felt hot against his skin, and he tried to imagine the moment he plunged the knife into the old man's chest.

Underwood took a drink from his canteen. He was a man of slight build, but the ordeal of the expedition had reduced him as it had the others to a wiry collection of muscle and bone. His face was the most interesting thing about him: heavy eyebrows above large blue eyes weathered and creased by the sun, eyes that showed a keen intelligence and were always searching the horizon for trouble, as if expecting pursuers to crest the hills at any moment.

As he studied the faces of the workers, recruited from the blackest holes in Khartoum, he could feel the eyes on him, and he knew they were afraid. The expedition was deep into the sacred Valley of the Departed, and the tribes in this region were known to be fierce and distrustful. He wondered if he had made a mistake in not hiring more guards. Perhaps, he admitted to himself. But the risk was worth it, and they were so close now.

Since their arrival two months ago, all the luck had been bad. Most of the camels had died, several men had deserted and the sand storms had nearly buried three others. Was it two days since the big Nubian had attacked him? Yes, two days, and he had shot him, cleanly, through the heart. It had happened so quick and the knife had only just missed his neck but the Nubian had taken Underwood's bullet through the chest and had fallen heavily into the sand. They had buried him without incident, but everything had changed after that and he had not slept since.

He closed his mind to the problem of the men, sat down in his tent and fought off the fatigue. Yes, this had to be it.

Soon they would break through the wall and find the tomb and he could pay the men and let them go. The markings were all there, identical to the ones he had discovered in the London museum archives that day in 1936. Now two years later, he could still remember the discovery of the dust covered box, forgotten for decades, and his excitement at opening that first scroll.

His reverie was interrupted by the approach of Mustapha, his overseer and the one man he trusted. Normally a cheerful, ebullient man, this morning he looked worried.

Henry fought to focus on something he was saying.

"Yes, Mustapha? What is it?"

"Mr. Underwood, sir. There is a problem, sir" said Mustapha in his sing song voice. "We have to stop. The men refuse to work unless they are paid. Some of them may cause trouble." Henry stared at the old digger and he saw the worry on his face and nodded.

"I know, I know, but tell them not until we get to the bottom of those stairs," he said, forcing out the words. "Then we pay."

"No sir. They won't work. They say this place is cursed. They want to go home. Much trouble."

Henry realized it was pointless to argue. He looked up into the dark face with its black tattoos and tried to remain calm, in control. The sun was getting low on the horizon.

"Give them these," he said reaching into his satchel to pull out a small leather sack.   Mustapha's eyes went wide. Among the ordinary trade beads were several made of a strange green glass, a precious commodity prized throughout the Sahara. He looked around. They were alone. He took the beads and put them away. "There is something else. This morning, one of the men found something, a door. Not where we expected. Far from here."

"How far?" asked Henry.

"Maybe 200 meters. 300. It is different from the others. Not sandstone. Something else. Like marble, very smooth." Henry wasted no time, and rousing himself from his lethargy got to his feet and put on his kit.

"Let's go," he said, and followed Mustapha out the door.

An hour later,   the two men made their way to the back of the dig and Henry waited as Mustapha cleared away the sand. There, peering out at them after 3,000 years was the outline of a large door. He brushed aside the dirt and studied the markings a moment, compared them with the ones in his journal. It was about four feet square and made out of bronze and it would not yield an inch, even when he and Mustapha put their shoulders into it. He banged on the door with his pistol butt and could again feel the heaviness and immensity of the thing. It must be several inches thick, he thought, and he knew that only the royal family could indulge in such devices. The markings on the door also revealed it to be of the Old Kingdom. Henry took out his pocket journal and began tracing the designs from the door. Mustapha looked at him expectantly. He could feel his heart pounding and tried to relax.

"Is this it?" asked Mustapha, leaning in to look

"Possibly," he said at last, his voice a dry rasping croak. "Probably. All right. Pay the men in the morning." He opened a leather sack and poured out the last of the money, a few coins and some green beads. "But I want them under guard tonite. We'll need more equipment to get this open. I'll go back to Banbuku with a few men. You wait here until I return."

"As you wish," he replied, and after a few minutes Henry was satisfied with his drawings and put the book away. The job of concealing the door, using a blanket and a tree branch to smooth the sand, took a further ten minutes and when they had finished, carefully sweeping over their footprints, the site appeared as if it were untouched for millennia. In a state of tremendous excitement, Henry went back to his tent and watched as Mustapha led the men out of the dig and up to the makeshift camp. He told them they would be paid, and there was weary relief on the face of the five survivors.

•   •   •

After the campfires had started, he tried to focus on his books but it was harder now. He knew he had to sleep but not long after sunset Mustapha returned. The men were all guarded, he reported. Nothing to worry about. Henry nodded, asked who he had entrusted with this job. "The new man, Casim," replied Mustapha. The name meant nothing to Henry, and he laid down on the cot and fell instantly into a deep sleep.

It was late at night as the men were sleeping that a silent figure seemed to rise from the sands, clothed in a black robe. Silently it approached the first sleeping man and knelt down. The curved dagger with the serrated edges raised high and then in one smooth, practiced motion came down into the man's chest just as the hand went out to cover the victim's mouth and muffle any sound. The man struggled for only a few moments and then was still. Four more times the scene was repeated, until there were none left alive and the wind blew sand over the faces of the dead.

It was the midday sun creeping over the edge of the wall and falling on his unprotected face that awakened him. Slowly, his senses began to focus. He realized there was absolutely no sound, none of the usual background noise of men at work. He tried to get to his feet and then realized that his leg was chained to a wall. His mouth went dry. He looked around for signs of life and then he saw it: bodies at the top of the shallow stairs. Several men were heaped together, some of them looking as though they died grasping at their throat. One of them was Mustapha.

A wave of fear came over him and he fought to control it, to stay rational. He remembered there was a knife in his backpack and looked around for it, but there was nothing. Whoever had done this had been thorough, he reflected. He was alone.

But not quite. As the sun began to burn his throat, he saw a shadow slowly enter the dig. Someone was standing above him. The shadow began to move, and then the man he recognized as Casim stood before him, carrying a jug of water.

"You!" said Henry, the voice a dry croak.

"Yes," he began, like a schoolmaster talking to a truant child. "Now. Where is the money for the payroll? Give it to me without delay and I'll leave enough water for two days. You might get lucky." Casim poured a little water into a cup and held it out. "You must have hid it well. If I had found it, you'd be dead already. This way, you get to live a little longer. You're a lucky man." Henry shook his head, tried to clear his throat but could only manage a crude whisper.

"Why should I trust you?"

"What choice do you have?"

"Water first," he croaked. Casim smiled, a malevolent smile that showed lifeless eyes. He shook his head and poured the water into the sand.

By mid- afternoon, Henry was laying on his back, and didn't hear the footsteps behind him as Casim returned. His breathing was a desperate rattle. The pain in his chest was intense, and as Casim sat down in front of him, he wondered if he had left the old man too long in the sun.

"Ready to talk about the money yet?" he asked. Henry nodded. Casim poured a few drops of water into a cup and held it out. The old man took the cup, drank it slowly, then raised a trembling hand and motioned for his captor to come closer.

"I want to know something" he whispered, barely audible. Casim came forward, bent down to his ear.

"What?"

"The men..."

"All dead. With this," came the reply as he lifted the long dagger. The words were spoken without any guilt or remorse and Casim smiled, enjoying the moment of triumph. Henry tried to focus on the knife, wondering how he would deflect the deadly thrust.

"Enough!" came the whispered cry of anger, and he bent down. "Where is it?" Casim held a pistol in one hand and in the other a handful of the green beads Henry had been using to pay the men. "Where did these come from? Where is the gold? I've searched the camp. You hid it, didn't you? Talk fast, old man, if you want to live," he hissed.

But Henry made no sign, merely went on staring into the lifeless eyes. He knew it was the end.

"No," he finally said, very quietly. "All gone." Casim began to laugh, a low, cruel laugh. Without further word he stood up, took aim with the pistol at the center of Henry's chest and fired. The older man's body jerked violently, twisted to his right and was still. The assailant stood up and walked out of the tent.

• • •

It was not until the next morning that the vultures appeared. There were at least 10 of them and they immediately began tearing at the flesh of the dead men, making their terrible sickening screech as they worked. One of them hopped over to Henry's body and was about to take a bite of his arm when it suddenly twitched and the bird flew out. His eyes opened. Slowly he rolled over onto his back and felt his chest. Underneath the shirt was a large, thick aluminum plate, about 7" square, and in the left center of this was a deep indentation made by the bullet. The pressure of the shot had knocked him unconscious.

An hour later he staggered to his feet and made his way to the gully a hundred yards away. He searched the site for any sign of life, but Casim had been thorough. Forcing himself to walk against the terrible pain, he counted off the steps into the desert until he came to a small mound next to an extinct stream bed. The secret cache of food and water was still there, untouched, and after eating he hurried back to the door he and Mustapha had discovered and verified it was undisturbed. He had to stop several times to catch his breath because the bullet had bruised two of his ribs. He knew well the signs, but after an hour the work was done, and somehow he loaded the water and food onto his back and began walking due east.

• • •

It was four weeks later. The village of Banbuku was one of those half-forgotten outposts on the Nile that were vaguely under British influence but in reality were little more than trading posts where British goods could be shipped without being hijacked by local tribesmen. It happened to lie on one of the ancient caravan routes that swung south of Cairo before turning west into the Sahara, and as such attracted every form of criminal activity known to man.

The main street was wide and smooth and along it stood dozens of small shops and a souk where camels and donkeys waited to load or unload their burdens and small boys chased chickens for sport. It was also a hub of smuggling arms into the interior, a heroin depot for the harems of

Arabia and on occasion a clearing house for the slave trade which had long since gone underground but which in fact was flourishing with the introduction of British money into the region.

The wealthier residents all built their houses along the river, some of which even featured elaborate Moorish designs and interior courtyards with fountains. At the end of the dirt street stood one of these, an imposing brick edifice belonging to a Sheik Ali, a friend of Henry's, with walls 20' high, tall minaret towers at each end and a collection of date palms filling the interior. There was a pleasant view onto the Nile. In the garden a woman sat under a palm tree, watching the river. A servant came out of the main house and bowed. This always made her smile.

"Miss Underwood, lunch is ready, and today we have a special treat. Fresh perch. You like?" asked the servant who smiled through bad teeth.

She wrinkled her nose at the thought. "Not hungry just now, thank you Saleh." The servant watched her a moment, wondering what this strange English girl was doing here on the upper Nile, debating whether to press the point. She had eaten poorly for days and he knew that there had been no word of her father for several months now, but she refused to return to England. It had become a matter of some speculation among the staff.

He decided that it wasn't proper to say anything yet, and so he bowed and returned to the house. He could have told her about the rumors he had heard, about the white man who had risked the wrath of the local warlords by entering the forbidden valley to disturb the tombs, but he thought better of it. Better to let others do it, he reasoned, and let them deal with her temper.

As always, it was too hot to stay out of doors for long, and he went inside, worrying about his failure to tell her that her father was in all likelihood dead.

It was not until night was falling that she stirred, and then she walked slowly to the great outer gate that led onto the dusty street and nodded for the huge Nubian servant to open the door. This was not done after dark because with the darkness came the threat of abduction, but she insisted and moments later stepped out into the cool evening air. The great doors swung closed behind her and she was alone in the African twilight.

She had spent years in the Sahara and other dangerous places with her father on his academic quests and by now had a simple routine in place. Underneath her khaki colored vest trimmed in red lace she kept a very flat 9-shot Mauser pistol in a sling she had made herself which was invisible under the vest. It was accurate to 100 yards and she had spent countless hours in places like Bolivia and the

Caucuses in target practice, and could now hit anything she aimed at with no more than 2 bullets. She had often been asked by her father to go and shoot their dinner when he was too busy to make other arrangements, and after her initial revulsion she had quickly developed a good eye for edible game and knew which animals she would merely enrage by shooting them.

She felt no fear that evening as she walked through the twilight toward the hooded lights at the end of the street and the old cafe where the handful of Europeans frequented and gambled and occasionally bedded each other. Incongruously, there was music tonight from the cafe and she was curious to discover its source. She had half given up on the idea of finding her father alive after so much time without even a letter, but there was always the chance that a trader might have picked up scraps of news. Besides, there were no other European women in Banbuku and she was lonely for the conversation of educated men.

And so the evening had passed under the endless stars and the great stillness at the edge of the Sahara. Above her she could see Orion and Scorpius, which the ancient Egyptians had called Ip. She listened to the conversation on the veranda and chatted about the latest movies from America and the odds that Neville Chamberlain would make peace with the Germans and about the river. And when politics became tiresome there was always news of the river, of its crossings and the strange men who came and went, their business generally veiled in secrecy. Her area of expertise was Egyptology and she loved the stories people told of the pharaohs and their wives and how they lived. It was generally not known or even agreed upon that they had reached so far up the Nile, but many local people speculated that they came here to hunt and to mine the jewels which still cropped up occasionally in the low hills beyond the river.

It was as she was walking back to the compound of Sheik Ali that she first saw something in the water, floating down with the stream. She stopped and watched as the object moved slowly, carefully to the river's edge. The moon was very low but in the dim starlight she could just make out the outline. It was a man, and he was trying to climb out of the water. Her instincts told her to run, because the abductors she knew often used similar tactics to lure their victims to the water's edge, where others laying in wait could overwhelm them. But there was no boat in sight and the man did not move, and so she began to climb down the embankment.

She had closed the distance to a few meters when the head rose slightly and she heard distinctly a voice call out in a hoarse whisper the word "Margaret." She ran forward to the river's edge and knelt beside him. It was Henry, and he was badly dehydrated. She helped him to his feet.

"Father!" she cried, unable to recall any of questions she had rehearsed for this moment.

"You weren't worried, were you?..." he gasped, and despite his exhaustion the overwhelming relief at seeing her again made him smile.

"You bet I am! Where have you been all this time? I was about to give you up for dead. This is so...so damned unfair!"

Henry had prepared himself for this moment, and before she could go on he kissed her on the cheek. "There's a plane leaving for Khartoum in two days. We're going to be on it, together. They always have a few empty seats," she said.

"Very impressive," he managed to get out.

"Thank you. Now you can tell me what happened out there, but don't forget: we're leaving."

The walk back to the house was uneventful. As he entered the front room and breathed deep the delicious kitchen smells he had to smile. She had grown up exactly as he had raised her, with a mind of her own and a keen sense of duty, but this was no time for reminiscing. He got up and went to the window and looked out at the night. If they're coming, he thought, it will be here. Still, he might have lost them. He had been very careful. The moon was high now, and all along the shore there was only the silent kiss of the waves against the thin rocky beach.

She could see something was wrong in the way he was groping for words, so unlike him. "Father, please. Tell me. You owe me that much, don't you?" As she helped him up, he kissed her cheek.

"You have every right to be upset, my dear. Every right. And we will talk. In the morning. But now..." and as he limped toward the bedroom he fell silent.

• • •

Three days later and he had not spoken of his adventure, but had slept most of the time and in his waking hours had made lengthy notes in his journal. He seemed irritable and short tempered, but he had regained his strength, and when he asked if she would like to talk she was eager. It was late in the afternoon and the sun was nearly down when they went out to the compound and for several minutes walked in silence. Finally he sat down under a rose trellis and took her hand and held it a moment. "I found it Maggie," he began. "Yes! I really did. After all these years and all the setbacks. It's there, out in the desert, just two weeks by camel from here. Everything I hoped for. We can prove that this senseless bickering between the three great religions is nonsense, that we're all brothers. It's just incredible, just..." He took a moment to compose himself. "But then, before I could begin the excavation, he murdered all the men. Killed them in cold blood! Even dear old Mustapha," and he suddenly became emotional and had to stop.

"Who?"

"That devil, Casim!" he shouted. "The one we hired in Khartoum. I never trusted him. It wasn't until it was too late that I learned he was working for this Massoud Al Hiri, the local warlord. But it's there! I found it, a great bronze door that must weigh two tons. The *Door of the One*, just as we thought. The proof is inside. I thought it would be alabaster or something and we could break through. I couldn't budge it. That's why I came back, to get the supplies and men I need. You understand, don't you?" and he looked at her, imploring. But she shook her head.

"You're not going back. You can't. It's madness."

"I have to. I have to finish it, even if it kills me. It's too important to stop now."

"But what about me?" she asked, and he fell silent. "It's a miracle you're still alive. We have to go home."

"I know that would be the sensible thing to do, really I do, but I have to go back before somebody else finds it. You see that, Margaret, don't you?" He looked at her imploringly, hoping for a sign of support, but she turned away, hiding her tears. In the distance, Saleh, the houseboy, motioned to Henry. He was holding up a satchel. Henry waved him over.

"I'm sorry," she said. "How did you survive?"

"Perhaps God protected me. I made my way to the river and then I floated for two days. I don't know why the crocodiles didn't get me. Just luck I suppose, like you and I and your mother and those sweepstake tickets she made me buy. Remember?" She nodded.

"There was a policeman here last week, asking about some men who had been killed in the desert. It sounded bad. He wanted to know if I'd seen you."

"What did you tell him?"

"Nothing."

He fell silent. Something was moving toward them in the shadows. He got to his feet as Saleh handed him his battered leather satchel.

"What are you doing?" she asked. Saleh began laying out two automatic pistols and several boxes of ammunition, and as they talked he stuffed these into the satchel.

"Father?" He took out a map and spread it out on the bench.

"I have to go back, Maggie, before they find it. They'll try, you know. There isn't much time. To them it's just money, an easy fortune but it's far too important for that. And I have an advantage. I'm the only one who knows exactly where it is." And he jabbed at the map with his finger to an unmarked spot that meant nothing to her. He turned to Saleh and motioned for him to come over. "Could you tell the Sheik I'd like to see him now if it's convenient. Ten minutes."

"Yes doctor," said the smaller man, and hurried off.

"You can't do that. It's a miracle you're alive now. Come back with me, and then if you want we'll come back later, with more guards." He shook his head.

"No, that's the mistake I made the first time. Telling too many people. No, it's got to be done fast and quiet, and quickly. The only thing is, I'm going to need help getting it out. It may be too heavy for the camels." He stopped and looked at her, hard, as if trying to remember. "You've always been so good, Maggie, always there. I know how hard this has been, but this is the end of the road. Promise. After this I'm not leaving England. There's only one more thing to do, and I'm relying on you."

"What"

"There's a man I know, in Lisbon, a good man named Joe McQueen. You haven't met him. He's a bit of a rogue, I suppose, but he's the only one for this job. It takes raw guts and brains and McQueen is all of that. Now take this." He gave her an envelope. Inside, there were two letters, one with a thick wad of pounds sterling, the other addressed to

McQueen. "You'll find him at the Lisbon airport, if he's anywhere. Give him the money in here and if he agrees, give him the other envelope. You understand?" She nodded. "Good. Can you remember that?"

"Yes, but..." Before she could go on, there was movement to his left. A houseboy came in with Saleh speaking in a language Margaret recognized as Urdu.

"What is it?" she asked.

"Master," said Saleh, "men coming, this way. From across the river. Many men. Guns."

Outside, in the moonlight, they ran up a shallow stairwell to the highest parapet and there, in midstream, was a boat and a dozen tribesmen. It was a ragtag affair and no attempt at concealment was being made. A moment later, Sheik Ali ran out to join them. He was a tall, distinguished looking man in his Hashemite robes and the beard, going to gray. He had a pair of binoculars and studied the boat a moment. When he put it down he was smiling.

Ali had been born in the slums of Cairo and had run away at 12 to make his fortune. The stories about him were endless and veiled in mystery, but somehow by the age of 35 he had become a rich merchant and had settled in Banbuku, where it was said he became a master of overcharging the British.

"Well, Henry, here we go again," he began. "It seems you have returned! And brought your friends with you!" Ali roared with laughter as he watched the boatload of men approaching. Margaret was appalled at the sight, and couldn't understand why her father and the Sheik were so calm. Then she noticed a group of armed men emerging silently from the edge of the building.

"They come across every week now, mostly looting what they can. This will be a good lesson for them," he said to Henry. One of the Sheik's men, the leader, looked up at Ali, who slowly nodded. Suddenly, the night was rent by the deafening sound of heavy machine guns opening up on the boat. Margaret gripped her father's arm but in a few seconds it was over. The makeshift wooden boat had been splintered to pieces and sank quickly, while the bodies of the soldiers began to drift slowly with the current.

On the opposite shore, the first crocodiles slipped into the water. They were the large Nile crocodiles, and for them a human posed no difficulties whatsoever. The few men who had survived tried to swim away, but the crocodiles were too swift and as the jaws closed around the hapless men their screams pierced the night. For a moment they struggled as the great predators rolled them over and over in the deathly embrace they used on wildebeest and antelope. Margaret could see Ali was enjoying the spectacle and wondered again how her father had come to know such a cruel man.

One of Ali's men ran up the stairs and had a word with him. Ali nodded and the man withdrew. He leaned over to Henry and spoke a few words, bowed to Margaret and waved to the men below, who shouted his praises loudly as they put away their weapons.

"A most excellent spectacle, Henry, but there will be more. Everything is arranged as you asked."

"Thank you, my friend. Once again I am in your debt."

"Go in peace," he replied graciously, "And now I have much work to do." He smiled at them both and was quickly gone. Henry slung the satchel over his shoulder and as if by prearrangement two porters appeared with packs on their backs. Margaret was too stunned to talk.

"Who are they?" she asked.

"They're for you, my dear. You're leaving the compound tonight. Too dangerous for you to stay here. These men will hide you at their home until the Air France flight on Tuesday. You'll be perfectly safe, but you must leave Africa for a time. Until we meet again."

"But. I thought we were going to go together."

"No time now. Get to Lisbon. Find McQueen. He'll know what to do. I'll see you in Cairo, on the 9th day of October. Remember."

"But what if I can't find him?" she wondered aloud. He smiled at her, gave her a quick embrace.

"We never talk like that, do we?" She shook her head and forced a smile. Saleh appeared from out of nowhere, wearing a field pack. "That's my girl. Besides, I've got the best man in the Sahara as my guide now." Saleh took a little bow. "Now go and pack quickly, before any more of Massoud's men get ideas. Wait for us in Cairo, at the Semiramis. We'll have a party to put Buckingham palace to shame. If anything happens and I can't get there," he hesitated a moment. "Well, if the worst does happen, I'll try to get back to Banbuku, to our secret place and wait for you there. You remember?" She nodded. With a final embrace and a smile he went to the stairs, was joined by Saleh and they slipped quietly out the gate. She watched a moment as they appeared at the river's edge, where a small ferry boat was waiting to take them across. As it went, Henry caught sight of her and waved.

· · ·

The lights were going out when she finished her story. "That was the last I saw of him. I may have left out some details, but now you know why I need help, why this is important. I want you to fly me down to Cairo. There may be trouble getting him out. I'm prepared to pay. But I must be there by the 9th of October."

"Yeah." For a long moment McQueen sat silent as he turned it over in his mind. He knew she was telling the truth so far as she knew it, but there would be much she was unaware of. Also, he might be walking into a trap.

"Here," she said, and handed him the envelope with the cash. "Is this enough?" He didn't look at it.

"Why did he need you down there?"

"He had to have someone to do the science, in case he found what he was looking for, to verify it was of a certain age and provenance. I have a degree in chemistry and physics. It's very convenient," she added ruefully. "Like everything in our life, so long as it's for the work. Actually, it was his idea that I study chemistry and anthropology. And physics. He always said a well educated girl is never at the mercy of an unqualified suitor." She laughed at this. "Kind of a strange mix. I used to get chemistry sets starting when I was 7, together with books by Margaret Mead and Newton. I think secretly he's been planning this for 20 years. Comforting to be wanted," and added with a smile." And I can't complain. It's the life I wanted too."

As he listened he knew he had to find out what the Germans wanted in the Sudan, if for no other reason than he owed Col. Campbell, the British officer who had gone out on a limb to secure his landing rights in Lisbon, and who had been reprimanded for it by his superiors. The British were in danger of losing the war, he knew. It had to be done. It was a question of honor.

He closed his mind to all issues of motivation and motioned for Eddie to come over. "See that Miss Underwood gets home safely. And lay in fuel and provisions for six weeks. We leave tomorrow morning. File a flight plan for Cairo. And make sure you get her money." He looked at her and tipped his hat. "Night," he said, and was gone. She handed the envelope over to Eddie, who winked at her.

"See," he said after McQueen had left, "didn't I tell you? Nothing to it."

Chapter 4

TWO DAYS LATER, after a long night spent in the harbor at Palermo to make sure they weren't being followed, the Goose and its collection of equipment and people followed a rain squall south to Cairo and touched down shortly after sunrise in a heavy mist that unnerved their passenger but which caused Eddie to whoop with delight. To him it meant a new adventure, a good excuse for going off his diet and the possibility of treasure.

As McQueen was counting on, no one had seen their approach through the low clouds. He had set the plane down expertly, just below the Qasr-el-Nil bridge where he knew the traffic would be light and they could tie up at Roda Island. As he feathered the engines and taxied to the dock, narrowly avoiding a very large dhow laden with sacks of coffee, McQueen motioned for Eddie to come forward. They talked for a moment about the supplies they would need and about how to avoid attracting attention. McQueen happened to catch sight of the girl. Throughout the bumpy decent she had sat silent, staring straight ahead. Now he could see that her knuckles were white around the seatbelt but that otherwise she was composed, her eyes closed.

As they reached the dock McQueen was relieved to see a very fat mechanic loafing around, brewing coffee. This was his friend Harry, formerly of the London docks, and after a cup of the thick black coffee preferred by Egyptians and pleasantries about the new British taxes and Harry's first year of married life - he liked the food very much - it was all arranged. Eddie would spend the night with the Goose, Harry would keep an eye out for intruders while Joe and the girl would find quarters in the city at the Hotel Semiramis.

Throughout the dealings Margaret had kept silent as she watched McQueen, so much at home in this strange land. It was partly out of curiosity and partly because she knew she was almost completely helpless in this bustling city with its endless children begging for food, the strange smells and sights and the feeling of being watched.

It was as they were climbing up the Qasr Al Nil that McQueen realized they were being followed. The street was very crowded and it was easy to lose sight of someone but he caught a brief glance of a tall, very thin man wearing a Western suit and a fez. It was an odd combination and it occurred to him that the man was unconcerned with whether or not McQueen knew he was being followed.

"Walk a little faster," he said.

"Is something wrong?" she asked, seeing the tension in his face and the quiet urgency in his voice.

"Not yet. Go into that shop, the one on the right, and pretend you're there to buy something. Wait for me." And without another word he turned off down an alley. He waited.

A minute later the man reached the alley and paused. There was something odd about him that troubled McQueen, watching from the shadows of a nearby store. The man wore the telltale sign of the British official in Mesopotamia: he had a pocket watch from JW Benson, in Ludgate Hill, London, which he kept checking. He decided to let him have a little more rope.

The man was cautious, but as he walked up the street and kept looking in every shop window, McQueen was closing in behind him. At the fifth store the man stopped and looked at his watch again. McQueen took out his 38 pistol and pressed it against the man's back. "Turn left down the side street. Don't look around." The man did as he was told, and in a few moments it was quiet and McQueen put away the pistol and turned the man around." I thought so. McAndrew, isn't it?"

"Yes. What are you going to do?"

"Nothing, but you deserve low marks for the fez. Bad idea. Speaking of which, whose idea was it for the tail?"

"Head of station. I mean, I can't say. It's confidential." McQueen grinned and waited. "All right. There's a report out that a German couple disguised as Americans were coming to Cairo. You fit the description," he added somewhat helplessly. McQueen read the young man's nervousness and decided to relent.

McQueen showed him his passport and McAndrew's shoulders slumped. "Wrong guy. You better get back to the docks. And tell Roland I said hello." McAndrew brightened up at this, realizing he wasn't going to be reprimanded, and smiled broadly as they shook hands and parted.

"Will do," he said and hurried off toward the river. McQueen, who would normally have been alert to the faces around him, didn't notice the middle aged man in the grey Homburg watching his conversation with the young English staffer, didn't hear the click of the camera as it took his picture, and didn't see the man hurry off down the street. The young Englishman had taken the bait and led them to the girl, that was the important thing. Now the mechanisms would be put into place. It wouldn't be long.

The Hotel Semiramis was a famous spot on the east side of the Nile where anything you wanted could be bought or sold for the right price. McQueen liked it because it was old and the sheets were clean, and because despite its poor reputation with the police it had an air of authenticity that appealed to McQueen, a sort of broken down charm in the way it recalled the great days when Cairo was the center of the known universe. They were still here, he thought, the intense imams, waiting for a call to action, circling in the shadows. He hoped he wouldn't be around when it erupted.

They checked in quietly at the desk and McQueen had a chance to look at the register and casually inquired of the desk clerk what was happening in the city. His Arabic was a little rusty but he made himself understood and they chatted amiably for a few minutes. When McQueen made a joke about the Germans and their parsimonious habits that included allusions to Hitler's sex habits, suddenly everything was OK. The manager came out and offered him a better suite, which McQueen declined, and tickets to a private room in the casino, which he accepted. He waited until the manager was talking with a guest before turning to his companion. She was scanning the register, going back several weeks.

"See anything? This is the 9th, isn't it?"

"Yes, and he should have been here by now."

"So what was the plan? We meet Henry, he's got the stuff hidden somewhere so we help him load it up and fly out. That it?"

"Something like that. He was very vague."

"What exactly was the cargo?"

"He wouldn't say. He was incredibly closed mouth about it. It could have been a few coins, or maybe a statue or something heavier." McQueen wasn't happy with any of this, but he was getting an idea as he watched a group of well dressed people enter the casino. Suddenly, the room seemed to grow silent. A young man, about 35 he guessed, had entered the lobby with an older man, chatting easily. The older man he recognized as a Wermacht colonel in the supply corps he had once met on a job flying parts into Bremen. But it took him a moment to place the younger man. Was it in Germany? No, Paris. That was it. A party for a group of German university scientists. He had been dragged to it by a woman he was seeing at the time. And the man? It escaped him. He turned back to her.

"All right, we wait," he said finally, still watching the young man. "In the meantime, there's some high ranking Germans staying here, probably playing at the casino. Did you bring a long dress?" There was a sign in the lobby announcing a luncheon hosted by the Goethe Society.

"What?"

"Evening dress."

Involuntarily, she laughed. "Oh, I always take one into the desert. No. Why?" She thought a moment. "If its important I can get one."

"Meet me here at one," he said, still studying the man in the library.

"I'm going to go look for Henry."

"Look terrific," he said, winking at the girl. Relieved to be free of her for a moment, he went directly to the house phone and put in a call to Eddie. Everything was going well, he learned, but there was something odd and Eddie told him about a small cargo ship loaded with crates guarded by a group of men who looked distinctly Aryan. McQueen told him to keep his eyes open and rang off.

Margaret followed the bellboy to her suite, tipped him and went inside. It was a large, comfortable room with a bedroom down a short hallway and a kitchenette. She had decided: she would search for her father, without McQueen.

In the lobby, the usual lunch crowd was starting to build, and it took a few minutes before he spotted the short Chinese waiter in his gold and purple vest, hurrying in with a plate of food. The waiter, who everybody called Sammi, had a friendly face that had seen much death and he loved his job at the hotel. As he came out of the dining room a few minutes later he was surprised to see McQueen waiting for him, grinning. The two men said nothing. Sammi nodded toward the service entrance to their right and hurried off.

Fifteen minutes later, outside the lobby, Sammi smoked his cigarette and listened to McQueen with the patience that only those who have known great hardship possess. McQueen showed him a picture.

"That the man?" Sammi asked.

"That's him," said McQueen. "Supposed to have passed through here a few months ago on his way up the river. Always liked to live high so I figured he might have stayed here. Name's Underwood. Seen him?"

Sammi looked at the picture and nodded. "May. Maybe June. Nice man, but very careful, not talk much. What you want him for?" McQueen smiled, knowing how Sammi's mind worked, already trying to get one jump ahead.

"Rescue mission, naturally. I'd pay a lot to know who he was travelling with when he left Cairo." Sammi thought it over. McQueen held out a small roll of Drachmas tied by a rubber band, he pointed to the young German through the window, now talking with several older men.

"See that guy? See if you can find out who he is."

"Friend of yours?"

"Strictly business."

"OK. Give me some time. Meantime, you be careful. Germans staying at the hotel, they don't like Americans. Bad people."

"Yeah. Everybody keeps saying that," he replied.

• • •

The day before McQueen and company arrived in Cairo, a kilometer away from the Semiramis, in a third floor walk up apartment, a different sort of rendezvous was taking place. The place was empty and in the kitchen was a single chair. There was a smallish Egyptian man tied to the chair, and there were fine rope bindings that ran from the chair legs to the man's feet and thighs, the bindings tight enough that they bit painfully into the flesh. His face and upper chest were covered in ugly bruises from the beating. He was gagged and as the frightened eyes darted around the room there at last came the sound of footsteps. At first all he could see was the boots, heavy black leather boots rising to a pair of striped trousers, a field gray tunic of heavy wool and finally the swastika and eagle insignia of the Gestapo. The Egyptian looked up in his agony and saw a strong, heavy featured face of a man in his 40s with black, evil looking eyes. The man spoke impeccable Arabic and leaned close to the prisoner's ear a moment, while twisting the tourniquet around his neck just a few millimeters, enough to cause the onset of panic.

"Now then. We want to know where you got these and who you stole them from. Remember?" The Egyptian nodded vigorously. He tried to speak but could not. The rope was loosened and he coughed violently for a moment.

"What is your name?"

"Saleh."

"Good. And where did you get these?" The Egyptian Saleh looked at the green beads, trying to focus his eyes.

"In the desert. In the desert. Please! For God's sake..."

"And where is Underwood?" The noose tightened again. Saleh looked up to the cold eyes and shook his head.

"I don't know! Please!"

"Well?" the dark eyes demanded of his companions, the voice now harsh. "Is this all you have for me, is this why I came to Cairo, to see one hysterical Egyptian?" The two younger men looked through their reports and one of them ran a thin finger down a list of names. The interrogator looked back at Saleh. He had passed out. "When he wakes up, start again. Find out where Underwood is. Use the needle if you must." As the interrogator was about to go, a junior officer stepped forward.

"Colonel. I know this is just routine, but..."

"Yes? What is it?" he said, washing his hands in the sink.

"These are new registrations for all the hotels tonight. This name, at the Hotel Semiramis. Joe McQueen. I know this man. We have had dealings with him. A cheap adventurer who lives in Lisbon, but he knows people. And you see this name, farther down the register." He pointed to an entry, "M. Underwood. That could be his daughter," he leered. Flush with triumph, the interrogator brought his fist down on the paper, making the pencils shake.

Ten minutes later, the Germans were all in another room, down a long hallway from the kitchen where Saleh was bound. He could hear them. He opened his eyes. He knew that the next encounter with the German would end in his death, and he had decided he would not die that way if he could prevent it. Across from his chair was a partially open window. During his interrogation one of the bindings on his legs had become loose, and with the strength that comes from desperation he was able to gain some freedom of movement and suddenly the chair moved. He stopped and listened to see if they had heard. When the conversation continued, he began carefully pushing the chair toward the window.

It took almost five minutes but he finally got to the ledge and stopped to gather his breath. He closed his eyes and hoped Allah would forgive him. Then, with one desperate move, he got to his feet and heaved himself through the window, fully expecting to fall the 8 stories to the ground. He closed his eyes.

At the moment of impact, the glass shattered and he could feel the tearing of his skin as the sharp glass sliced through his shoulder, and then there was only the blissful moments of silence as he fell, weightless, into the hard black abyss.

As soon as their prisoner had escaped, the Germans had gone to the window. The body was sprawled awkwardly across some boxes. They had no doubt he was dead. What they hadn't seen was that a large bale of cotton, not visible from above, had cushioned the fall and the prisoner was alive but unconscious. A crowd of children had quickly formed and based on standing orders they had made the decision to immediately abandon the apartment before British police arrived asking questions. The three German officers all left by separate entrances and in five minutes the apartment was again empty. Even the blood had been cleaned up.

But the crowd of children had quickly grown bored and dispersed. They had seen death before and it held little fascination for them. Perhaps someone would come and take him away, they said, and immediately ran off to other things.

The next morning, a street cleaner was at work when he noticed the legs of a broken chair sticking out of some boxes. He went closer to investigate, thinking he might be able to sell the chair. What he found instead was the body of a man, bloody but alive, under some bales of cotton. He helped him up and offered to take him to a hospital, but the man merely mumbled his thanks began walking unsteadily in the direction of the Semiramis hotel.

• • •

For Margaret, the search had produced little. She had talked to several members of the staff in case Henry had registered under an assumed name, then looked at two nearby hotels reasoning that he might have changed his plans, but there was nothing. The effort had taken most of the morning, broken only by the chore of finding a plain black sheath dress at a souk not far from the hotel, and now she was unpacking in her room and getting dressed when she heard something.

Someone was knocking at the door.

"Who is it?" she said at the door.

There was a long hesitation. "I have a message for Miss Underwood, please," was the reply, in a labored, halting English. She finished getting dressed and opened the door a crack. Her first instinct was to scream, which she suppressed with a hand over her mouth.

"Saleh!" she whispered. His eyes looked at her pleadingly. There was dried blood on his face and fresh bruises everywhere, and he was bent over. In fact, two of his ribs was cracked and he was in excruciating pain, finding it difficult to breathe.

She threw open the door and helped him in. With great difficulty, she got him to a large arm chair and he sat down, unable to speak. She hurried to close the door, making sure no one was watching in the hall.

"Saleh, what happened?" she breathed. He looked up at her, unable to speak. She ran to the bathroom, called room service for some bandages and food, and returned with a wet towel and some tissues. When she came back, he had fainted. She got him to the bed and for the next five minutes she worked in silence, cleaning his wounds. When she had finished he opened his eyes and even managed a pained smile from beneath the bandages, although the effort cost him. She noticed his breathing was becoming more strained, a hoarse rattle.

"I'm going to get you to a doctor," she said, but he reached out a hand and gripped her arm, shaking his head.

"No. Listen now..." he managed to say. He closed his eyes and there was another pause. She could stand it no more.

"Saleh. What happened to you? Have you seen my father?"

He nodded his head. "But you must leave Cairo, Miss, leave today. They are coming... they know. A man with black eyes," he managed to get out. And so the story came out, in fragments and whisperings from the bloody remains of the man laying on the bed. They had journeyed far into the desert, following Henry's secret map to the site with heavy equipment and dynamite, when a sand storm caught them in the open. Two of the workers had died. The map was destroyed and they became lost for weeks. When they finally reached the site it was being guarded by men loyal to Casim.

"I think Mr. Henry he got a little crazy then, started yelling and shooting. Very bad, Miss. Big argument with one of the men. He shot him," said Saleh. It was too much for the small party, he explained, and Henry had finally agreed to send Saleh to get more supplies, then to Cairo for more men, but three days ago he had been betrayed to the Germans.

He held out his hand to Margaret. Inside it was a string of green beads. They had a curious look. "Don't know. They want these, Miss. They know you're here," he said, trying to rise from the bed. She ran to the telephone and picked up the receiver to dial for a doctor, then realized she had to talk to McQueen and fast.

"Saleh, wait here. I'm going to get a doctor," she said as she came back to the bed. She tried to help him up but the effort to talk to the girl had been too much and with a sudden gasp he fell back, dead. She didn't cry out but picked up the beads after covering the body. With a last look back, she walked quickly to the door. The tears would come later.

Promptly at 1 pm, McQueen walked into the casino wearing a dark suit and a tie borrowed from Sammi. He looked surprisingly at home in the pale wool suit with the polka dot tie, as if he had just stepped out of a meeting at Whitehall.

It was a small room with a roulette wheel, a baccarat table and three poker tables. He estimated the crowd at 80% European and most of them either wealthy or dying to become. His passenger had not yet arrived so he busied himself by walking around the room and observing the players. The play was quiet, hushed and discreet. He recognized the placards as being 5,000 francs each. The men looked grim and purposeful, he reflected. The young German was now wearing a tuxedo and was playing roulette with friends. Several women were on hand as window dressing, a collection of the usual pretty young things that frequent high stakes gambling parlors around the world.

The young German caught sight of McQueen and held his eye a moment, then with a quizzical expression returned to the game. Apparently, he too could not remember.

McQueen was nursing a drink and trying to remember when Sammi came over with a plate of drinks.

"Got something for you. Cost you extra."

"OK. Let's have it." Sammi placed a drink in front of McQueen and when he withdrew his hand there was a small slip of paper, folded, under the drink. He bowed slightly and moved off. McQueen took the note and went around a palm tree. There was just one word: Oedheim. Of course! Suddenly, it all came back to him. Rheinhard Oedheim, the quiet scientist with the intense eyes. That night in Paris, the German professors. They had been talking about physics and the possibilities of fission from uranium or something. He hadn't paid much attention to the details, which were far beyond his grasp anyway. But the leader of the group, the impassioned firebrand was this man Oedheim. But what was he doing in Cairo?

McQueen was starting to put the pieces together when Margaret walked in and every man in the room looked in her direction. She wore a low cut green satin dress and a string of what might have been a diamond necklace from Cartier. She stood beside him a long moment while he tried to remember. What had they been talking about? A weapon. That was it, some sort of theoretical device, one that didn't require dynamite. There had been a lot of discussion about the work of Fermi and others, he recalled. He was trying to concentrate when he became aware that she was standing next to him.

"You look beautiful in that dress," he said, meaning it.

"Thank you."

"You didn't get that at the souk, did you?" he asked, somewhat annoyed at having lost his train of thought.

"Of course not, but a girl should always be prepared." She looked around, lowered her voice. "We have to leave. Now." He glanced at her, not understanding.

"In a few minutes. The Germans want you for some reason, and we're going to let them get a good look and then pick off the stragglers," he responded.

Her attention was diverted to the movement of three men at the far side of the room. They were Germans, they were watching her intently. The senior man issuing orders matched Saleh's description.

She caught up to McQueen as the crowd bunched up near the ornate portico. They slipped through and went to the elevators.

"They've spotted us," she whispered. "They know who I am."

"Who?"

"The Germans. Saleh is dead. He told me ... I know where my father is now. But we have to get out of Cairo and go up river about 600 miles."

They started walking out. "Wait a minute. Who is Saleh?" Over his shoulder, McQueen could see that the three Germans were now hurrying toward them, that they were undoubtedly armed. His instincts told him the situation was about to go very bad.

"Can we talk later?" she said.

"All right," he said. "Let's go. But this will definitely cost extra."

"Fine!"

"Know how to use one of these?" he asked, and held out a thin .25 caliber Beretta pistol. She took it from him and checked the magazine, then slammed it back home and glanced up at him with a knowing smile.

"I might have known. Stay close." He looked around then headed to the stairway door and immediately was taking the stairs two at a time. She was behind him but in the high heels had to keep stopping. At the second floor landing he looked through the glass window in the door, then they hurried down the hall and into her room. "Be back in three minutes. Be ready."

"Three minutes!" He was gone. She began to throw her clothes into the leather suitcase. She debated only a moment about some of the souvenirs she had bought, and tossed them into the trash. With a final look at Saleh's body she went to the door and listened.

The attack on the hotel had all the earmarks of a well rehearsed commando raid. As Margaret was opening the door, a man nobody had seen in the hotel that evening quietly came up behind the house security guard, clamped a hand over his mouth and crushed a potassium cyanide pill beneath the man's nose. There was a brief struggle, all the more horrible for it's silence before the man finally had to take a breath. Death was near instantaneous. The killer then went to the control panel and removed the fuses for that floor, plunging the rooms and hallway into darkness. Simultaneous to this, three men in black overalls entered the hallway and began checking doors.

From her side of the door, she could hear some of this and instinct kept her frozen behind the door. With a start, she realized the latch was turning. She suppressed a scream and started to back away from the door. Almost stumbling over her suitcase in the dark, she turned in time to see the silhouette of a man entering her window. The .25 pistol was in her hand and as she started to raise it there was a quiet voice. "It's me. Don't shoot."

"Prove it," she said shakily.

"I don't have to," the voice said. "That's my gun." she relaxed as he came to her side and listened. "All right, here's the plan," he began, but the words were cut off by the blast of a shotgun, very close, that shattered the door and threw them back against the bed. The girl screamed once, helping the killers locate their target, who they were instructed not to kill. In the distance there was the sound of distant yelling, and of heavy footsteps approaching, then gunfire followed by screams. McQueen knew he had only moments before they were overwhelmed and took the only door left open to him.

"Scream, honey!" he yelled. She did as she was told. The dim light spilling in from the emergency lamps silhouetted the killers against the door. It was enough. With a Colt .45 in each hand, each one with a flash suppressor, he began firing in a rapid sweeping motion across the door, hoping to catch at least two of the men before they returned fire. It was a calculated risk. The killers had automatic weapons as he knew they would, but McQueen had the element of surprise. Caught between their instructions not to harm the hostage, they hesitated just long enough, and in a few moments the three gunmen lay dead on the floor.

McQueen grabbed her hand and they ran. There was a small fire burning at one end of the hallway. They ran to the opposite end, found an open window and looked out. It was a 25 foot drop onto a blacked out patch of what might be cement or shrubs. Too great a chance, he realized, not with the girl. The sound of angry, threatening men's voices yelling in excited German began to get nearer. A frightened guest opened one of the doors and dropped in a hail of gunfire. More screams. McQueen realized now that the Germans, not taking any chances, were methodically opening doors and shooting anyone inside. It was fast becoming a killing jar. In the distance, sirens began to sound, then more. A searchlight played against one of the windows. The footsteps were getting nearer.

She looked at him and somehow he appeared to be calm, which surprised her. It occurred to her this was all in a day's work for McQueen. Across from them was a door.

"Shoot the lock off," he told her, then ran to the hall and began firing shots down the hallway. A burst of automatic fire answered him and he fired back. The bullets hit home and she could hear two men scream briefly and then the sound of bodies hitting the floor. By the time he ran back, she had the door open and was inside.

The room was empty, but there was an open suitcase and clothes on the chair. He noticed the dresser, where a bottle of perfume and a can of lighter fluid had been left. They ran to the back window and opened it. Outside was a fire escape, and 10 feet below them the roof of another building, but perhaps 12 feet away. Footsteps were approaching.

"Grab the sheets, tie two together!" he yelled as he ran to the dresser, grabbed the perfume and lighter fluid and poured it on some pillows all in one fluid motion. He produced a silver cigarette lighter and in a moment the pillows were blazing. He poured the rest of the lighter fluid onto a blanket, tossed the pillows on it and carried the burning bundle out into the hallway, throwing it on the carpet. Instantly, smoke began to fill the corridor. He ran back into the room and they got to the fire escape as more gunfire broke out. He tied one end of the sheet to the railing and looped it around her legs.

"What are you doing?" she yelled as he pushed her off the ledge. "Wait a minute!," she cried out as she swung freely in the air once, twice, and as she was approaching the other roof he took out his knife and cut the sheets just as she swung over the roof, falling the last 5 feet onto the flat surface. There was a muffled cry and then she was on her feet. "You son of a bitch!" she yelled.

By now the smoke was thick everywhere. The door of their room suddenly disintegrated in a hail of bullets as McQueen grabbed the remaining sheet and swung out into space. He landed on his feet and as they ran down the roof toward freedom she looked back in time to see the building engulfed in flame.

Five minutes later, on firm ground again, he pulled her into a shop alcove and caught his breath. The 3rd and 4th floor of the hotel were on fire, the fire engines were starting to arrive and a large crowd had gathered, including several pickpockets. She looked at him a moment, then kissed him on the lips, hard.

"What was that for?"

"Saving my life," she said. Several people were now ignoring the fire and watching them. It was only a matter of minutes, he calculated. They were in a part of old Cairo where the streets are narrow and crowded. It wasn't going to be easy. They needed a car.

As he was beginning to wonder which street to run down, a taxi came around a corner and dropped off a passenger. It was an old woman with a camera, and she had come to see the fire.

"Wait!" she yelled to the taxi.

They pushed through the crowd and into the back seat. The driver started to argue but when he saw the 1000 piastres note, he took it, closed the door and they tore off down the street with the old woman screaming in the rear view mirror.

Two motorcycles now joined the procession, driven by dark men in black masks and heedless of pedestrians. As they rounded a corner, shots rang out and the driver clutched at his throat. The taxi veered left into a news stand, scattering books and souvenirs over the street. McQueen got into the driver's seat, pushed the wounded man aside and put the old Fiat into gear as one of the riders came up beside them and took aim.

"Find something to bandage his throat!" he yelled to a startled Margaret as the taxi bounced down the rough cobblestones leading back to the Nile. Bullets continued to ricochet off the coachwork as she tore off a piece of her blouse and wrapped his neck wound, which was superficial. Behind her she could see the two motorcyclists hurrying through the traffic, 50 feet behind them.

"Get your head down!" he yelled but it was too late. She heard another shot, then her shoulder exploded in pain as a bullet grazed the skin, tearing into the muscle. McQueen looked back. She was bleeding badly. He knew the type of weapon that had been used: even a surface wound would quickly spell death if not attended to immediately.

Up ahead of him was the river, and in the distance he could see the Goose, tied up at the dock, but there was something wrong. A throng of police were marching down the pier toward the Goose, followed by what looked like an angry mob. He could see Eddie standing guard holding a rifle. A shot from behind him broke through the rear glass and narrowly missed his head. In the rear view mirror he could see one of the riders was readying an automatic rifle. They were about 20 yards behind, with only a few pedestrians separating them. In a few seconds they would pull up beside them and it would be over.

He stopped the car suddenly, putting all his weight onto the brake pedal as he pulled up on the emergency brake. Margaret and the injured taxi driver pitched forward, out cold. As the first bullets started to rake the taxi he reversed gears and floored it. Caught between the taxi and the crowded, now screaming, the assailants tried to keep firing while getting out of the way. The rear bumper of the taxi caught the first man just above the knees, broke both legs and as he was dragged under the car yelling for help from his companion, the second motorcycle tipped over and before the man could run the bumper pressed him against the wall of a shop.

McQueen calmly got out of the taxi, shot both men twice in the head and removed their wallets, then got back in and drove off. Pieces of bodies clung to the undercarriage for a few yards before falling off. The last piece to go was the first assailants hand, which had a swastika tattooed on the back.

He parked the taxi near the pier up an alley being used by produce delivery trucks. The driver was alive but he would need medical attention. Margaret had lost some blood and had fainted from the pain, and he knew she would improve when they could lay her down. He wrapped a bandage around her shoulder and asked a passing woman about a doctor. A crowd of onlookers was gathering. It was time to go.

Leaving a few ten pound notes in the driver's pocket, he picked her up as easily as if she were a child and carried her across the street onto the pier. After a few moments she opened her eyes.

"Take it easy," he said. "You've lost some blood but you're going to be OK." She could see the crowd now, the police and the Goose beyond.

"What happened?" she asked finally. " It's bad, isn't it?"

"Maybe. Can you walk a little"

"I think so."

As the dock appeared she witnessed a transformation. McQueen was no longer the tough guy she thought she knew. Instead, he was wearing the biggest, silliest lopsided grin she'd ever seen as he waded through the crowd, talking in Arabic and patting everyone on the back. In moments a large crowd had gathered around him to listen to his story, which she could only guess at. Soon they were laughing. He pointed at something across the street and the crowd went marching off, followed by the three policeman who had come to maintain order without really knowing what was the problem.

"All right, Eddie, let's cast off, quick," he said quietly. "Did you gas her up?"

"Only half a tank. They ran out. I figured we'd have more time."

"You figured wrong."

When they got to the Goose Margaret was bursting with curiosity and as he helped her aboard and onto the long seat that ran down the starboard side of the cabin, she stopped him.

"How did you do that?" Margaret demanded and he grinned the same oddball grin again and despite being in pain she had to laugh. He was embarrassed. If she hadn't been in so much pain she would have laughed out loud. Eddie came over with a syringe of something and slipped it into her arm.

"Hey. What's that?" she asked as he put the needle away in his well-worn leather first aid kit.

"Oh, just antibiotics, some morphine. In this business it's called 'You'll feel swell in a minute'."

"I'll bet I will." She turned to McQueen, who was obviously enjoying it. "Well?"

"OK, it's like this. I just told those guys that there were two dead communists across the way who had tried to impugn the name of Allah and if they wanted to see him before the crowds tore 'em apart they better hurry."

She lay back and could feel the morphine taking hold. "Not bad at all, for a human blowtorch who... never.." and with that her eyes closed and she was out. Eddie strapped her in and they climbed into the cockpit. The pre-flight check was kept to a minimum, and the engines turned over easily.

It was as they were taxiing out into the river that the first bullets started landing in front of them. McQueen could see that the mob had turned, and someone with a rifle was firing and getting closer. There was debris floating in the river ahead.

"Say, what if we hit something, like maybe a submerged tree or something?" asked Eddie, suddenly worried.

"Well, we're no worse off than we'd be if that mob catches up to us." He pushed the throttles all the way forward and the engines roared in response, shaking the airframe fore and aft as the engines reached their peak torque and they began plowing through the river. The plane was heavy at all times, what with the ammunition McQueen always carried, and even with half a tank of gas and supplies it was going to be tricky lifting her off, as McQueen knew. He swung the ship into the wind and they both could see the Abbas II bridge looming in the distance.

"You're not gonna try to jump that thing, are you?"

"Why not? We've done it before."

"Not with this much cargo aboard. And remember, I got a lot to live for."

"Such as?"

"Such as I got a lot of property in Lisbon and I don't want my ex-wife to get her hands on it."

"You always were a greedy SOB," McQueen muttered.

"Dammit, Joe, why don't we taxi under it? That's the sensible thing to do. What's wrong with that? Plenty of room on the other side!"

"Because we don't have time. Look!" yelled McQueen over the din, pointing at something on the far shore. A contingent of Germans had arrived and one of them was aiming a heavy caliber gun at them. Eddie gulped once and hung on.

With the throttles fully opened, the ship began to gather speed. Almost immediately, gunfire began to erupt from the Germans, but it was wide of the mark and now they were up to 70 knots and the stick was beginning to respond. Eddie knew it was no use reasoning with McQueen when he was like this, but it was going to be close. The air temperature was cool but Eddie's forehead was covered with cold sweat as the plane began to climb up to the wave tops.

A small explosion detonated in the water to their left at about 9 o'clock, then another to their right at 2 o'clock. At 85 knots and full flaps McQueen pulled back on the stick and the Goose rose slowly into the air, cleared the bridge and its startled pedestrians by five feet and slowly banked away from the city.

"Now what?" asked Eddie.

McQueen looked at his map of Egypt. "Up river was all she said." McQueen had a look at Margaret, who was still out.

"South it is," said Eddie, and as the Goose dipped her wing toward the south, he began calculating their fuel range and possible landfalls.

Chapter 5

THE NUBIAN DESERT stretches from the Red Sea halfway to Libya, a landscape inhospitable to man and beast. The sand had been blowing for almost a week now, and the old man with the sunburned face covered in sores carefully tried again to work out map coordinates, but they were useless. Henry held the sextant in one hand as the sun climbed to its zenith and again tried to calculate their longitude. But the delirium was worse now and he was having trouble controlling his shaking. He stopped and sat down in the sand underneath the cliff face where there would be some shade.

It was now four weeks since he had sent Saleh away for more supplies and the last of the men had run away. He cursed again out loud his poor luck with hiring workers and his own poor planning, but there was little time to indulge in such diversions. His chief problem was that the water was running low. He had calculated how much longer it would last and he was now down to a matter of days. The sandstorm had hidden the wells that he knew of, the ones the Bedouin had dug ages ago and which sometimes still had water. He took out his battered pocket journal and looked again at his notes from the first discovery of the site and tried to remember. Yes, the low hills were on the left. That much he had right. And he knew the dry river bed was nearby but had been unable to find it. With some effort he got to his feet and began to search.

And then he saw it. In the distance, perhaps a hundred yards away, was a tall stick protruding from the sand. On top was tied a red cloth. He remembered that Mustapha belonged to a tribe that buried their dead with such a marker to ward off evil spirits. He remembered too that after Casim had left him to die, he had buried Mustapha as the last act of the ill-fated expedition. This had to be it. He began walking. Involuntarily, he shouted for joy.

An hour later he stood on the spot and tried to remember. The shallow ravine had been close by, perhaps 50 yards away, that's right. Only 50 yards, he reassured himself. Down the long slope where the men had camped out, then turn right and into the desert. It took another 20 minutes but it was still there. The sand had buried most of the site, but the ledge was intact and he fell to his knees and began digging with his hands. An hour later he felt it. The brass door.

But he could do no more today, and it took all his strength to return to his pack and drag the leather satchels he had salvaged after the mules had died. Dragging them to the door, he closed his eyes with his face on the sand. It had to be there, he told himself. He would find one of the wells and it would be alright. His mind went through the long checklist he used to keep himself sane, to maintain a semblance of purpose, but the answers would not come and at last he fell into a dreamless sleep.

The next morning he indulged himself and drank a full cup of water and ate some of the dried Egyptian peaches he had saved, and with new energy began to clear away the sand from the door. It was backbreaking work. The sand had to be carried out of the site and up a narrow ramp. Moving the last of it took all his strength and he had to stop for 30 minutes to let his heart stop laboring. When he had cleared away the edges he removed one of the sticks of dynamite, cut it in half and wedged it into the corner, trying to judge how close to the door he should go. He only needed a small hole. He lit the fuse and staggered away. He hated to destroy the door because it was so beautiful, but there was no choice now.

The explosion knocked him off his feet, even though he was 50 feet away around a wall of the cliff face. He prayed that the blast hadn't simply re-buried the entrance in rocks, and hurried back to wait for the dust to settle. The door was still intact, but now there was a large hole in the stone wall next to it and he could see inside for the first time. His heart began racing as he pushed the stones inside and, tying a rope around his waist and securing it to a nearby boulder, peered into the cave.

The cave-as Underwood thought of it - had lain untouched for more than 5,000 years now, and in all that time no trace of sunlight or air had entered the tomb. He could smell the aroma of wood and the dust and a kind of sweet smell he couldn't identify but which might have once been fruit. The space was about a hundred feet deep and twice that wide, and there was a pile of boulders that looked like they had been left by the workers as a staircase to the entrance. He wondered what had happened to them, because the Egyptian custom often called for the entombment of such unfortunates, but there was no sign of bones or other human remains. He located his torch in the leather satchel and began to climb down. It took almost 20 minutes to reach the bottom.

Dropping to the floor, he was surprised to find it was made of polished stone, of a dark grey material, and that the edges were flawlessly joined and immaculately clean. Around the room were bas relief images of very tall figures, he estimated 50 feet high. In the dim light he could not distinguish their features, and he had a fleeting image of a rich career of continual visits to the site to mine its historical treasures and the lecture tours which would surely follow. But most of all he felt the thrill of vindication for a job long undertaken against tall odds. Whatever happened now, he had come to the end of his journey.

The room he stood in was a kind of entrance chamber, essentially a large foyer, and he could see the outline of a very large door, about 20 feet high, on the far wall. It was inlayed with gold and precious stones. He imagined that this once lead up some kind of ramp, perhaps richly decorated for ceremonial purposes, and then when it was freshly built the site had been lushly planted and the entranceway would have been clean and wide.

There was also a second door, much smaller, on the adjoining wall, and to this he now walked. He could see there was another, much larger chamber beyond the door, and that it was a few feet lower than where he was standing. As he approached it some sixth sense urged caution, and it was just as well because, hidden from the light of the torch was a narrow slot in the floor where the four broad steps went down at the entrance. He had nearly overlooked it, so cleverly was it disguised, and he could see that it was about 5 feet wide. Peering into the darkness, the abyss seemed to stretch to infinity.

Jumping over this, the light now cast shadows on a vast room that stretched for hundreds of feet into the darkness. He recognized from his research what this room must be, and stood for some minutes in simple awe of the fact that he was in the king's audience hall; that no living man had stood here for at least 50 centuries. There were more statues encased in the wall, and at the far end an enormous throne.

Outside a warm wind was now blowing, and the hole in the entrance made an eerie moaning sound. He approached the throne, his footsteps echoing against the polished granite walls, their blue and green paint now faded but the glory of vanished days plainly evident. They showed dozens of scenes: of a great man, being rowed on a river, the king driving an early chariot into battle, slaying a tiger. Others depicted family life and a large single sun in the sky. There were benches set on either side of the great hall, and the ones in front were covered in the remains of what would have been tiger skin, which looked strangely vibrant in the flickering light.

Beneath the throne was a white marble bench, enormously heavy and wide and set at the height of a man's waist. On it was a singular item, a black onyx box. With trembling hands he put down the torch and opened the box.

Inside was a single papyrus scroll, about 1 foot in width, wrapped in a leather sleeve. It was surprisingly heavy. He lifted it out and sat down on the smooth marble steps. The heaviness was explained: the scroll was wrapped around what looked like a solid gold core. It occurred to him that the value of the artifact was beyond his ability to calculate.

The moaning of the wind was less now, and his nerves began to ease up. He took a sip of the precious water and carefully began to unroll the brown scroll onto the floor. After he had revealed about 30 centimeters he realized that the scroll was too brittle to read here and would have to be taken to a museum with proper restoration facilities.

Still, there was the first few inches waiting for him, and carefully placing small stones at the corners, he began to read. The language was that of the Old Kingdom, a mixture of cunieform and heiroglyphics, and it was only haltingly that he was able to reconstruct the message. As the words materialized on his journal page his jaw slowly dropped and he was aware of a tingling in his fingers. It was all there. In his deep Midlands baritone, he heard himself slowly reciting the words. "I Nester, Pharaoh of the two Kingdoms, write this scroll to my brother, known to men as the prophet Abraham."

"My God," he whispered. Quickly, fearing the ancient leaf would crack, he deciphered the next few stanzas, not sure of what the words meant. When he came to the end and tried to open more of the scroll, there was a sharp crack and a piece of the edge dislodged itself and fell to the floor. He carefully rolled up the scroll and replaced it in the sleeve.

He was suddenly weak from hunger. He knew the signs. He would have to return to the surface for his pack. But no matter. The find of a lifetime was within his grasp.

The next two days were spent cataloging what he had found, which he stacked up neatly on the marble bench. Several times he had to stop himself from hyper-ventilating, as each new find added to the staggering revelation hidden in the sand for 50 centuries. There were coins, some of them quite large, small golden pieces inlaid with precious stones and the scroll. All of this he carefully wrapped in oilskin and then placed into waiting leather cases. In all the booty weighed some 50 pounds, but it was manageable.

After five days the work was finished. He emerged one last time from the outer chamber, carefully filled in the blast hole with rocks and covered everything in sand. He stared at it a long time, and could see no sign that would tip an intruder to the location. Then, after a light lunch, he loaded the camels, consulted his compass and moved off due east. With luck he would reach Banbuku in six days, just about the time his rations ran out.

• • •

About one hour flying time south of Cairo was a small trading post called Wadi Halifa. It was seldom seen by

Westerners since there was nothing there but a few huts providing provisions to some of the large farms that grew cotton by the banks of the Nile. It normally kept a small inventory of gasoline on hand for the few vehicles that plied the dirt roads leading away from the river into the desert. The prices at these trading posts were ridiculously high.

McQueen knew all this as he glanced at his fuel gauge. They were flying at 7,000 feet and their passenger was still unconscious.

"I'm gonna put her down. Get ready!" he yelled.

"What's the rush?" said Eddie. "You know what happened last time." McQueen merely pointed to the gas gauge. "We gotta get organized around here," muttered Eddie as McQueen cut back the throttle and the Goose began to circle for a landing.

Ten minutes later they were taxiing up to the small jetty. McQueen took a handful of cash and handed it to Eddie. "Pay 'em quick before they remember. I'll get on the pump." As they touched the dock, Eddie tossed a line to a dark man in a dashiki with a rifle over his shoulder. The man stared intently at Eddie but tied off the bow line. Moments later Eddie was on the planks, hurrying toward the little shed where he knew his nemesis would be waiting. McQueen began filling up the tanks as he listened to the men arguing.

It was as he was manning the pump that he noticed their passenger getting unsteadily to her feet. She almost fell over before finding her way to the open hatch and looking out.

"Where are we?" she asked.

"Place called Wadi Hafifa."

"Where?"

"Trading post. If you've got some idea of where we go next, this would be a good time to tell us."

"Why?" she mumbled, not feeling well.

"Because in about 10 minutes that man at the hut up there is going to start remembering a little problem we had here a couple of years ago, and he's going to want money. A lot of it. I'd just as soon leave before that happens."

"Good idea," she allowed. She rummaged through her pack, found a map and came out onto the dock. The day was blazing hot and she didn't have a hat on. McQueen lent her his ball cap. "Thanks." She looked over the map.

"And while you're at it, I want some answers about why the Germans find you and your father so interesting, or we're turning this thing back to Lisbon," he added with a hard stare. She found the man alternately charming and appallingly blunt. This was one of the blunt moments.

Despite the urgency of the situation, while he was talking she began to think again about poor Saleh, who had been her only friend in Kordafan, and the image of him made her want to weep. He had been a good man, a good friend, and she had reached the age of understanding in which those qualities are known to be all too rare.

The loud arguing with Eddie and the trader had stopped and Eddie was hurrying back down the jetty. It didn't look good, she reflected. "All right. I'll tell you what I know," she began, and the story, which she dreaded having to tell after Cairo, poured out of her more easily than she imagined, the missing pieces of the puzzle seemingly finding their way into the slots. The full story, she knew, was too long for now, having to do with her father's motives, which he largely shielded from her but which she had long guessed. The abbreviated story she told McQueen was enough: they had been searching for months when the first German "trader" had contacted them on one of their resupply missions to Banbuku. They had been in the desert two years by then, searching in various sites, and the locals knew them as English and apparently well financed. Her father always carried cash and the so-called African trading beads with him, and was able to quickly settle for supplies or services in any village. Of particular value were the beads. They were bright green, and in some lighting conditions glowed slightly in the dark. In truth, they were much more valuable than gold by weight, and in time the word had gotten around that the Englishman had an unlimited supply.

When the first German, a very pleasant man named Hahn had arrived one day on camel, they had given him lunch and Henry had freely given him a few of his green beads. Months later, Hahn had returned, this time in the company of two men who looked like soldiers. Gone was the politeness. They wanted to know the source of the green beads and were prepared to pay well for the knowledge. For reasons she never understood Henry had dodged the issue, complaining that they were a trivial thing, of no real value, and that the man who made them was a friend of his and wanted to remain anonymous. He wanted to know why they wanted the beads and they told a story about wanting to recruit local workers for a rail line they hoped to build that would connect the remnants of the old German East protectorate in Tanganyika and the western territory in Zambia. Henry ridiculed the idea.

They had then talked into the night, and the Germans had brought excellent brandy with them, knowing that Henry had a taste for good brandy. But despite all the liquor, they could not get the secret from him, and when they left in the morning, there had been words exchanged, which she had not heard but which left Henry shaken. Shortly after that they had moved to another site, and Henry began to take greater care to mask his movements.

Then six months ago they had come back, and as Henry was now close to his find, he wanted nothing to do with menacing Germans over something which he considered nonsense. The Germans had been searching for the source of the green stone without success, and now offered more money for the secret. There had been an argument, and the Germans had killed several of Henry's men before he had driven them off.

After that encounter, she explained, she had joined him and the work had continued. She had seen Saleh, and learned that Casim had gone over to the Germans, that they were again searching for her father, and that her only hope now was to find him and remove him, by force if necessary, from Africa.

She paused in her story and looked at McQueen. "Why all this interest in the Germans? You're an American, a neutral. What is it to you?" He finished the refueling, put away the gas hose and looked at Eddie, who had listened to most of the story in silence. He seemed to her suddenly troubled by something.

"He just wants more money," interrupted Eddie with a wink before McQueen could speak.

"Yeah. Excuse me," McQueen said pleasantly to her. "Eddie, get ready to move fast."

She watched McQueen walk away. "I don't understand," she said.

"It's like this. Up until two years ago he was a Navy pilot."

"U.S. Navy?"

"That's right. Lieutenant Commander, sea planes. I was his mechanic. We flew recon flights out of Pensacola, but when Congress passed the Neutrality Act, everything changed. Went right to hell. Suddenly we were a bunch of paper pushers. When we ran into the Japanese or the Germans they told us to back off. Had our hands tied but good. Well, Joe didn't want any part of that. Me neither. There's a war coming, Miss, sooner or later, so he went over to the admiral and..." he suddenly stopped, realizing he was going too far. He took a bite of chewing tobacco, stuffed it into his cheek. "Anyway, the rest I can't talk about, but that's kind of why we like to keep an eye on our Aryan friends."

She thought about this for a long moment and made no sign except a barely perceptible nod. McQueen returned, looking relieved and happy. "We made a deal, but Kaviz says there's some kind of revolt going on up river. Somebody's stirring up the locals against the British. Said the Dinka tribe is behind it, and we should avoid the place at all costs. You know anything about the Dinkas?"

"No," she said.

"They enjoy killing people. It's like a sport with them. And they hate the British."

"Not too keen about Americans neither," added Eddie.

"Would this have anything to do with your father and his expedition?" he asked as he got in behind the wheel. He looked at the girl and waited. She shook her head.

"I don't know. Probably."

"So, where to?" Eddie asked. "I got plenty of work lined up in Lisbon, Joe. We could be back in a couple of days."

McQueen nodded and looked at the girl. It was a common occupational hazard. Plans changed, objectives became fluid, and with it the margin for error got smaller. He knew all this, but he also knew it was too late to turn back.

She put her finger on the map. "There. He said that if he couldn't come to to Cairo, he'd try to make it to Banbuku. There's a rendezvous point, on the edge of town. If he's there, we could be in and gone in a few minutes." She looked at him hopefully.

"This wasn't part of the deal, Joe" said Eddie.

"I know," he said.

"That's right in the middle of the fighting," noted Eddie, taking out a small ledger book. "Means another 800 gallons of fuel, supplies, ammunition probably. Good chance of getting killed."

"That's what we're being paid for, isn't it?" snapped McQueen.

"I guess so."

"All right. Set a course for Banbuku." He turned to the girl. "Then what?"

"I have a plan."

"Let's hear it," McQueen said as Eddie started going through his pre-flight check list.

"Well, if you're gonna talk I wish you'd hurry it up, because we got company," said Eddie, pointing to something off the port bow. It was a large dhow in full sail, rapidly approaching them, and well positioned to block the only route they had to open water for a take off.

"What's that?" she asked.

"Pirates most likely," said McQueen. "They're going to want to shoot first and loot second. Eddie, take the wheel. You, get strapped in. We're leaving." McQueen ran to the back of the plane and brought out a Browning M2 machine gun, fed an ammunition belt into it, mounted it under the window on a bracket built into the bulkhead and started opening a window.

Eddie fired the port engine and as it shuddered into life he looked outside. "Hey, we're still tied up! Somebody go outside and cast off!" he said. Seeing McQueen was busy, Margaret clambered out the door onto the dock as the second engine coughed to life and the prop wash almost blew her over the edge.

"Sorry," he mumbled, watching the pressure gauges climb. She had just cast off the line when the plane lurched forward and began moving down the dock. Shots began coming in from the dhow, now about 50 yards away and closing. She ran with the plane to the end of the dock and jumped. Her hand barely caught the edge of the open door and she screamed once.

"What was that?" asked Eddie.

"What the hell are you doing?" yelled McQueen, "Swing to the left," and he now had the attackers in his sights and began to fire short bursts. As the plane began to move he looked around.

"Hey! Where's the girl?" he asked, but Eddie didn't hear him. Then McQueen heard another scream, this one fainter than before and looked out the starboard side. She was clinging to the open door frame and calling out. McQueen cursed softly under his breath, reached across and pulled her inside as the Goose began to build up speed, heading straight at the pirates.

Eddie swerved the plane again, giving McQueen a good angle, and he raked the pirate ship with the Browning again, knocking holes in the wood. Most of the men on board jumped into the water as McQueen fired again. Eddie banked to the left and brought the Goose into mid stream, checked the wind direction and pushed the throttles all the way forward.

Margaret was laying on the floor and McQueen went to her, took her in his arms and picked her up. "Are you all right?" he asked. She nodded and he got her onto the seat and ran forward to the cockpit. They were picking up speed but something was wrong. Eddie throttled back and got into the co-pilot seat as McQueen scrambled behind the wheel and looked at the gauges. He flipped a switch.

"You forgot the flaps," was his deadpan response and with the throttles pushed forward, the Goose quickly mounted the small waves and became airborne. Behind them, the dhow was beginning to sink. McQueen brought out a map, showed Eddie where he wanted to go and went aft.

She was drenched and shivering when he got to her. He found a blanket from behind the seat and wrapped it around her shoulders. "That was a gutsy thing you did back there. Thanks."

"Don't mention it," she said and as Eddie banked the plane heading for their next landfall, near the sixth cataract, she tried to calm her breathing.

Chapter 6

IT WAS LATE afternoon and there were storm clouds moving in when McQueen began to drop down. Margaret was crouching behind him and they had been discussing what they would do when they entered a break in the clouds and the river valley was suddenly visible below. The Nile was slow moving here at the mouth of the Obeadah Valley, and the sharp distinction betwen desert and grasslands was clear to see. In the green distance she could see a range of hills rising into the west, but closer to the river all was desert. It was a desolate place, like much of the Sahara, alleviated only occasionally by the presence of civilization and she looked forward to seeing Sheik Ali again and her friends in the compound.

The first sign she had that something was wrong was the tall pillar of white and black smoke in the far distance. It reached about a mile into the sky and already she could sense the smell of burnt wood.

"What's that?" she said.

"That's Banbuku," said McQueen.

The plane did a slow flyover of the town, much of it shrouded in smoke. Whatever had happened was recent, they could see, and there was not a single person to be seen.

"I say we turn around and go back to Cairo," said Eddie, floating his trial balloon. In response, McQueen looked at Margaret.

"Well?" he said. "what do you say? It's your party." She thought for a moment and nodded. That was enough for McQueen. He cut the engine and began the long descending turn that would bring them to the west bank of the river. As he did so, Eddie went to the back and brought out the heavy case that contained their hand guns and ammunition and began checking the arms.

The landing was uneventful and with a light breeze blowing away the smoke, they could finally see the blackened buildings clearly. There was a British flag pole bent at a crazy angle, the flag partially burned and touching the ground. Several bodies were laying in the street and these had been set on fire. Small fires continued to smolder and the stench of burning flesh was everywhere.

The dock was only partially destroyed and Eddie jumped out and tied up the Goose without incident. Outside it was quiet, not even the usual sounds of birds could be heard.

McQueen got out of the plane and looked around. Whoever did this was both ruthless and thorough, he reflected.

Ten minutes later they had reached the end of the dock and stood where the small trading post had been. There was no sign of life. The windows had been broken and the mud bricks scorched, but it had not been looted. That was a curious thing, thought McQueen. If an African tribe had done this, looting would have been number one on the agenda. Margaret looked around the desolate scene and wept.

"Why?" she asked of no one in particular. They began to walk. Everywhere they looked it was all the same. A few bodies, blackened buildings, the odd goat or chicken wandering around. They walked slowly down the riverfront road to the compound of Sheik Ali. Like the rest of the town it had been burned, but here there were signs that the defenders had put up a fight. Several of the dead still held their rifles, and along the upper level of the tower there were bullet holes in the walls. As elsewhere, the scene was deserted.

"I'd say this happened yesterday. What does it look like to you?" said McQueen to Eddie.

"Like a big force of men moved in and rounded up most of the people. Some of 'em put up a fight, but not many. See those tracks over there?" Eddie pointed to a line of tracks leading off into the desert. "They were in trucks, some of 'em."

They walked through the compound but found no one alive. Margaret called out to Ali. They found the barracks where Ali's men were quartered. Several men had been lined up against a wall and shot. McQueen stared at the scene a few minutes.

"Did you know him?" she asked.

"Ali? Yes, I knew him, slightly. Good man," was all he said. He took Eddie aside and they talked for a few minutes while Margaret went on searching around the compound. She hoped her father might have come here, but there was no sign of him and his upstairs bedroom showed no signs of visitors.

When she came downstairs McQueen and Eddie were still talking. Eddie had found a few expended ammunition clips and was examining them.

"German all right. Probably Mauser," said Eddie.

"You said there was a rendezvous point near here?" McQueen asked. She nodded.

"It was the home of a friend of my father's, on the outskirts of town - if it's still standing. It was a place where a man could hide for a long time."

The wreckage on the edge of the town was more intact, as if the invaders had run out of time or patience and had simply marched through. There were a few children wandering around, but they hid when McQueen and company approached and nothing they could say would bring them out of their hiding places. They found the small stone house without incident but it was empty. There was a trap door in the center, leading to a large cellar and this too was vacant.

McQueen seemed to make up his mind when they climbed back to the surface. "It's like this. I've got to find your father. I can't explain everything now, but it's more than just rescuing a man. We also have to find out where they're going to. If the Germans are up to something, my friends in Lisbon are going to want to know about it. OK?"

"I understand."

"Good," he grinned, looking relieved. "Eddie is going to fly you back to Cairo. You can catch a commercial flight from there. You'll get your money back. And if we find him alive, I promise we'll get him out somehow. Oh, and I'll be needing that little map you carry around." He smiled again and started walking toward the river with Eddie. The conversation was over.

"I'm not going back," she snapped. The men stopped. "I came here to find my father, and I intend to, with or without you."

"You know what this means?" McQueen snapped back.

"I do."

He hesitated a long moment. "All right. We have to find a guide."

• • •

20 miles south of Banbuku was the small village of El Hafin, and later that afternoon, the Goose tied up and camoflaged, they walked into the souk and made inquiries. It was market day, and there were several camels being auctioned off. They bought six of these from an old man with no teeth who was openly suspicious until he realized McQueen was an American, at which point all difficulties melted. His nephew, Benny, he announced, would be happy to be their guide, for a small additional fee. Margaret showed him the area they were going to and the old man said there were wells in that place and that he would draw a map for Benny. It was the best deal they were going to get and they paid for the camels and asked if anyone knew what had happened at Banbuku. But whoever they asked merely looked away.

For the next two days, while the camels were readied and supplies assembled, McQueen and Eddie busied themselves with preparations for the trip and with long discussions of how best to protect the Goose. Eddie suggested he fly it back to the relative safety of Cairo and perhaps recruit a few guards, but in the end decided to stay in El Hafin when he saw - to his great relief - that the locals were friendly and only wanted to be left alone.

On the third day they left the village. Eddie watched the tiny procession from the river for a long time as it wound up the hills into the desert and then finally vanished.

For six days McQueen, Benny and the stubborn English beauty traveled in near silence. Hoping to escape detection, they avoided camels and caravans and detoured around two small villages. The job was made easier by the fact that most of the traffic swung farther south where the water was plentiful. They were following one of the ancient caravan routes her father had shown her, but which soon reduced down to a single rut and then disappeared from time to time.

As to their ultimate destination, Henry had written her two letters during his absence, and there were clues as to the location but that was all. McQueen didn't like it but there was little he could do until they got closer. It was, in fact, a poor plan, but if there was a chance of catching the Germans red handed he had to press on.

It was on the 7th day that the robbers came. Benny had seen something in the distance and they had spent time looking for it, but when the dust cloud failed to reappear they dismissed it as a mirage. That night they took extra precautions with the camels, even tying them all together with tin pots hanging from the lines. McQueen sat up that night, his rifle inches away, but finally fell asleep.

When they awoke in the morning three of the camels and most of their water were gone. The thieves had taken only the animals without the alarms hanging from them. McQueen and Benny searched all that morning and found the tracks of several camels, but it was windy that day and the prints soon vanished in the sand.

During the march that day there was almost no talking. They rationed the water carefully and talking only meant a further drain on their resources. But that night, as he sat by the fire, staring into space, he could hear her crying. He waited until Benny had gone to sleep and went over to join her.

"Doing OK?" he asked. It was a statement of fact. She knew there was little room in McQueen's world for pity.

"I'm all right. Really." She dried her tears and forced a smile. "We're not going to make it, are we?"

"All depends on how fast we find one of the wells. The Bedouins hide theirs pretty good. I talked to Benny. He thinks he knows where one is, not too far from here."

"It's all my fault. I was a fool to try and find him. He always shows up, fit as a horse, no matter what I do."

"Maybe not this time. Say, I brought you a present," he said, and handed her a small jug of water. "Just a small sip."

She tipped it back and felt the cool liquid on her tongue an instant, then handed it back to him.

"You've been holding out."

"You have to plan ahead out here. I was saving it for a special occasion."

"Thanks. What special occasion?"

"Well, I figure you're the only one who knows where we're going. Gotta keep you alive. How special is that?" He grinned at her and got up. She watched him walk back to his blanket and lay down and tried not to think about anything but surviving another day.

•   •   •

The monotony was finally broken on the tenth day. McQueen had stopped to take a sighting off the sun when he noticed Benny had also stopped and was pointing at something in the distance. Both men watched in silence as the slow moving cloud of dust crawled across the horizon. Margaret joined them.

"What is it," she asked.

"Caravan, Miss," Benny answered. "Big one." McQueen got down from his camel, took out his binoculars and had a look.

"I didn't think there were any more slaves in this part of the world," she said.

"A few," said McQueen. "It's all quiet now, not like the old days . They get the girls from Cairo and Beirut, then run 'em by the old caravan routes south, away from the French patrols, and into the big markets in Morocco."

The caravan was about 500 meters long, and was travelling slowly. There were innumerable camels, some laden with dashikis for carrying passengers, and several dozen horse drawn wagons. McQueen rode over to Benny.

"This is very bad men, sir. Very bad. I know these men. We wait here until they pass."

"No, we go and do some trading. They've got water and we don't." He rode over to Margaret. "I want you to put on everything you can, and then wrap yourself in a blanket. Do it now before they spot us."

"Blanket? In this heat? What for? I'll burn up," she said

"Better a little hot than getting taken as a slave," he said. She started to argue but he stopped her. "Margaret, we don't have any choice. They get one look at that body of yours and we'll have the sheiks in a bidding war, and that can only end one way. Either I'm dead or you are. They have at least 50 guns on their side. Go over behind the camel and put on those clothes. Try to look like a boy." He chanced to look up. There were two riders approaching them. "We don't have much time." She nodded and hurried to the camel, which was now kneeling down. Benny and McQueen walked out to greet the riders and to distract them from the girl.

The two were of the Azande tribe, which means they were horse traders and nomads. They wore the long green and purple robes of the tribe plus the gold tassels that indicated they were members of the sheik's immediate family. McQueen could see that they each carried a heavy pistol and the traditional curved dagger, and he guessed that they knew how to use both. They had the hard, distrusting eyes of the nomad and their beards were trimmed short for the desert.

The taller of the two men approached McQueen and bowed shortly. "I am Nazir," he said in Arabic. "This is my brother Mekram. Are you only two?" he asked in a raspy voice, the words slow and carefully chosen. The other man was scanning their camp and had caught sight of the camel and the girl. She was standing up now, wrapped in a blanket and a low hat that obscured her figure. McQueen noticed that Nazir was also looking at the strange figure, that his gaze was more than casual. He wondered how many times this man had encountered similar deceptions.

"I am McQueen, this is Benny. Our companion is a slave boy we bought in Khartoum at the tent of Omar the Arabian.

"Yes, I know him," said the man called Nazir. "A good man. How much did you pay?"

"Fifty pieces of gold," said McQueen, trying to remember the going rate.

"We have many slaves. Our prices are very good and our terms are generous. Would you care to be the guest of Sheik Ibrahim at our table tonight?" said Mekram, smiling. "Perhaps we might have something that would be of interest."

"Perhaps," said McQueen. "Please give our thanks to the Sheik and say that we would be honored." The men bowed and McQueen watched the two Arabs ride back to the caravan, which had stopped a mile away. Margaret walked up and watched them go.

"Well, that does it," said McQueen. Margaret was sweating heavily now and took off the heavy blanket.

"What does that mean?" she asked.

"It means they know more than they're saying," he said, and began cleaning his pistol.

•   •   •

The sun was going down as they rode up to the slave caravan. It was still very hot and Margaret was sweating profusely. McQueen wanted to be early and to get a good look at their numbers. On each of the three camels were empty water casks and skins. Benny was very nervous and tended to twitch at every shout or random sound. The girl, dressed now in a flowing robe and headdress borrowed from

Benny and her face roughed up by sand and dirt, concentrated on what McQueen had told her, which was to avoid talking at all costs. She was trembling slightly and hoped it didn't show.

"What do I do if someone demands an answer or something?" she thought suddenly. McQueen never altered his gait.

"Just remember, our only job is to get water and leave. If you get in a spot, make out like your throat is all raw and make a funny noise." She thought this was preposterous but said no more.

The caravan was like a small city. They had made camp for the night and there was music coming from several tents. The smells were a mixture of sweat, perfume and what might be roasting goat. As they passed the tents she could see inside some of the larger ones. There were great rugs on the sand forming a floor, and sitting on these would generally be a collection of men in robes talking and watching the entertainment. In each tent there was a slave girl, nearly naked, dancing to the sound of an Arabic stringed instrument called a *sintir*. The girls were generally young, no more than 20 she estimated, and very attractive.

What she was soon to learn was that Sheik Ibrahim had a reputation as the purveyor of the finest harem girls in all Africa, and his fame even extended to the royal houses of

Arabia and beyond. In general his girls were all well treated and could play an instrument and tell marvelous stories. They tended to command very high prices and some had even married into the houses of wealthy merchants and royalty.

As they rode on, passing tent after tent and seeing the large number of girls, he hoped that perhaps there was little to fear from the old trader. One look at Margaret told him she was clearly flushed from the heat.

They were nearing the head of the caravan, where one very large tent had been set up, guarded by several very tall sub-Saharan African tribesmen. They eyed him carefully and were about to unshoulder their rifles when Nazir rode up, all smiles, and welcomed them.

"Come in, friends, and make yourselves welcome. We have food and drink, and perhaps you will then tell us about your adventures in Khartoum with the good Omar," he said, pulling back the ornately embroidered flap of the sheik's tent. McQueen bowed to Nazir, as did Benny and Suleiman, which was the name McQueen had given her.

Inside was a spectacle of luxury she would have thought impossible. The walls of the tent were covered in rich Persian tapestries, with matching rugs covering the sand which had been raked smooth. There was fresh fruit overflowing a table, jugs of wine and what looked like a freshly roasted pig.

Ibrahim himself was something of a rascal. A fat, jovial man with a quick wit and a quicker dagger, he had risen over the years to the top of his profession by being both discreet and opportunistic, a talent highly valued by his customers. It was sometimes said that he wept at the prospect of selling some of his favorites, but after all, business was business. All of this, plus the fact that he told wonderful jokes and could put anyone at ease, made him welcome from Casablanca to Tehran.

Most of this history was well known to McQueen, who had had dealings with the Sheik once or twice in his other capacity as ad hoc negotiator. In their last encounter McQueen had been able to trade a used refrigerator for a girl belonging to a friend of his in Tripoli, and Ibrahim had always respected McQueen's resourcefulness. But there was a ruthless side to the man, seldom seen but held in check just beneath the surface, for the situations where good manners and money are not enough. McQueen didn't relish getting on the man's bad side.

"Come in, my friends, come in!" the voice boomed as the Sheik came forward and greeted McQueen warmly. "It has been many years. Too long. You must tell me what you've been up to, my friend, and I mean everything," he said, shaking with laughter. Margaret could see why he was so successful. This was a man whom few would say no to.

McQueen took a seat. "My companions, Benny and Suleiman, also thank you, Sheik. I would be happy to tell you more but we have met with ill fortune and have lost most of our water."

"Water is very scarce out here, is it not?" said the Sheik.

"Indeed, and we would trade with you for a few jugs. Benny?" he indicated to the guide, who immediately brought forth a jeweled box for just such a purpose. "A rare box for books, from the silk markets of Khartoum," he added. Ibrahim looked it over for a moment and set it aside without comment. All the while, his eyes had been returning to the girl, as if to penetrate her disguise were a form of entertainment to him. He smiled at McQueen's gambit.

"Thank you, but I have too many such boxes already. Is it not possible you have other gifts with which to tempt me?" he asked, and his smile embraced them all. McQueen realized that the game was up, much quicker than he had expected.

"But let us not decide such weighty matters on an empty stomach," and the sheik clapped his hands once. Instantly, three slave girls entered the tent, bearing platters of food. McQueen thought he had seldom seen such beautiful girls before, all of them dressed in gossamer thin silks that barely concealed the swell of their breasts and the rounded curves of their stomachs.

As McQueen was debating his next move, there was a brief but vivid interruption, a reminder that the Sahara was ever home to the unexpected. The calm was broken by the sound of a noisy crowd approaching. The entrance to the great tent was pulled back and in walked a man McQueen had never wished to see again. His name was Tarik, an English speaking renegade Algerian rumored to have interests in girls, gold, diamonds and guns, and his business with the sheik was the procurement and sale of southern European slaves, almost always female. He had with him two such specimens this night, and they were high spirited and fighting their captors to the end. Tarik spotted McQueen and turned aside for a moment.

"Joe McQueen. What was the last time?" said the man.

"Malta. '36. You were trying to abduct a woman from the British ambassador's guest house as I recall."

"And you stopped me. I remember. You're in my world now, Yank. Remember that. If you're alive after this maybe we'll talk over old times." There was a nasty sneer as he spat the words out. Tarik's group gathered before the Sheik. McQueen thought he caught a sneer of triumph on Tarik's face as he glanced at him.

"Noble Sheik! Men of the Sahara," he began boldly. "What am I bid for these two perfect specimens of womanhood? The first one is from a prominent family in Italy." With that he tore off the covering of the girl, revealing a slightly plump body and blue eyes.

"And this one! I acquired her from the gardens of Tunisia. Behold, she is French, and greatly skilled in all the arts. Her hair is like silk, her teeth as pure as pearls, and she speaks three languages. What am I bid?" The second girl held her head up high, and as Tarik recited her virtues she never blinked or showed any fear. "As a bonus, I offer you the rarest of trade goods, suitable for commerce on the great African continent. Behold!" he said, and with a flourish opened a small jewel encrusted chest. Everyone leaned forward. Inside were hundreds of trade beads, including a special section with the highly prized green glass beads used by many of the traders in human inventory. He knew his offer would draw interest and waited for the fish to swim to the bait.

But as the Sheik stood up, his tone was desultory. "Alas my friend, we do not trade in such things. If the girl is truly French, the Legionnaires will be looking for her. We prefer to conduct our business in peace. Help yourself to food and drink." It was a sharp rebuke, but Tarik took it gracefully and bowed low.

A glass of wine materialized at McQueen's left, held out by a graceful hand belonging to an equally beautiful face. Was this one of Tarik's tricks? He muttered his thanks and looked around for Benny. The guide had already drank half of his goblet and Margaret was sipping hers, trying to quench a thirst that needed water more than wine. McQueen knew that if this continued, he would soon lose the services of Benny for the evening, complicating the job enormously

With a start, he got to his feet and appeared to sway back and forth. "Your pardon, sheik, but have you any water? This wine has gone to my head," and he smiled at the sheik in his best imitation of a drunken tourist.

"Outside you will find casks of water. Refresh yourself," the sheik said, and as McQueen slipped out the front, he could see Nazir rise and sit down next to Margaret.

In the bright moonlight, the water casks were unguarded and it took him a full 5 minutes to refill their waterskins and return them to the camels, now sitting asleep on the sand behind the tent. Not for the first time he vowed never again to work for a woman, particularly a beautiful one. Then he heard a loud cheer from the tent and hurried to the entrance.

The scene inside the tent had changed little as he returned, except that in the center of the tent a juggler was tossing lighted torches into the air and catching them behind his back. Two of the slave girls were sitting on either side of the sheik, panting for attention while the sheik merely applauded each new twist of the juggler's art.

Margaret and Benny were where he had left them. Benny looked somewhat drunk and held out his cup to one of the girls for more. She had other things in mind, apparently, and whispered something in his ear which made Benny go red in the face. Next to him, Margaret was doing her best to ignore Nazir, who made a show of watching the juggler while stealing glances at her face, hidden under the headdress.

As quietly as he could, hugging the shadows, McQueen moved around the perimeter of the tent and finally came up behind Margaret. Benny noticed him and leaned over.

"Do you know what she said to me?" he started before McQueen cut him off.

"Later. We got the water. Let's get out of here," he said.

"How did we pay for the water? Margaret wondered, skepticism growing.

"Oh, I signed a marker with one of the men. Helps to have credit." They rose to their feet, Benny very unsteadily, and as they made their exit McQueen bowed low to the sheik, who was now focused on the two girls and waved his hand cheerily at the departing company.

Outside, the stars glowed brightly as they mounted the ill-tempered camels and began the trek back to their camp.

Within a few moments the dust from the camel's hooves had settled and only the dark figure standing at the tent's entrance took any note of their passing.

No matter. It could wait.

•   •   •

When they got back to the camp a warm wind was coming up from the south, and after organizing the packs McQueen gave orders to leave in an hour. The sky was clear and he could tell from the stars the general direction they needed to go. They would swing to the south, away from the caravan, and resume their base course to the east in a few kilometers.

He had no wish to insult Ibrahim but with two slave traders so near it would be better not to take chances, he told himself. Besides, Benny was beginning to sober up and could help guide the camels on foot if need be. As for the girl , she had remained silent on the ride back and now busied herself with packing her bags onto the remaining camels.

As they worked, McQueen climbed to the top of a large sand dune not far from the camp to get a look at the caravan. Any hostile action should be easy to see from here. A trace of music drifted to him on the night wind and the smells of the feast that was now going on, but in all respects the scene was as peaceful as before. Of Tarik there was no trace. No doubt he had joined Ibrahim for the night, McQueen reasoned. After all, they were friendly competitors and it was a good night for resting. McQueen's little company was now entering the general area where Margaret's map indicated Henry's dig might be, and as he chewed on a snack of dried apricots he tried to outline a plan for beginning the painstaking work of finding the explorer. But he was tired and decided it would have to wait.

With these and other thoughts revolving around his head, McQueen walked slowly back to the campsite. He looked at his watch and realized he had been gone 20 minutes. He started walking faster and had gotten to the bottom of the dune when his instincts told him something was wrong. There was absolutely no sound from the camp. The camels should have been snorting at the late hour and the smells from the caravan. He gripped his pistol and moved forward slowly. Entering the small depression where they had camped, he stopped.

They were gone. It had happened quickly and in absolute silence. Apart from a few scraps of clothing, there was nothing to indicate anyone had been here except the few tracks leading off into the west. A brief search of the area turned up nothing. He cursed his carelessness and knew he had underestimated Ibrahim. The thought made him ill. The girl would now be on her way to Tangier and Benny might be dead. He would have to sneak into the caravan and steal a camel.

He had walked a few paces toward the caravan when he suddenly sensed something behind him. But there was no time. The attacker, walking silently in bare feet, raised his rifle and fired at McQueen's head. Some instinct caused him to turn to his left, and that tiny margin was what saved his life. The bullet struck the back of his head behind the ear and glanced off. McQueen fell unconscious to the sand and was still. A few moments later a short tribesman came up and would have stripped the body but for the presence of a rider out of the east. Unable to identify the intruder as friend or foe, the attacker fled, leaving his quarry for the predators of the desert.

Several hundred yards away, Tarik rode through the night with his bundled and gagged captive behind him. She would bring a fortune, he thought. And he had gotten even with that bastard McQueen. It was a good night and he began to sing.

Chapter 7

IT WAS NOW a week later and the slave caravan had traveled far into the central Sahara, following a route known only to Sheik Ibrahim. Margaret had long since recovered from the ether that was used to abduct her and now after riding for days in the cramped horse drawn cart she was becoming accustomed to the life of the caravan, if no less furious at her captivity. There was a routine for everything, and this included breaks for meals and for the men to talk about their journey and the prospects for selling their cargo.

On this day they had not eaten since morning and her head hurt and she was hungry. The oldest slave girl, a dark eyed beauty from Lebanon named Mira, came over to her.

"How about some food?" she asked in a rough French dialect, and handed her some bread and what looked like a sack of wine. Margaret ate the bread hungrily and without comment. The taste of the coarse wine burned her throat, but she was alive.

"Where am I? Is this Egypt?" she asked in French and the other girls laughed. Getting to her knees, she looked out the grating at the long caravan stretching out in front of her. They were moving slowly and from the look of the sun their direction was south, as it had been for several days. Earlier she had thought about escaping but there were locks on the grates and the driver kept a constant watch. Mira explained to her that as a prisoner, she was lost to friends and family and must forget all hope of freedom. The best thing to wish for, she was told, was to be sold to a benevolent man who would not beat her very often.

Besides Mira, her companions were two young girls from Bombay. How they had gotten to Africa she never found out because they spoke only Hindi. But they were well mannered and seemed to accept their fate with a stoic calm. Mira knew a few words of Hindi and they sometimes talked about their captors.

One day Margaret had noticed the girls playing with a few green beads.

"What are those?" she asked. Mira brought over a string of the polished glass beads.

"These are trade beads. Very rare. They are used for money. If you had only a hundred of these you could buy your freedom." Margaret looked them over carefully.

One of the Hindi girls came over and showed Margaret some more. She said a few words to Mira. "She says that there are Germans on this caravan, and that they covet the beads." Margaret handed them back.

"In my country this is called uranium glass. But I've never seen any with this much color before. Why do the Germans want them?" she asked. The Hindi girls talked to Mira for what seemed like a long time.

"They say that what they want is to find the place these come from. They say that they will offer much money for this knowledge." Margaret sank back into her thoughts, trying to understand the riddle of the trade beads.

With the setting of the sun the caravan stopped beside an ancient oasis. There were several wells here, all of them with markings of the owners, and a large pool where the camels were watered. The Bombay girls had been whispering to themselves but suddenly stopped. There was a man outside the cart, and he was unlocking the door. It was Tarik.

Seeing him now in the daylight she was taken with the sheer debauchery and vitality of that face. He looked to be in his late 30s, very fit and tall, with dark features and jet black eyes that seemed to be always laughing or about to. His smile rarely left him and he seemed to take particular pleasure in looking over the girls in cart number six.

"I apologize for the manner in which you were invited into our little group, Miss. I hope your travel has been comfortable," he said with elaborate politeness and moved on.

. . .

Late that night, after the girls had gone to sleep, Margaret arose from the bed and, waiting until the guard had passed by, slipped through an opening and alighted softly on the sand. In the distance were the lights of a small village. She had a water sack and a few scraps of food and was intending to make an escape when she heard the sound of German voices. Crouching in the deeper shadows outside the tent, she drew closer to a large tent.

Inside, Colonel Walser was looking at a sack of the green beads. He was a short man, no more than 5'6", and the distinguishing feature was his eyes, which showed the whites all the way around the pupils and which gave the impression of madness. Across from him sat Sheik Ibrahim and Tarik. Between them was a low table, on which were several of the green beads, plus several raw chunks of the green glass. A fervent Nazi, Walser was smiling. He had with him a small chest, which his assistant, an unctious man named Kruger, placed on the table and opened. Inside was a small mound of golden coins and two heavy gold bars stamped at the corner with the legend "Reichsbank."

"So," began the Sheik. "I understand you would like to travel with us. Very interesting. Why may I ask," said the sheik in his patient, officious voice.

"Actually, no Sheik" said the colonel, smiling broadly as he relished the moment. "We would like to hire you, and your men, at a very handsome fee, to guide us to the place where you found these," and he picked up the largest green stone and turned it over. "We are prepared to pay very well for your help." He spread out a map before them. "We believe the mine is located about here," and with the point of his SS dagger he indicated a spot on the map in northeast Congo, not far from the border with Kenya.

The sheik thought it over for a moment, masking his confusion. "But, uh, my dear Colonel, you realize this is the most dangerous part of the Congo. Tell me, why is it so important for you to find something as... forgive me, but trivial as these little beads? They are little use to anyone except us, and that for trading with some of the tribal peoples who value these things. What can that be to a great nation like Germany?" The sheik felt he had summarized the point nicely and sat back against his cushions and waited.

Walser knew all this, had been expecting this question. He had no intention of bending to the will of this savage, however and his voice became blunt. "Sheik Ibrahim, no doubt you have observed that we have with us a force of 20 men, heavily armed with automatic weapons, grenades and even flame throwers. We are very serious people. What I have asked you is in friendship. The truth is that we have learned that in this mine there is a great store of a brown substance, from which the glass is made."

"That is correct," said the sheik, amiably. "I myself have seen it."

"Good. Well, we only wish to buy some of this ore. We are willing to pay you handsomely for your services, which will include the use of your men to haul out the ore and take it to the seaport at Kameroon, where we can load it onto ships. You know the territory better than anyone. You are the obvious choice." Walser's smile appeared to be genuine, and the Sheik could see how he had become feared throughout the old colonies of German East and German West Africa.

"And if I refuse?"

"Germany is entering an exciting new time, Sheik, in which she will be the dominant power in Europe and Africa. It would be well for you to join with us now, voluntarily. Later on we may be forced to take what we want, without compensation." The big smile was still there, but now there was a hint of undisguised malice in the voice and the eyes.

"Colonel, we do not have such weapons as you speak of, but we know how to use the ones we have. For instance, earlier today we discovered one of your men trying to defile one of our women. This is a very serious offense."

"I can understand that. What was his punishment?" Walser looked around, then his eyes settled upon one of the Sheik's men bringing in a small canvas bag, which he set on the table. The man opened the top of it, revealing blonde hair and a face whose eyes were wide open in death. The man bowed to the sheik and withdrew.

"So, Colonel," the sheik began, "we both have our methods. Your proposal is not without interest, but the hour is late and I must have time to think. Perhaps we can talk tomorrow. In the meantime, would you like to take with you anything? The head of your sergeant for instance?" The sheik's steady gaze in the now silent room bore into Walser's eyes. He got to his feet and bowed.

"Thank you, no. Let us talk tomorrow. Good night, Sheik," he said and with his assistant quietly left the tent.

Outside, Margaret had heard the story and pressed herself into the folds of the canvas as Walser and his man came out. Walser needed a moment to compose himself. "That bloody savage," he said quietly in German as they began to walk away. "He will pay for this. We leave in the morning.

Radio to camp that I wish to see Dr. Oedheim as soon as we return."

    •   •   •

The vultures found McQueen after an hour. The body was alone and looked to be dead, and in a few minutes half a dozen of the giant birds were circling, waiting for confirmation. There was a small trickle of blood near the head and this had attracted the attention of one of the Sahara's most fearsome predators, a large black monitor lizard. With it's acute senses, the lizard had detected the scent of blood and when there was no sound had ventured out of his cave and into the open. It came close to the body, but the presence of the vultures circling overhead was too much risk and it had crawled back to its hole. The giant vultures, able to strip a dead camel in minutes, had no such compunctions and a few minutes later the largest of them began to descend.

They would have begun tearing into the body within minutes had not McQueen opened his eyes and rolled painfully onto his back. He could feel the large knot on the back of his head, covered in blood. The bullet had torn through the skin but had missed any veins and despite a blinding headache and a mouth full of sand and swollen from dehydration he knew he would live if he could only stop the bleeding and rest.

Getting to his feet he saw the vultures as he staggered back toward camp. There was almost nothing left, just a few scraps of clothes. He remembered his emergency precautions and felt for his leg. The curved whisky flask was still there, taped to his calf, and he took a drink. Finding a piece of cloth to bandage his head only took a few minutes and he was left with the choice of direction. He knew he could follow the caravan and eventually might catch up, or he could resume the search for Henry.

Being on foot in the desert forces one to contemplate death, and as he set out now in the direction of what Benny had described as the best well in this region he knew that his end was at hand. He was not an introspective man, but he knew he had to maintain his rationality as long as possible, and to take his mind off the heat and the hopelessness of his situation, he thought back to where it had all begun.

He had been a brash 18 year old that winter of 1921 in New York living with his widowed mother, and was on the verge of getting in trouble. Remembering it now made him laugh. A strong youth, he was generally well mannered but when faced with insult had no hesitation about settling the issue with his fists. A natural and cunning fighter, he found he could hold his own with bigger men and was soon being courted by a boxing promoter of dubious reputation. His mother heard of this, and after one particularly bloody brawl had written to an old friend of her husband's.

A few days later a curious older man appeared outside their door.   Navy Commander Dawson Davies (ret.) was a character straight out of Charles Dickens.   He was old enough to remember when the American navy had been comprised of 3 masted cutters and brigantines and had served in the Civil War as a midshipman with Admiral Du Pont at the blockade of Charleston.   Later he had been a gunnery officer when the Merrimack had been sunk, and had remained on active duty until shortly after the Spanish-American civil war. He had an enormous white beard, bushy eyebrows over deep blue eyes and for a man nearing 90 was amazingly virile. Only the slight stoop from arthritis and a cane betrayed his age.

He walked into the living room and greeted the mother warmly, whom he had known for many years.

"Elizabeth. Good to see you," he said in his gravelly baritone voice.   He spoke with a faint Irish brogue - his mother had been born in Dublin - and when he laughed, which was often, the room seemed to shake.   Her son stood quietly watching as the old man straightened up to his full 6'3" height and took off his coat, then gave her a warm hug. He had been the best man at their wedding and as he trudged up the sand dunes McQueen could still remember how the old man had squinted at him, like measuring a distant squall.

"You must be young Joe. All grown up now, I see. Aye, you're the spitting image of your grandfather, and a fine man he was. He could throw the overhand right, believe me!" he laughed, rubbing his jaw. "Well I'm glad to know you, lad," he said, holding out a big paw of a hand. "Sit down and let's have a talk. Tell me all about yourself." Shaking the hand, young McQueen thought he had never met anyone who radiated such warmth and wisdom. Here was a man who had lived, he realized.

Even now McQueen could remember the scene. They had talked long into the night after Joe's mother had gone to bed, and the fire kept the room warm as rain played upon the windows. From time to time the old man took a sip of the whisky his mother had brought out, savoring it deeply, and young Joe began to feel a kinship with the old sea dog and his curious talent for painting pictures with words to illustrate this point or that idea and who seemed to have an endless list of stories tucked up his sleeve.

"I'd still be at sea," he often repeated. "But the pencil pushers in Washington said I was too old. Can you imagine that? Too old! No man who can do his duty is too old, I say. So here I am now, on the beach, and wishing for one more turn on deck." He took a sip of whisky and his eyes seemed to light up. "Say, would you like to hear the story of old One-Legged Moses Hamm, second mate on the Cutty Sark, that was a tea cutter, and how he saved the ship during a gale off the coast of Maracaibo when they were escorting merchant ships around the Horn, and how all the other ships were lost with all hands, and how the King of Spain himself made him a prince for saving his son?"

"Have you had too much to drink sir?" he said, shifting uneasily in his seat. "I mean, how could something like that happen?" he asked, incredulous.

"How?" he roared. "Because a strong man can do anything, that's how. And well I should know! I was there," he said, and held out his arm. "See that scar? I got that by falling out of the rigging that same night the ship was almost lost," and off he had went into the lurid story full of details of how a young American navy had fought to survive one setback after another, how they were hounded by the British even after the war of 1812, and of the skirmishes with the remnants of the Spanish empire off the waters of Guatemala and Venezuela. On the stories went, into strange ports of call and stranger characters, and the women they knew, both virtuous and otherwise. He had the gift of a natural storyteller, and soon one story led into another, emerging out of the smoke from his pipe like a genie from a bottle.

He had been a friend of Joe's grandfather and his father, a rising officer in the Army until he was killed in France at Verdun in 1918, and had been keeping a distant eye on the boy for some years as a favor to his family. Joe had not known this, which made the revelation all the more startling. The old man listened patiently as he talked of his plans for the future, how he loved boxing, but it was clear he considered the sporting life to be beneath the dignity of the McQueens.

"Well and good, lad," he replied, "but it's only a bit of sport, not a life. Find yourself something that's real, I say" he had said, and seemed to remember something important, because he got to his feet and walked around waving his pipe. "I remember now! There was a young man, much like yourself, with us the morning when we surprised the rebels at the mouth of the river as they were loading up cannon for General Beauregard, the black hearted devil! He was a lot like you. This won't take a minute," and off they went, into the early days of the Civil War, when the Navy had faced down the threat from a British packet trying to resupply the South. As the hours ticked away, the boy had begun to feel that nothing could possibly be as adventurous or exciting as a life in the Navy.

By morning he was ready to enlist and later that summer a letter of recommendation from Vice President Cromwell found its way to their third floor walk-up apartment. To his mother's great relief, he had been accepted to Annapolis. He could still recall his bitter regret that the Commander had died shortly before his graduation. They had become great friends, and the old man had taken the place of the father he had lost so early.

McQueen had been a top student in his class, and his rise through the ranks had been steady but not spectacular. The late 1920s had been a time of drift and rust for the Navy. The transition from coal to oil fired ships had been completed, the country was at peace and budgets were kept tightly in check. He had been assigned to a battleship, the Farragut, and as he learned his trade on the seas he could see nothing of the adventurous life the Commander had talked about.

• • •

The sand was burning through his shoe as McQueen walked up another dune, half in a trance. He knew such wanderings were dangerous and took a minute sip of the precious water. Despite everything, he smiled to himself. If only old Davies could see him now, he thought. How he'd laugh.

But the heat was at its worst and as he reached the top of the dune he could see nothing in any direction except more sand. He was trying to remember something. What was it? Oh, yes. Then had come Lindbergh. The trans Atlantic flight had rippled throughout the Navy as it had the country, opening up new thinking about the possibilities of Naval aviation. McQueen had had several conversations about tactics aboard the battleship in the off watches, late at night, when the senior officers were not around. Some of the junior officers were experts in metallurgy and munitions, and it became clear to him that the day of the capital ships was ending. A single plane, it was argued, carrying a single heavy bomb could sink a battleship. Although many argued vehemently against the idea as heresy, McQueen understood that his world was about to undergo profound changes, and that meant opportunity.

He had gotten a transfer the following year to the fledgling aviation unit, based in Norfolk, and graduated first in his flight school. There was a freedom to this life that he found appealing and which had no conflict with his loyalty to the Navy. Because everything was so new, he was able to fly everything the Navy had in the air, and because of his skill soon became an instructor. Those were among his best days. He was not yet 30, he could fly as much as he wanted and he enjoyed helping the young cadets learn aerial combat.

By the mid 30s he had risen to the rank of Commander and the Navy had built its first aircraft carrier. He was, at heart, a fighting man and a patriot who yearned to be where the action was, but America was at peace. The various wars that sprung up in Asia and Europe didn't touch U.S. interests, and so there was little opportunity to hone his skills. When the Japanese invaded Manchuria in 1931 the Hoover administration had done nothing about it officially, invoking the Stimson Doctrine of non-recognition of confiscated territory. However, it gave McQueen his first taste of the life he had dreamed of.

When the U.S. ambassador to China had decided to see for himself what had happened, the State Department had suggested a military escort, and McQueen was one of the few officers qualified to fly the new long range deHavilland sea plane with enough range to ferry the ambassador to and from the war zone. They had met in Shanghai and for the next two weeks, avoiding the press and under strict rules of non-engagement, the ambassador, his assistant and McQueen toured the devastation wrought by the Japanese army in Manchuria.

It was a nauseating experience. McQueen had never seen the full effects of what an occupying army can do to an otherwise peaceful civilian populace. The slaughter in Manchuria was but a precursor to the larger tragedy of 1937 when the Japanese 3rd Army Group landed at Guanghou, but it taught a young McQueen the importance of mobility. On more than one occasion, the ambassador had found himself cut off by advancing Japanese troops, and only McQueen's insistence that they stay close to rivers and lakes suitable for fast takeoffs had prevented a larger tragedy. The ambassador had tried to evacuate some of the wounded to Peking, but in the end only three children had been rescued. McQueen also learned that the signs of an imminent invasion were obvious for weeks before the event, but the Manchurian government had done little to prepare. The point was driven home: information, applied in the right quarters, can avert or minimize conflict.

Back in Washington McQueen had tried to interest his superiors in the idea of a Naval intelligence service but had gotten nowhere. He was too young, and the anti-war sentiment too strong. When Hitler became chancellor of the Reich, the stage was set for another rung in the ladder.

Italy invaded Abyssinia in late 1935, and shortly thereafter Germany marched into the Rhineland. The world was lurching toward war, and Franklin Roosevelt was not a man to sit passively as events pushed America toward the abyss. The Italians had used a mechanized force to subdue the Ethiopians and this gave FDR the excuse he needed. He had heard about McQueen's exploits in Manchuria, and although neutrality was very much the official position of his administration, he was restless.

The call came as McQueen was testing a new dive bomber prototype built by Chance Vaught in Pensacola. His boss, Rear Admiral Virgil Enright, a pioneer in naval aviation, took the call and listened calmly as the CNO explained to him the nature of the "unofficial request" from the White House. Ten minutes later McQueen was sitting in the admiral's office and an hour later was on his way by train to Washington.

The meeting at the White House was brief and brisk. Harry Hopkins, the President's chief aide, was present, and explained to McQueen that they wanted to simply find out how the Italians had overwhelmed the Ethiopians so quickly, what they hoped to accomplish there and to assess the fighting capabilities of the Italians. As an aside, if there was any way the U.S. could work with Haile Selassie, Emperor of Ethiopia, to broker a peace, that would be a welcome bonus. It was understood that McQueen would be out of uniform and that the entire operation should be kept to 4 weeks.

Arriving by boat in LeHavre, he had made his way to Cairo, chartered an airplane and flown directly to Massowah, on the Red Sea, as a military observer and the guest of the Italians. It had taken a full week to shake free of his hosts, and flying out under cover of night he had arrived at the besieged capital of Addis Ababa early the next morning. Everywhere was chaos. The cities of Adowa and Axum had fallen, and now reports were coming in that the Italians were using some terrible new weapon. After a quick meeting with the Ethiopian chief of staff, McQueen was given a jeep and an escort, and the next day set out for the front.

After the emperor had ordered a counter-attack against the Italian commander, Badoglio, the Italians had responded by firing chemical weapons at the defenders. It was a new type of mustard gas, and to the unprepared Ethiopian troops it was devastating. Wholesale retreat had begun as McQueen and his escort arrived.

He could immediately smell it. It was distant, and it combined with the smell of burning flesh, but the gas had an odor he was never to forget. Everyone was covering their mouths with rags and it was only when they were inside a makeshift command center that anyone could talk. The center was also being used as a crude first aid station.

"What happened?" shouted McQueen over the sound of shells exploding in the near distance. The young lieutenant looked bewildered.

"The gas, the gas," was all he could say, as a dozen armed men demanded his time. Three soldiers were brought in, still wearing their ceremonial ostrich feathers indicating the Emperor's ceremonial troops. They were clawing at their throats, trying to breathe, as other men tried to tie their hands to the stretcher. But there was no medicine to give them, and as McQueen waited for the lieutenant to return, the three men died in that terrible way that only poisoning causes.

They drove for an hour along the front, seeing through binoculars at a distance the phenomenon of gas shells bursting and of troops turning and retreating wildly. Apparently they had not been told what to expect.

It went like that for the rest of the day, and into the early evening. The Ethiopians on this front were being slaughtered, and they were the last line of defense before Addis Ababa.

A week later, he was on his way home. On board the ship he heard that Pope Pius XI had congratulated Mussolini on his conquest.

• • •

On the third day in the desert he began to hallucinate. At first it was nothing more than sounds. The wind began to sound like voices, and as he struggled forward he tried to imagine who belonged to the voices. But now he was beginning to see images of random shapes on the horizon. The wound on the back of his head was still sore and he recognized the early signs of hemmorage, but there was little he could do about it except wrap the bandage tighter.

He looked at his compass and took another bearing. He had been moving steadily north for the last 2 days, which was where he thought Benny had pointed out the well, but even that memory was now hard to call up. When the water was gone, the end would come quickly he knew.

The dunes had given way to a faint track, which might have been an old trade route or merely a herder's shortcut through the northern desert. It wound its way through a series of small hills covered with scrub brush. He remembered something from his days in Ethiopia about finding water in the desert, how an oasis is often preceded by traces of vegetation which can easily be seen from the air but which from the ground are often confusing in their randomness.

He struggled to the top of the tallest hillock and looked around. It was just after noon and the sun made it difficult to see. His face was badly burned from exposure and he tried to control his shaking long enough to scan the horizon. Yes, there was something over to his left, a shadow. It was the thinnest possible lead.

By the time he had covered the two miles to his goal he was almost crawling from delirium. Never a man given to self pity or introspection, he nonetheless thought it amusing that for a Navy pilot his grave was going to a pile of bleached bones 200 yards away from an oasis. He looked around. The sun was starting to get low on the horizon. He knew that if he were near an oasis the predators would be coming out soon. He had to get to a defensible position and hold out for one more day.

With thoughts of survival spinning in his head, he stumbled the last 20 yards down the track, much more defined now, and suddenly there in front of him was a small tree. He laughed out loud. It was a jacaranda, such as grow in profusion with any water at all. Looking up, he could see more trees marching up a little rise, and in the center a rock-lined pool of water. He had found the only oasis within a thousand miles.

• • •

McQueen sat by the small pool of water, feeling human again and cursing the day he had met Clayton Ellison. It was only the normal reaction to near death, and he quickly got about the business of finding a way out. All oasis in the Sahara are in constant use, and it was only a matter of time before a small trading party or caravan passed by. He wondered about what had happened to Margaret and for a brief moment regretted that he had failed to protect her, but he knew it was a waste of time to look backward.

Later that afternoon a few camels appeared in the distance, moving slowly across the horizon. He watched them for a few minutes but they turned away. He was beginning to wonder if this was in fact the lost oasis of legend when the sound of camel drivers and bells came to him on the wind from the south. It was a party of traders, who are rare in the Sahara and who are usually marked by their use of extra camels for packs, and the presence of rifles hanging from the camel bags. He was weak from hunger and as he got to his feet he was surprised to see a familiar face.

Archibald Mehmet, who everyone called Archie, was a mongrel Egyptian trader whose mother had been an Englishwoman. He was a terrible and unrepentent liar, a dealer in questionable goods and an outcast, although partly by choice. Fluent in Arabic and English, rejected by both cultures because he respected neither religion, he had learned good manners from his mother and sharp trading from his father, and had set out on his own at 18 to conquer the world. After a series of mishaps involving the Emir of Dubai, he had fled into the desert where he discovered he could make a living buying and selling anything that could be carried on a camel. It was a frequently unforgiving life, but it suited Archie, who despised the benefits of civilization. Over the years McQueen had encountered the bearded rogue many times, and they had always been friendly.

McQueen waved at him as the portly trader rolled into the oasis and got down from his camel. "I say, McQueen, is that you?"

"How have you been, Archie? Can you spare a bite of food?"

"Haven't seen you since that night in Tripoli. What the devil are you doing here? You look like you've been beaten by one of Ibrahim's camel drivers, may his name rot like that jackal's leftovers. What will you have?" he asked in a surprisingly cultured voice that McQueen had forgotten. "We've got salted camel meat, salted horse meat and salted monkey. The monkey is really quite good." McQueen held out a hand.

An hour later, refreshed and wearing a new Hashemite robe sold to him on credit by Archie, he was again himself and they began talking - meaning that Archie, talked and McQueen mostly listened. Like any good traveling salesman, Archie was full of gossip, much of it hilarious, and with his belly full and a half bottle of very cheap wine under his belt, he could have told stories all night long had McQueen not fallen asleep in the middle of one of them.

After a breakfast of figs, the two men got down to business. "If you want to find the girl, I passed Ibrahim's caravan two nights ago, heading south, just outside El Obeid. Gave him a wide berth, I can tell you. But you'll have to hurry, Joe. I can sell you my best camel for 50 pounds. A bargain, believe me."

McQueen knew he was being cheated, but ignored it. "No, I have to find a man. Archeologist. He might be anywhere between Umm Badr and En Nahud," and McQueen showed him the area on a map.

"Important?"

McQueen was all business. "Very. The girl can wait. But about this camel..."

"Oh, he's a very fine camel. I practically raised him from a baby." McQueen suddenly remembered something.

"Don't you still owe me a hundred pounds for that shipment of liquor we landed in Kampala last year. I distinctly remember getting shot at and you riding off before we settled up." Archie thought it over a moment and then laughed loudly, slapped his friend on the back.

"Good memory for one so near death! Ha! But after all, can you blame me? How was I to know they were thieves. But yes, you are right. I had forgotten. For that, you can have my second best camel for nothing. I bought her from a camel herder who lived in this very same area you seek. She'll probably lead you right to it. For a small additional fee, I could throw in the saddle."

"All right, all right, second best it is," he said, growing tired of Archie's serpentine logic. "But why is it only second best? Is there something wrong with it?"

"Oh, no, no. Not at all. But when I tell jokes, the other one winks at me."

•   •   •

With a ten day supply of food and water and a promise from Archie to deliver a message to Eddie if he should fail to return, he rode out that afternoon heading northeast. The trip was uneventful and on the morning of the fourth day he arrived outside the ancient Nubian city of Nyassa, long since reduced to ruins. It was the spot Margaret had indicated as the likely center of her father's dig, and he searched the area all that day for a trace of Henry's camp but found nothing. The next morning he realized he had reached the end of his journey. He would have to make his way back to Eddie and the Goose empty handed, and the prospect made him angry. The next morning he set out for the river. He had bought dates from some nomads in Nyassa and had plenty of water.

He had traveled about 50 miles when he realized he was being followed. It was no more than three camels, he estimated, keeping well back, and he could only occasionally catch a glimpse. He had his pistol and two clips of ammunition, but otherwise was in no condition to withstand a determined assault if they were intent on robbing hm. That night he made his camp near a cluster of stunted baobab trees and bedded down 50 yards away. He kept awake until well past midnight then fell asleep.

The next morning, with no sign the camp had been disturbed, he pushed on again. He thought the followers had turned aside, but at about midday as he passed over a high khor, he could spot them again about a mile behind. It was becoming too risky to play the game again, so that afternoon he stopped early and concealed his camel in a narrow wash and waited. An hour later, the shadow finally reached its source.

It was Henry, barely alive. He had tied himself to his mount and appeared to have been badly beaten. His eyes were swollen almost shut. There was dried blood on his face and neck, and his left arm was wrapped in a crude sling. His breathing was labored, and McQueen guessed he had run out of water. When he stopped he would have fallen off the camel had McQueen not helped him down.

He gave him a drink of water, then cleaned up his bruises using a little bit of the precious liquid and a scrap of soap Archie had given him. It was 15 minutes before the old man was able to talk.

"Who are you?" the older man mumbled at last. "Where is this?"

"Where do you think? You're in the Sahara, Henry, and it means I've fallen into another one of your fouled up adventures," he said bitterly. Henry sat up, looked hard at McQueen.

"Wait a minute. I know you. Sure. You're the pilot, aren't you? Joe McQueen, that crazy guy out of Lisbon."

"Look who's talking," he said. "What happened to you?" Henry smiled and sat back.

"Just like old times, huh?" The color was coming back into his face and his eyes regained their focus, as if he had just won the lottery. "I did it, Joe. Found it. A fortune! They tried to steal it from me, but I fought them."

"What are you talking about?"

"There were... five of them. I killed four, I think. The other one ran away. I told Margaret you were the only man alive who could help me and I was right. Just like old times." Henry was about to say more, but the talking had taken a toll on him and he laid back against the sand and closed his eyes. McQueen went to get some food and when he returned the old man had fallen asleep.

The next morning Henry was better and had some breakfast and was able to walk. He looked around expecting to see McQueen, but the other man had more pressing matters to attend to. He was standing on top of a dune 20 yards away, watching something through the small binoculars he always kept in his pants pocket. Seeing Henry awake he hurried back to the camp. The reunion would be brief.

"There's three of them, about a mile back, coming this way."

"Who?"

"Whoever did that to you, that's who. We'd better get moving." McQueen started loading the camels, tying the knots securely as Henry tried to puzzle out what was happening.

"Wait a minute. You're supposed to be in Cairo, waiting for me. Or Banbuku."

"Banbuku was burned to the ground. I came here because you've got some information I want." They packed in a hurry and five minutes later the tiny expedition set out toward the west. It was late morning. If McQueen's plan was going to work, he needed all the time he could get.

By the early afternoon they had reached the fringe of a range of low hills bordering Obeidah plateau, which meant they were getting close to the river. The pursuers were still following them, and the gap had closed by half. He knew from having flown over the region for years that there were a cluster of Nubian pyramids not far off now, and that they were sometimes inhabited by tourists or nomads moving down the river toward Khartoum.

It was called El Maedok, the place of the skull. Five hundred years after the pharaohs built their great pyramids, their vassals in the Kush had learned the craft and started building pyramids to house the bodies of their kings. The pyramids had long since been plundered, but like a magnet the site continued to attract the curious.

As McQueen and Henry came over the crest just after midday, the scene appeared to be deserted. They rode silently into the necropolis and found shelter in an ancient chamber attached to one of the larger pyramids.

"Fascinating. Do you realize that these people actually conquered Egypt and became the pharaohs in the 25th dynasty," said Henry, as McQueen watered the camels. McQueen watched for 20 minutes but there was no sign of their pursuers.

An hour later, Henry found McQueen inside one of the smaller pyramids, stretched out on the floor, his hat over his face. "Well this is a fine thing. What about those bandits? What's our plan?" he said. McQueen sat up. All he wanted was a bath, but it would have to wait.

"Relax."

"Huh?"

"Didn't you see the sign back there in Acholi?"

"No."

"That's the local dialect. This place is forbidden," McQueen said as calmly as ordering tea.

"Why?"

"Purple fever. That's their word for dengue fever. Nobody in their right mind would come near this place."

"Then what are we doing here?"

"We're desperate. Just don't drink the water." Henry looked outside. The camels were drinking at a shallow pool that looked a little yellowish.

"What about the camels?"

"Oh, they're OK. Immune."

"Where did you learn all this?"

"Oh, us crazy pilots get around. Get some rest." McQueen lay back and replaced the hat.

The sun was going down when they woke up, refreshed. McQueen liked the quiet but there was work to be done. He knew the men pursuing them would be waiting outside the necropolis, and that meant they had to leave by night. He lit a small fire and they ate in silence.

"By the way, thanks for saving my life," said Henry. The water and food and a long nap had brought him back to his normal self, which meant curious. "How about the rest of the story?"

McQueen nodded. He noticed that Henry had a string of green beads around his wrist. "What do you have those for?" he asked.

"Oh, they were a gift from a friend of mine. Owns a great big mine on the edge of the Congo. It's called uranium glass. Worthless, really, but they come in handy when you want to pay a native. I forgot I had them."

McQueen got to his feet. Like a veil suddenly pulled away, it became clear. The scientists in Cairo, the meeting in Paris. They were talking about uranium. Then the Germans had come to Banbuku. All the clues began to fit.

"That's it. The Germans are here because they know where to get more of that stuff, and whatever it is, it must be important. We have to get back to Banbuku. Show me where the mine is." Henry had a battered fold up map of Africa, and pointed to a spot in the northern Congo, near a large river.

"There. Not two miles from this river, the Irrigati."

"And you say the man that runs it is a friend of yours?"

"Oh sure. Dutchman, name of Olaf. Been working it for years. Sometimes when you get an electrical storm the stuff glows in the dark. But what do they want it for?"

"That's not my job, but I'll bet it's got something to do with the war."

"Roosevelt says you're staying out of it."

"Maybe. I have a friend in Lisbon who thinks otherwise. I need to get to a long range radio, and fast. Pack your stuff. We're leaving."

"In the dark?"

"Don't you think your friends are waiting for us out there? In the dark we've got a chance to slip past. A chance. After we get some backup, I'm going to find Margaret." He tried to say it as casually as possible.

"What about her?

"Well, it's a long story."

"Isn't she in Lisbon?"

"Uh. No. Last I saw of her we had a little run in with a slave caravan."

Henry jumped straight up. "A what?" he shouted.

"Now take it easy. As far as I know they haven't sold her yet. Who knows, they might keep her around. Or some merchant might have bought her, somebody who wouldn't beat her too much.... I was going to tell you about it. Later." Henry put down his bags.

"McQueen. You were supposed to leave her in Lisbon! It was all in the letter."

"What letter?"

"She didn't give it to you?

"No. All she gave me was a lot of go there and do this."

Henry thought it over. "Where were they going?"

"Didn't say."

"Well, this changes everything. You realize what you've done? I'll have to break my journey back to England to find her. There's only a couple of places you can sell a white woman in this part of the world."

"Don't you think I know that," McQueen barked back at him. "Let's get out of here." They packed hurriedly and left the rude shelter just as the moon was going behind the clouds. A few minutes later they were mounted and riding toward the east. They rode in silence. The moon cooperated just long enough for them to leave the necropolis and disappear into the the long valley that descended steadily to the sea.

Chapter 8

A WEEK LATER, Colonel Walser walked into the Semiramis and shook the dust off his clothes. It had been a long plane flight from the ruins of Banbuku to Khartoum and then Cairo and he was itching to close the battle with these African *untermunchen* and return to Europe, where the real glory lay. But he was first of all a German officer, and when he had received the radio message that a Blohm-Voss seaplane was flying down to take him to Cairo, he assembled his notes and waited at the deserted dock. Promptly at 10:15, the big four-engine plane made a perfect landing on the river, taxied to the dock, and in 10 minutes they were airborne. It had been done with German efficiency and at 9:00 the next morning they touched down on the Nile in Cairo.

He took the stairs to the first floor and walked to room 106. The door was opened by a very tall blonde man in a plain gray suit he assumed was a Wermacht officer. The slender man at the table rose and held out a hand.

"Colonel Walser. So good to see you." Oedheim was much as Walser remembered him. Quiet, observant and intensely curious. But there was something else now, an air of resignation. A pioneer in quantum mechanics and the Nobel prize winner of 1932, Oedheim would have been happy to remain in Berlin where he had offices, but with the military takeover of his research project two years earlier, all of his efforts were now directed at the so-called *Uranprojekt*, which was the military application of nuclear fusion. Walser had only heard the vaguest of rumors until a month ago when he had been detached from his position under General Holzenherein.

Sitting with them that afternoon was a colonel from the Waffenamt, which Walser knew was the Wermacht unit behind the top secret Uranverein, or uranium club. Oedheim was the principal scientist in the club and if he was in Africa it could only mean something important.

The angry little man with the maniacal stare sat down on the sofa next to Oedheim, whom he noticed had very pale skin, almost translucent. He waited in silence while the Wermacht officer eyed him dispassionately. The silence grew heavy. Finally, he leaned forward.

"Colonel Walser, what I am about to tell you must never leave this room. You understand?" he asked.

"Certainly."

"I want you to tell Dr. Oedheim everything you have learned in Africa about these," and he produced a handful of green uranium beads. Walser had come prepared. He extracted the thick sheath of documents from his briefcase and began.

•　•　•

The slave caravan continued its long roundabout route to the south, avoiding the occasional French patrol and seeing no one. Margaret had followed for three days after her expulsion but her legs were beginning to cramp up and on the third night she slipped quietly into one of the carts that held the girls.

With no customers in sight, the caravan settled into a routine. Mornings were for washing and feeding the animals, then the caravan loaded up the camels, hitched the horses to the carts and moved off. During this time Margaret was careful to stay out of sight. The caravan did not stop or slow down until nightfall, unless they spotted a French patrol and were forced to hide themselves in the sand dunes as only Arabs know how to do.

At night the women helped prepare food while the men amused themselves with those of the slave girls they found appealing. She had learned that her overseer was a dim-witted ox named Dodi who barely looked at the women. Some said he was a eunuch. Margaret only knew he had a price: for 20 drachmas a week, he agreed not to tell Ibrahim there was a stowaway aboard.

Occasionally the monotony was broken up with fights over the women, which always included betting on the outcome, and once a Bedouin had been found with a dagger through his heart after a heated argument, but in general Ibrahim was a benevolent if wholly untrustworthy master.

The wild card in the deck was Tarik. A distant cousin of the sheiks, he was loud, boisterous, frequently drunk and very much wanted to be his own man. Several times he had come by the cart where Margaret was riding, and seemed to have his eye on her. She couldn't understand this, because several of the girls were truly beautiful, but each night after the caravan had gone to bed and the gambling boards had been put away, Tarik would stop on his way back to his tent outside the bars of her cart, always silent, always smiling. She had to admit he was a handsome enough brute, but romance was the last thing on her mind.

"Tell me the truth," he finally said in his deep baritone voice. "You find me a little attractive, don't you?"

"Not in the slightest."

"Not even this much," he asked, holding up two fingers.

"You know what you can do with those fingers, don't you?" she snapped back, and he laughed long and quietly to himself.

"Hey. Why don't you join me one night after the games. Must be awfully cramped in that little cart. We have lots of food, and maybe you don't want to go where I think you're going," he smiled. It was infuriating. He knew something, she was sure. Life was complicated enough.

"Better decide soon," he said. "We're getting close to the sea. Just a few more days. They say a French patrol is following us. If they catch us, they might have to kill you to cover up the evidence, but that wouldn't happen if you were with me."

"No thank you."

"Suit yourself," he said, smiling. She noticed that some of the men were beginning to roll up the tents.

"What's going on?" she asked him.

"Orders from the sheik. We're moving out. Think about what I said, huh? We'll be at the port next week," he smiled and was gone.

One of the new girls who had come aboard at their last stop had been watching this exchange and moved over closer to Margaret. Her name was Malieva, she was 19, and had dark eyes. More importantly, she possessed the gift of telling amusing stories and had a stunning figure that made her one of the sheik's favorites.

"Don't worry about him," she said casually. "All he does is talk." She had been born in poverty in the desert near

Abeshr, and had been sold by her family into slavery for the equivalent of one cow. At first it had shocked Margaret when she openly declared that she considered her lot to be better than it had been working under the hot sun helping her family raise goats.

"He sold all of my sisters before me, and all he has now is six goats," she said of her father. "Not one cow. The man has the brains of a water buffalo," she added for good measure, although she used a tribal name for the animal, and they both laughed. It was good to laugh.

"But you can't be serious about this life, a prisoner on display for these drunken sheiks," protested Margaret. She truly wanted to understand.

"At least here I have plenty to eat and something to wear," said Malieva. "And they don't beat me. I know how to control men. Besides, I will not be a slave for long. I speak many languages. I will escape, as you did, but I will be smarter and pick my time, and I will take much with me, enough to start over, as a free woman," she had said with great dignity on their first day together. Despite their differences, Margaret admired the diffident girl from the Sahara and they became friends. As the days stretched out they had spent many hours together in the rolling cart, trying to keep cool by eating pomegranates and learning about each other's culture. Margaret had never encountered this kind of poverty before and she was surprised to learn Malieva had a very dry sense of humor and a love of all things American.

"Some day when I go to America, as a free woman, I will own a pastry shop. And I will be fat and happy," she had said with a melodic laugh. "But first we must survive what is coming."

"What is that?"

"Oh, I forgot, you do not know. One of the girls told me. We're going to Port Sudan, just north of the old slave market at Suakin. The slave dealers there are very cruel. They buy for the sultans and the houses of the East. Very dangerous, even if you are beautiful as we are."

"Why do you say that?"

"Because they may want to sell us for any price in Port Sudan just to have a fast money. Then the life will be very hard. If they wait till we get to Jeddah we will bring a greater price, and we will be treated better."

"How do you know this?"

"The other girls told me," she said. Then the strange girl had gotten hungry and they ate in silence as the caravan rolled on into the night.

It was hours later when Margaret woke up. The caravan was still moving and she guessed it was about two hours before dawn. She woke up Malieva.

"What is it?" said the younger girl. "I'm sleeping," and turned back over. Margaret woke her again.

"I have to get a message to someone. He's at Banbuku, on the Nile, about a hundred miles west of here I think. "

"Is it important?"

"I have to tell them where we're going. They'll rescue me. I'm sure of it. And you too." for the first time, Malieva was alert.

'You promise?"

"I swear it." Malieva went to her little bag of possessions and searched for something, careful not to wake the others.

It was not until the next day that she got her chance. The caravan had stopped for water and there was an old trader with only three teeth asleep next to his camel. Margaret slipped out of the cart when the guard wasn't looking and ran to the old man. He didn't understand her poor Arabic, but her French finally got through and she learned that the man was on his way to Wadi Jebel, which was only a few miles from Banbuku.

"Could you take a message to someone in Banbuku?" she asked. The old man smiled and shook his head.

"Very dangerous now. Can't do it," he said as he reached out and tried to squeeze her arm, as if testing a peach. She pulled back.

"Please. It's very important. Here. I'll write instructions in the letter that the man is to give you ... 500 drachmas. He is very rich," she added, and wrote the instructions on the back of the note, then handed it to the man. The caravan was getting ready to move. Before the old man could object, Margaret thanked him and ran back to the cart, careful to mix in with the confusion of some animals being fed.

As the caravan pulled out, the last thing she saw was the old man puzzling over the note.

"Why is this so important, this message?" asked Malieva.

"Because the Germans are at war with England, and if they're here it means trouble."

"I do not understand such things," said the young woman. "But if this is your wish, you could have picked a better messenger."

""Do you think he'll do it?" she asked Malieva. "That message has to get through." The young girl looked back at the old man and waved. She shouted a few words at him and his face suddenly broke into a toothless grin as he waved enthusiastically at the girls.

"Yes, I think so."

"What did you say to him?"

"I said if he did it, I'd screw his brains out the next time he's in Port Sudan."

Over the next few days Margaret learned that Malieva was more than capable of carrying out her promise. Every night a different sheik would arrive at the cart after the caravan had settled down for the night, sometimes bringing liquid refreshment with him and sometimes not. After a modest bribe was paid to the guard, she would slip out of the cart, generally wearing a harem outfit constructed of the sheerest silk and designed to highlight her perfect breasts. One only had to wait a few minutes before the moaning would start. With the older men it was very brief, and she would walk back to the cart alone, toss a coin to the guard and crawl into bed. With the younger men, the moaning sometimes lasted a half hour and became a duet. Apparently she was very good. Then she would come back arm in arm with her young suitor, who would cast a lustful eye toward Margaret before strolling off to his tent, drained of all erotic impulses.

The days also had their rhythm and dragged on, cut off from news of the outside world and monotonous except for the occasional fight. Tarik was looking increasingly unhappy, she thought, and she began to hear rumors of an argument between him and the sheik over the commission to be paid him at the slave market for the girls he had found. Money was generally at the root of the dispute, she learned. Both men were very greedy, they all agreed.

By the end of the week it was becoming obvious that it was only be a matter of time before Margaret was compelled to join in the evening fun. Twice Malieva's "date" had showed up with Tarik, hoping to make it a party. This in turn required still more creative excuse making. A product of English schools, she was adept at this but it only seemed to whet his appetite, and it was reliably reported that there was a wager among the men as to which one would be the lucky winner of her affections.

Then one night a figure had walked out of the darkness toward the cart and called out to Malieva. Apparently she had raised her prices and only the most prosperous of the sheiks could afford her now. But this was no sheik. The man wore the khaki uniform of the Wermacht, a junior officer, and his blonde hair and handsome looks had evidently gotten Malieva's attention. He was slightly drunk and whispered something to her through the bars in German and she laughed as he paid off the guard and helped her down. They walked out into the desert and soon the familiar moans began, very loud this time. It was almost an hour before she returned, looking sexy and satisfied. The young Army lieutenant, carrying a bottle and weaving, gave her a tip and then looked around to see if anyone was listening. Margaret pushed herself back into the deeper shadows of the bedding. Satisfied, he came close to Malieva and took her hand.

"I see you again, ya?"

"Why?"

"We will be coming back here a lot."

"Oh?"

"Ya, we find something, a big mine on the river Arumnui, 400 kilometers from here. You know it?"

"Sure. Almost to the Congo. Near Jebel."

"No, farther inland. No towns. Just jungle, where it joins the Congo. We found it. Now we'll be there a long time, so I can come see you all the time, ya? You take care of me."

"No. I must go to Port Sudan. The slave market." This seemed to depress the young man.

"But, I have money. Look," and he produced a handful of green beads. He gave her a few. "Soon, we will rule the earth, you'll see."

She laughed. "Not enough. Those are just trade beads. How you going to rule the earth with those?" But the man suddenly put a finger to his lips.

"Secret. Only the scientists know. Maybe I go to Port Sudan and buy you there, set you free. How would you like that? I'll bet you'd be very grateful, huh?" She smiled and kissed him, a kiss that seemed to go on forever. The drunken German, his head swimming with visions of a private harem, finally turned and staggered back up the caravan. He didn't notice that his wallet was gone.

The two girls talked until very late. Margaret had her draw a rough map of the rivers of the Congo, and she traded away her compact for some of the beads. At the next oasis, after a small sandstorm, she decided to risk another escape. She waited until the guard had turned away to light his pipe and slipped out of the cart with food and water she had been hiding. They had stopped on the outskirt of a small village and she planned to find the first friendly face she could and barter for a camel to take her to Banbuku.

As she slipped out of the cart and ran for the safety of the village, she thought she could hear something behind her. She stopped for a moment and listened, but there seemed to be no one. About one kilometer away she could see a few lights from the village, and set off again. As she reached the crest of a low hill, there was a dark figure waiting for her. It was Tarik. She had no weapons. As he stepped forward she noticed he had a heavy pack over his shoulder and was carrying a Martini-Henri bolt action rifle.

"We meet again."

"What are you doing here? Malieva is back that way. Isn't she your favorite?"

"Maybe. I decided it was time to leave." She started walking again for the village and he fell in next to her.

"Oh?" she asked. "Why was that?"

"Well, in my business, information can be valuable. It seems the Germans have found something important. I wonder how much the British would pay? Or the Americans? Maybe the Russians. Germans have lots of enemies," he laughed.

"Well I'm going to Banbuku. If I see any buyers I'll be sure to send them your way." This made Tarik laugh.

"You don't get it, do you? You and me, we travel together now. For one thing, a woman alone in the desert wouldn't last two days. You think you can walk into that village and they'll help you? The women will take one look at you and put a knife in your back."

"I don't believe you," she snapped, irritated as his smug confidence and the way he looked her over.

"You'd better, because you're going to need me," he said and came over to her. She tried to ignore him and when he took her in his arms and kissed her, once, very hard. she fought for a second and then was shocked to find something awakening deep inside her. She broke free and started to slap him but he was smiling and she thought better of it and started walking again.

"Where are we going?" she asked.

"The Congo, of course. The Germans will never find the true mine, high on a mountainside that overlooks the river.

You see, I know who gave them the information and his information is wrong by 50 miles. I, Tarik, I know how to find it, I know all it's secrets. And when the Germans come looking, and then the British, they will pay a fortune for the information."

She tried to get away, but he held her fast.

"Let me go!" she cried, and tried to scratch his face, but he only held her tighter.

"They told me about you. An educated woman, chemistry and physics. I will have need of you, my beauty. Besides, with you at my side, your friends won't try anything. Be good and I'll split the fortune. Now come," he said, with a commanding tone that would brook no dissent, and five minutes later they came to four camels, fully packed and ready.

"It will be a long journey. But I promise I will return you to your father. And then you will see that Tarik is not a bad man and when we are rich, maybe then you will think different and be my woman," he added with a laugh, and turning the camels to the southwest, they moved off at a steady pace into the cold and silent darkness.

• • •

The remains of Banbuku had not improved when Henry and McQueen finally rode in two weeks later. Most of the city had burned to the ground, and what was left the scavengers had soon cleaned out. It was a cursed city. People said that a devil had come to dwell in Banbuku. The villagers who had not been killed by the Germans had escaped into the surrounding hills, and it was only now that a few began to return, looking for food and anything they could sell.

Henry, ever fearful of losing his treasure to robbers, had gotten very little sleep and clung to the camel's neck as they entered what had once been the main street. The skeletons of the old souk and its shops stared back at them, and the wind blew the dust freely down the road and out toward the sea, where they hoped to catch site of the Goose, and Eddie.

But the town was not completely deserted. Here and there they could see eyes in blackened faces looking at them, and when people saw that they were not Germans a few beggars appeared and asked for bread, but McQueen was in a hurry, and they did not pause until they had reached the remains of the dock. Only a few charred pylons remained, and what little shelter there had been from trees along the shore was gone.

"Why did they do this?" wondered Henry, half to himself. "What was the point?" He was still pondering the question when an old man, so thin his ribs showed through his skin, wandered up to them without a word and merely waited. McQueen found a piece of rabbit from their last night's meal and held it out to the old man. He smiled at them, bowed deeply, and accepted the priceless gift. After he had eaten McQueen got down from the camel and sat next to the man.

"What happened here?" he asked in Bantu. The old man looked around and gestured with a sweep of his hand.

"Soldiers come. Say all village boys go with them. We hide the boys. They kill many, then start fires," he answered in a slow, dignified voice devoid of anger and dulled by hunger.

"Where did they go?" asked McQueen. The old man pointed. He was pointing toward the west. McQueen gave the man some more food and they rode on.

"Now what?" asked Henry after they ridden a short way.

"Now we look for Eddie and the Goose."

"You think he went back to Cairo?"

"Eddie wouldn't have done that. We'll find him."

But after two days of searching the ruins for any sign of Eddie or the Goose there was no sign. Henry thought there had been a radio at the trading post but it had been looted several times.

The banks of the river were lush with tall trees but there was no place you could hide an airplane that size. They talked to the fishermen who plied the river fishing for perch but it had been some weeks since the Germans left and no one had seen anything.

The most dangerous time came at night, when they made their campfire and cooked whatever scraps of food they had salvaged from the trip. A few minutes after the fire started, they could see the eyes of the survivors watching them from a distance. The men slept in shifts, but even so it was sometimes necessary to fire a couple of rounds when the ghost-like creatures came too near. McQueen would have preferred to help but there were simply too many of them.

By the third night the situation had become untenable. After they had eaten Henry took an inventory of their food. It was almost gone.

"I have to go find her," he began.

"Where?" asked McQueen. Henry scratched his head and wiped away the sweat.

"In the old days it was Suakin, fifty miles down the coast, but now it's Port Sudan."

"How you going to get there? It's 700 miles to the sea. That's Beja land, all the way to the sea. They'll cut you to pieces."

"Maybe."

"We'll try for Sennar."

"On the Blue Nile?" He got up and waved to a large dhow putting in for the night not 100 yards away.

"Come on," he said, and started walking. "Let's make this fast." An hour later they had made a deal. It had cost Henry his Patek Phillipe watch, for which he had complained bitterly, but the dhow owner would take nothing less and with three camels to carry plus the threat of the starving survivors at their heels, it seemed like a bargain to McQueen.

They crossed the river with no difficulties and by morning were on their way east, toward Eddie and rescue - or a hot grave in the desert sands.

• • •

Eddie had not been idle. McQueen and Margaret had been gone for six weeks by the time the Germans appeared one morning on the horizon. It was a flotilla of six boats, each of them crammed with soldiers. He had taken the precaution of moving the Goose under a stand of tries on the river bank, and when a quick look through the binoculars showed these were not British soldiers, he knew it was time to go.

The Goose was fully fueled, and it took only a few minutes to break camp and load the essentials into the plane. The pre-flight check was usually a matter of professional discipline to Eddie and he hated to rush it, but the boats, now two kilometers away, would soon be in range for small arm fire. He cast off the mooring line and put it aboard, secured the hatch, powered up the gasoline pressure tanks, checked the flaps, buckled himself in and hit the ignition switch. There was a sickening moment where nothing happened. Then he remembered that the fuel lines were probably dry from having sat idle.

Finally, after priming the carburetors, the port engine fired, then the starboard sputtered to life, paused and quit. He tried it again with the same result, then re-checked all his instruments. Just as he was looking at the manifold pressure gauge the first bullets struck the trees above him. The lead boat was now less than a mile distant and there was a plume of white water coming from the stern. He had a momentary flash of two riflemen in the bow firing short bursts from machine guns when he realized he had not yet open the fuel valve to the starboard system. After adjusting switches the engine at last turned over and the plane began to move through the water.

She was a better target out in the open, and the firing of the distant guns grew more intense. Eddie gave both engines full throttle, which was dangerous at any time in a seaplane but particularly so when the pilot doesn't know of any submerged hazards. But a few seconds later he was racing across the water, then climbing up to "step" for a few more moments, then with a final bounce the Goose was free of the water and climbing, the engines drowning out any sounds of gunfire.

It had been very close, and he resisted the temptation to go back and shoot up the German boats with the onboard canon. With a steady hand on the stick the plane banked to the left and took up a heading of 11 degrees east. With luck, he would be at Sennar on the Blue Nile in time for a proper breakfast. The thought of it cheered him. He was very sick of eating Nile perch.

Eddie was well aware of the history of Sennar. Once part of a mighty empire stretching from Suakin on the Red Sea almost to the Pacific, it had been explored by the Romans in the third century B.C. when it was a part of the Beja lands, who were originally Christian. In the 16th century it had passed into Ottoman control but declined sharply after the Portuguese discovered the sea route around Africa to the Indies, thus bypassing the Red Sea. The Ottomans tried to stop this trade, were unsuccessful, and the port of Suakin was a virtual ghost town by the 18th century. Kitchener used it as a headquarters during the suppression of the Mahdi in 1897, but the decline continued.

Two hours later he landed and settled in for the duration after verifying no damage to the plane. Working through friends he had found help while haggling with the owner over a Roman artifact of dubious provenance at the general store. The man was a a French trader named Fayer who regularly made trips between Sennar and Kandohar. He was greying and nearly deaf but for a stipend of 1,000 francs, the fat little man had agreed to go and have a look around the town. Eddie hadn't liked it but he had no choice.

Weeks later the man had sent only one message: "Town decimated, no white men seen, send more money." After that Eddie had heard nothing more from Fayer but word was beginning to filter out that indeed the Germans had gone away to the east. The time had come for action.

It was an overcast morning when he eased the Goose out into the main channel and turned her into the wind. It was a risk, he knew, to go back, but he could wait no longer. For McQueen to have sent no word in nearly a month meant there was trouble. He knew he could expect no fuel at Banbuku, but the Goose had been designed with long range tanks and it was his plan to push on toward the last place on the map McQueen had shown him. It was a poor plan but he could think of no other.

An hour later he was flying at 2,000 feet toward Banbuku, keeping his altitude low enough to see the ground but high enough to be out of rifle shot. When he chanced to look down and saw the ambush, it was sheer luck.

•   •   •

McQueen and Henry had been averaging 50 miles a day for the first few days, but the camels were too old and tired to keep up the pace. They had encountered a small hunting party of Beja tribesmen and had scared them off, but they had shot one of the camels and they had had to transfer the food and water to the remaining two. It was nearly too much, and they were now reduced to traveling no more than 15 miles a day.

They had stopped to eat near a grove of baobab trees and had made a fire to cook a small pig they had shot when McQueen heard the distant sound of men shouting. They had been spotted. A dozen mounted tribesmen came into view, all of them armed.

"Are they the same ones from yesterday?" asked Henry, getting to his feet and checking his pistol. McQueen was already looking through binoculars.

"Uh huh."

"Can we run for it?" he asked, looking at the far horizon where a range of low hills rose out of the desert.

"Doubtful. Too far to the nearest dunes. They'd close the distance before we're halfway there. Real problem is they've got the new Mauser longbore. Friend of mine at Khartoum told me he knew who they got it from too."

"Germans."

"Yeah. They'll probably surround us, then pick us off from long range. Best bet is to try to slow 'em up till nightfall, make a run for it. You get over there to the right, behind the camels."

As he finished talking, there was the sharp report of a rifle and a bullet narrowly missed his head. Then more started coming in. McQueen checked his ammunition and was about to sprint for cover when the drone of engines stopped him and he looked up.

It was the Goose. She was banking hard and McQueen thought he could just make out the muzzle of the heavy caliber automatic cannon that Ellison had installed pushing forward through the small door in the nose. Moments later he could hear the engines of the Goose pushed to full throttle to counteract the recoil of the heavy cannon as it began spitting out death. The first few bursts were short of the mark, but as the plane finished its bank two more followed, cutting in half two of the camels and scattering the tribesmen like ants. The Goose made another turn and this time three more of the men fell. The rest turned and galloped back the way they had come.

As McQueen and Henry waited, the Goose came down very low and flew over them at 50 feet. As it passed, the wings dipped and it came back around. There was a flat grassy plain about a mile away and after doing two reconnaissance sweeps Eddie sat the Goose down flawlessly and she rolled to a stop.

McQueen came to the cabin door and opened it. "Man, that thing is nasty. Where'd you learn to shoot like that?" he asked with a grin as the two men shook hands.

"What else is there to do? Why don't we haul our tail out of here."

"Good idea," he said as he and Henry started hauling their goods to the plane. Eddie noticed Henry taking special pains with the 50 lb. treasure box.

"What's in there?" asked Eddie.

"My life's work," said Henry.

"Can I have a look? I'm always in the market for something different."

"Maybe later. How was it in Banbuku?"

"Just as bad as bad can get," said a disappointed Eddie. "They showed up on a Tuesday, and by Thursday the whole town was on fire. Tried to come back once but they had guards all along the river. Figured you and Underwood here were not gonna be stupid enough to try and take on that mob."

"Right you are, my friend," said Henry. "Have you heard anything from my daughter? She would have tried to come back this way if she was free, I'm certain of it." Eddie could read the anxiety in the older man's voice, but there was no time for commiserating. On the far ridge he saw the remaining tribesmen had regrouped and were watching them.

A few minutes later McQueen released the camels, partial payment to the tribesmen for the ones shot up by Eddie. McQueen loosed a few rounds at the tribesmen, who again retreated, and climbing aboard he turned the Goose into the wind and pushed the throttles forward. The huge Lycomings roared in protest and a minute later they were soaring over the would-be attackers, who watched in silence as the plane disappeared into the east. They would accept the camels.

Aboard the plane it was all business. McQueen climbed to 12,000 feet, the service ceiling of the Goose, and handed Eddie a message form. "Send that out to the Ambassador. Use today's code," he added as Eddie looked over the long hand written sheet. There was a code book hidden in the dash panel of the Goose, and Eddie retrieved it and began transposing words. In 15 minutes he had finished, and with the Morse code keyblock on his lap began sending. It took a full two minutes to transmit the lengthy report.

"OK, Joe. Now we wait for a confirmation?"

"Right." During the transmission Henry had sat silent, holding the treasure box. Now, like a reluctant gambler leaving a hot hand, he came forward.

"Where are we going?" he asked. McQueen checked his headings and listened on the headset a moment.

"Port Sudan. If she's there, we'll find her."

"But what about this business with the Germans?" At this question, Eddie stopped what he was doing and listened.

"I signed a contract to bring you back. What happened at El Fashr is my fault. Until we find her, everything else is off the table. OK?"

Henry was greatly relieved, clapped him on the shoulder. "OK, I just thought..." He was cut off as Eddie held up a hand for quiet. Transmission was coming in and he hurried to keep up with the incoming message. He tapped out a brief reply, there was a final few characters and it was over. Eddie looked a little surprised, and grinned his gap-toothed grin that McQueen had so often seen and that meant major news. McQueen cocked an eyebrow at him as he finished decoding the message. Henry inched forward to hear.

"And I quote: 'Message received stop marine detachment Khartoum at your disposal stop endeavor prevent Germans seizing the asset stop godspeed Ellison endit." Eddie pushed back his cap. "You know what this man is talking about?" McQueen shook his head and stifled a chuckle. It was just like the ambassador to cut to the chase without embellishing, but even for him this was impressive.

"It means," began McQueen, consulting a map and then trimming the nose down 5 degrees for the long descent to the afternoon's landing, "that the Ambassador, in his usual indirect manner, would very much like some more information." He glanced at Henry. "After we find Margaret. Signal the Ambassador: Proceeding Port Sudan. Will advise. McQueen."

Chapter 9

IT WAS THE MORNING of the next day when the great Red Sea came into view. They had camped in peaceful solitude the evening before on a small tributary of the Blue Nile, and had been able to refill their water casks and relax for a few hours. Eddie had found a small herd of Thompson's gazelles in the next valley and had shot one, providing them with the first hot meal in several days.

McQueen knew that the German navy generally stayed out of this part of the world but he nevertheless had Eddie and Henry maintain a lookout on both sides of the aircraft. Seeing no threat, he began the long descent toward the sea. Henry came forward and looked out at the huge expanse of water.

"That's not Port Sudan."

"No, it's Suakin. We stop here to refuel and to ask questions about conditions in Port Sudan. If anybody asks, were a bunch of wealthy tourists out for a joyride. OK?"

"Sure, sure. You don't take many chances, do you?"

"Not if I don't have to. Both of you, pistols only, and keep them out of sight."

The plane made a pass over the deserted island city of Suakin, once a place of unimaginable riches but now reduced to a ghost town full of crumbling monuments to the many civilizations that had made the walled city the center of central African commerce for centuries. Felled by technology when Port Sudan proved to be a more hospitable port, it now held only a scattering of farmers and fishermen.

They set down easily in the harbor and taxied to the deserted island as the sun was getting low on the horizon. It was not as deserted as McQueen had remembered. There was a presence here, he could sense.

He cut the engines as they drifted to the stone quai and Eddie tied up the nose line to an old pillar.

"I don't like this place, Joe. What you figure to find here besides gas?"

"We'll see. Let's move before it gets dark."

It took nearly an hour before they found what McQueen was looking for. There was a small ferry boat operated by an Englishman that supposedly ran between Jeddah and Suakin three times a week, McQueen knew. As it turned out, the man was an expatriate Englishman named Blakemoor, which in Arabic had been shortened to Ben-Bala. After growing a magnificent beard and learning a few words of Arabic he'd found that there was plenty of money to be made by anyone with a boat, which he had won in a game of *tarneeb*, an Arabic game of chance. The boat proved to be barely afloat, and after spending a small fortune making it seaworthy, the newly anointed Ben-Bala had vowed never again to play card games with Bedouins.

McQueen found him at the dock, trying to nurse a diesel engine back to life by adjusting the carburetor valve. The engine kicked over, wheezed, and stopped. This was repeated three more times, with the same result. McQueen listened politely and waited.

"Yes, what is your business here, effendi?" he said in broken Arabic, bowing politely to McQueen as is the custom. McQueen had a look at the diesel.

"Oh, just doing some fishing. Fairbanks-Morse, model 104. Right?"

"You know your engines."

"Sounds like your plugs are fouled. Try filing off the electrode where it's burned through." Ben-Bala stared at the stranger a moment, took out a wrench, unscrewed a small cover and removed the plug. With a broken file he chipped off some black debris and reinstalled it. Moments later the diesel was purring.

"So. Who are you and what are you doing in this God-forsaken place?" Ben-Bala extended a hand. McQueen liked the firm dry handshake and the man instantly.

"Name's McQueen. Like to buy some gas if you've got any."

"All you want. Damn Italians are trying to muscle me out of business. Haven't had a passenger in weeks. What are you sailing?" McQueen pointed to the Goose and Ben-Bala was impressed.

"You flew from Banbuku to here in that?"

"We did."

An hour later the Goose was tied up at Ben-Bala's dock, next to his rusting ferry, being refueled as Eddie did routine maintenance on the Lycomings. McQueen had paid for the gas in English pounds, which Ben-Bala appreciated, and since then had been keeping an eye on the quiet American, waiting for some hint as to his business. But none was forthcoming and the refueling was almost complete, so he walked over to the plane as McQueen was reloading the magazine that fed the nose cannon.

"Interesting. Do a lot of fishing with that?" he asked with a quiet grin, enjoying the moment. "If it helps, I recently was in the British army. Major. Married an Egyptian girl and we moved down here."

McQueen disliked having to explain himself, but the man seemed honest and he was in a hurry. He hoped he wouldn't live to regret his decision.

"We're on our way to Port Sudan. The slave market. Trying to find an English girl. That's her father over there." McQueen returned to his work.

"Oh. I see. Pity. The chances of pulling that off are about the same as me finding new customers in Suakin. You know that most of the slaves go to Jeddah now."

"Yeah, so I heard."

"I used to ferry a few carloads across until I learned what they were up to. Now I'm blackballed up and down the Muslim coast. Can't be helped. Anything I can do?" McQueen got up, looked at the man a moment and decided he was OK.

"You can do us a favor, if you care to. We keep running into Germans, and it's usually trouble. Heard anything about the situation there?" McQueen asked.

"Follow me," said Ben-Bala. Eddie took over the refueling as the two men retired to Ben-Bala's tiny office hut. When the refueling finished it was dark. An hour had gone by and Henry and Eddie were eating when McQueen came out of the hut and looked around. He did not look happy.

"She's gassed up and ready, Joe. What did he say?"

"It's not good. The Germans are using Port Sudan as a staging point for some kind of expedition. Keeping it quiet, everything disguised as Dutch. I guess they're pretty good at it. He says there's a rumor of scientists all over town, bringing in equipment, usually at night. The Brits are getting suspicious, but Whitehall won't lift a finger against Hitler as long as he stays out of Poland, so all they can do is watch and try to throw a few monkey wrenches their way. On top of that, he says they've paid off most of the Arabs within a thousand miles. Gold bullion. Promises to end colonialism. Now they've got spies all over the port and from what Ben-Bala says they never ask questions after shooting. A couple of Englishmen were murdered last week in broad daylight."

"Is that all?" asked Eddie.

"I guess so. What does that sound like to you?"

"Sounds like a pretty good way for us to get killed, doesn't it?" mused Eddie with a careless grin as he checked again the port engine wiring through an inspection port. Henry came over to McQueen and took him aside.

"Look, McQueen, this isn't what you signed up for, I know that. She's my daughter, I'll take the responsibility. Why don't you go back to Lisbon? We'll settle up and I'll make my way to Port Sudan all right," he said without fear.

"Besides, one old man with a grey beard in a dashiki, who's going to notice that?"

McQueen thought it over. He knew Underwood had a point. But it was too late for that. It had been too late the minute McQueen had shaken hands with Ellison. It was a question of honor. He looked at Eddie.

"It's up to you, Ed. This figures to end up with somebody dead."

"Sounds like it."

"But I've got to go," said McQueen as he tossed his bag into the plane. He looked at his two friends and waited. Eddie tossed his bag into the Goose.

"From what I remember of Port Sudan, a night landing on the Nile is just about the craziest thing anybody could do, what with all the sand bars inshore. They'll never expect that," and without further wasted breath he climbed aboard. Henry shrugged.

"You're both crazy," he noted barely aloud. "Of course, what does that make me?" and a minute later all the bags were aboard and McQueen leaned out of the cabin to shake hands with Ben-Bala.

"Anything we can get for you in Port Sudan?" he asked of the tall Englishman.

"Well, we haven't had any fresh vegetables down here for a month or so."

"See what I can do!" yelled McQueen and he waved as the engines turned over.

•   •   •

The late summer moon was three quarter full as the Goose flew up the coast, standing well out to sea to minimize the chance of being spotted. The navigation was going to be tricky, and Eddie had to wait until he could get a good fix through the roof with the sextant, but after 45 minutes they banked West and there were the lights of Port Sudan in the distance. McQueen immediately dropped down to just above the waves. Looking out the window Henry thought he could see a large herd of dugongs, the manatee-like creatures, feeding on sea grass in the shallows. There were a few freighters playing the waters between Suez and Aden that night, but none of them caught sight of the Goose and no radio messages broke their cover.

The difficult part was coming, and McQueen knew that he had only one chance to slip into the port unnoticed. When they were five miles out he climbed to 10,000 feet and at two miles out he motioned for Eddie to leave his navigator's table and join him in the copilot's chair.

"What's up?" he said.

"We're gonna have to do this dead stick, Ed. I'll need you to help me hold the wheel and operate the flaps. We only get one chance at this. We're at 9800, 140 knots. Glide angle 8 to 1. How far out do you figure before we pull the plug?" he asked. Eddie swallowed hard and tried to remember his algebra as he took out his pencil and did a fast estimate based on their height and the angle to the lights. He tried to push aside the thought that coming in dead stick meant that if they guessed wrong on the landing path they would lose the plane. At a minimum.

"I make it two and a quarter miles out, and we go in... about 30 seconds. The more height the better!" Eddie wasted no more time and got back to Henry fast. "Hey partner, you'd better strap in real good and get something soft around your face. This is going to be rough."

"OK," yelled Henry. "What are we doing?"

"Trying to imitate a flying fish!"

At two miles McQueen cut the engines, went to half flaps and dropped the nose. It immediately became quiet in the Goose, so quiet Henry was sure he could hear his heart beating. The lights of the port were clear now. The city spread out along the sea for about a mile. To the left was the commercial docks, and in the moonlight they could see four freighters tied up.

"Over there," said Eddie quietly. To their right there was a scattering of houses and a few darkened buildings, and McQueen banked gently.

"Keep an eye on the speed and altitude for me," he said as the plane continued to drop at a steep angle.

"135, 130, 127.... stall speed is 85," said Eddie.

"I know," answered McQueen as he peered into the blackness looking for smooth water. "What's that on the right?" Eddie raised his binoculars.

"Sand bar. Big one!" McQueen banked hard to the left. "120, 4000 feet."

"OK."

"Wind looks like it's offshore."

"OK."

And then they hit the turbulence. The Sahara produces tremendous thermal energy during the day, which translates to rising air, sometimes to as high as 10,000 feet. At night, particularly over water, that heated air falls, often causing violent turbulence. The Goose shook like a roller coaster as they passed through 3,000 feet, and Henry, sweat pouring down his face, concentrated on staring straight ahead.

Where the sea meets the sand in Port Sudan there are generally waves of no more than a foot high, and the small boy who was out playing with his knife stopped in mid throw, his mouth open, as the Goose silently swept over his head at 100 feet and touched down moments later with a tremendous splash. He ran to the edge of the water and watched as the plane finally emerged from the geyser of water and came to a stop, bobbing gently on the waves.

Inside the Goose, despite having tied everything down, everything was chaos. There were charts and bags all over the cabin, but they had survived the first crash, the leap into the air and then the sickening feeling of pancaking hard into the water which could have broken the plane's back. McQueen was immediately up and went to the hatch.

"Break out the oars. We'll row ashore."

"OK," said Eddie, and handed an oar to a still gasping Henry. "You OK?" he queried.

"Oh, fine. Tell me, have you two ever done anything like this before?" The two men started to row as McQueen climbed out onto the nose and then up onto the wing, looking for damage.

"Only once that I remember. It was off the Azores and we had run out of gas. There was sharks in the water, too. Great story. Care to hear about it?"

"Some other time, thank you."

An hour later, three very weary men were able to move the Goose a hundred yards down the beach to a fallen branch which was jutting into the water. There was a scant amount of trees sheltering the plane and they unfolded a light parachute cloth camoflage and covered the Goose, but

McQueen knew they would be in danger of discovery every minute in Port Sudan.

Port Sudan was at that time laid out in a grid around the harbor, comprised of winding streets made of rough cut stone with shops on the ground floor and apartments above. From its roots as a railway terminus built by the British in 1909 linking the rich cotton and sesame seed growing regions around Khartoum, the city and its port had grown into the chief entry point into both Saharan Africa and the rich lands of the Congo basin. Consequently, every imaginable commodity flowed through the city's seven main docks and the usual collection of agents, forwarders and criminals thrived off the rich trade.

It was also the home of the largest slave market on the Red Sea. Beginning in the 8th century A.D. the area had been a transit point for Arabian traders dealing in gold, slaves, ivory and cattle. After Suakin was eclipsed by Port Sudan in the early 20th century, the clandestine trade destined for Arabia moved quietly up the coast. Because of its illicit nature it was conducted by particularly brutal traders, and strangers were never welcome even if they could find one of the closed markets where business was done.

McQueen knew all about this trade and had a good idea where he could find the girl if she was still alive. The presence of Henry was the complicating factor. Without him they could do as they pleased, but Henry would give the captors the leverage of potential retribution against the girl. He didn't look forward to the dealings that had to come.

They had dressed themselves in robes of one of the ethnic Nilotic tribes that they might blend in easier, and after encountering no suspicious looks they entered the Street of Abdulaziz where the small souk yielded its secrets to those with money and the right answers. Several times they passed small detachments of British soldiers on patrol.

"Well, it looks like the British are not entirely asleep after all," said Eddie.

"Thank you. We've been managing the empire for a few hundred years, you know," said Henry.

"No argument there," said McQueen as they started up a shallow hill toward the souk. The actual slave market was down a long, narrow passage lined with lime trees and dimly lit. At the end was an iron grate guarded by several armed men. As they walked silently down the passage Henry pulled McQueen aside.

"You've been here before," said Henry, a little intimidated.

"Yeah. It'll be OK."

"I know this isn't the time, but someday tell me about it. In the meantime, how do we get past the guards?" In answer McQueen held up a finger to his lips. They walked to the gate and McQueen handed the first guard a bank note for 5 Sudanese pounds, a small fortune. He whispered a word to the guard and the door opened.

Inside was a scene not unlike that found in Rome 19 centuries earlier. There was a small dirt floor, like a stage, surrounded by curving walls above which were rows of seats. The slaves were led out and the bidding was brisk and businesslike. While they watched, a group of Nubians were sold, then what looked like four pirates. The guards worse heavy embroidered robes and long scimitars. It was a serious business and everyone strained to hear as the auctioneer called out each new description.

As they watched, Sheik Ibrahim entered the market with four female slaves. They passed through a thick cordon of armed men and arrived just outside the lighted stage area and waited for their turn to be called.

McQueen turned to Henry and lowered his voice. "When the trader comes this way, let me do the talking. His name is Hasan. Used to be a rug merchant in Cairo. Looks like he's moved up in the world."

"You're the expert. Just don't get too friendly. I'd like to shoot the lot of these bastards." McQueen glanced at him and nodded. As he looked away, he caught sight of a slave girl, very close, staring at him with eyes wide apart. She was very beautiful and there was a chain around her left ankle. McQueen might have been moved to pity had he been given more time, but to his surprise the girl motioned him over. The prior lot had just been sold and their party would be called any moment.

"You wanted me?" asked McQueen. She looked at him again, closely.

"Are you the pilot McQueen?"

"Yes."

"She described you. The blue gray eyes, the handsome profile, and that other man with you, the one with the cigar in his mouth, that must be the father."

"Who are you?" whispered McQueen. By now they had attracted the unfriendly attention of two of Ibrahim's guards. It would be only moments now.

"Her name is Margaret. The one you seek. My name is Malieva. I have a message..." But before she could continue the gate opened before Ibrahim and the guards pushed her forward. McQueen moved to the rail and watched as several buyers crowded in, excited by the unusual beauty of the four females. With a vicious swipe of his hand, one of the guards ripped the silks off the girls and they stood naked. The room became hushed and then the high, almost feminine voice of the auctioneer floated up in the smoky air, listing the virtues and skills of the girls. McQueen could see Malieva blush at the mention of her name. He had a good idea of what the auctioneer was describing and by the looks of the predators around the room, leaning in and out of the light like moray eels coming out to feed, he also knew the girl's ultimate fate. From somewhere, music began to play, slow and suggestive, one of the guards clapped his hands, and the girls began to undulate to the music. The room was hot and after a few moments of this lascivious display McQueen could feel the sweat begin to gather at his armpits.

"Whatever happens next, keep smiling," he said quietly to Henry and Eddie. "Watch my back," he added to Eddie, who nodded silently. Eddie felt for his pistol, although in a room with so much firepower he knew it would be no more than a gesture. Still, better to defy death, he thought.

The auctioneer had just finished his peroration and clapped his hands loudly, three times. The music stopped. The women were allowed to dress. "Men of the Hajj!" he cried. "For all four of these magnificent specimens, what am I bid?" There was a tremendous roar as hands went up and the bidding began. It opened at a thousand dinars and went up steadily, cautiously to twenty thousand, a huge sum. The high bidder, a young hellion in white robes with gold trim and an entourage of three men, smiled.

"Twenty thousand dinars!" As the auctioneer was about to clap his hands, ending the bid, McQueen stepped forward.

"Forty thousand dinars," he said slowly, and held up a leather sack. The auctioneer swung around to face him and smiled.

"Ah, the American adventurer wants to play, eh?" he said with a barely concealed sneer of anticipation, glancing now back at the young Emir. There was a moment of hesitation. The Emir could not match the bid and made a gesture of disgust as he turned away. All around the room the bidders began to laugh. Apparently the young Emir was not popular and now the American had humiliated him. McQueen turned to Henry.

"Give me a thousand pounds."

"What!"

"You heard me. You've got it. And don't stop smiling or we're all dead." The auctioneer was approaching. Eddie and McQueen kept smiling while Henry reached into his pocket for the calfskin pouch he always kept on his person and discreetly withdrew a handful of gold coins. McQueen reached in and grabbed one.

"That'll do," he said and prepared to hand it to the auctioneer. Henry stopped him.

"What are you doing? That's my gold florin, issued in 1344 by King Edward III. It's worth at least ten thousand guineas!" he added plaintively.

"Yeah, but just now we need their goodwill." McQueen smiled and held it up for the auctioneer, who took the coin and looked it over.

"Ahhh, a gold florin, exceedingly rare. But this is worth at least twenty thousand pounds in Zurich to a collector. I believe only five of these are known to exist. I don't understand."

"If you could make change, we'd be very grateful" said Henry with a straight face.

"Merely a small token of our thanks," said McQueen.

"Four!" shouted Henry, "Only four exist." He looked at the smiling auctioneer and at the guards who were not smiling, then inclined his head. "What I meant was, you're welcome your excellency." The auctioneer bowed deeply and spoke a few word to McQueen, who nodded and shook his hands. Moments after the auctioneer had gone, two guards delivered the girls to McQueen, who handed them over to Eddie. He took Malieva aside and the two of them talked for a moment.

"All right. Tell him," said McQueen, indicating Henry.

"We met on the sheik's caravan, outside El Fashr. Margaret and I. She wanted to get word to you but she was taken by the one known as Tarik. They are on their way to the Congo."

"What?" said a startled Henry. "The Congo. Why would they do that?"

"The Germans. Tarik wants to trade a secret to them. For the green stones." Comprehension began to dawn on Henry.

"I know where it is," he said aloud to himself. "I know where they're going." He turned to McQueen. "We could get their first." He wanted to talk more but noticed four armed men had arrived and were watching them. The auctioneer was with them and had a word with one of the guards, who nodded gravely.

"All right, let's fold it up," said McQueen to Eddie. "You go and get the girl's things. They're in the back. Meet us at the plane. Hasan is supplying us with an armed guard. You'll be OK, but don't waste any time."

"You know me," Eddie replied. "But what are you going to be doing?"

"Henry and I have some work to do." He turned to Malieva. "You're coming with us. Put this on." McQueen gave Malieva his jacket and hat and took her arm. She looked like a short man. With Henry following they quietly negotiated the gate and were gone.

Eddie turned back to the three slave girls who were watching him intently. "Moves fast, doesn't he? Anybody speak English?" he asked. They shook their heads. "French?" One of the girls nodded. He switched to broken French as they started walking away, followed by the guards. "Did you ever hear the one about the tortoise and the hare?"

As Eddie and his entourage left the souk and headed toward the sea, he was in the middle of telling a story to his guests and noticed briefly two uniformed British soldiers watching the scene. What he didn't notice was the blonde haired man pressed into the shadows across the street who was watching him. Careful not to attract the attention of the soldiers, the man stayed motionless as Eddie passed by, and when the group had reached the end of the block, the blonde man started following. A few moments later McQueen, Henry and Malieva stepped out of a shop.

"What was that about?" asked Malieva.

"I was afraid of that. It was a trap. We've got to get back to the Goose before Eddie does."

"I don't understand," said Henry.

"The Germans were in there. They put two and two together pretty fast, and now they know we're on to the plan. There's too many British soldiers here to try anything in the open, so they'll probably try to stage an accident." He turned to the girl. "I wish we had more time, but you're free

now. Will you be all right? You've got some place to go?"
She nodded slowly, letting it sink in.

"I don't understand. I'm free?" she asked.

"Yes," he said with a smile. "Good luck." He reached
into his pocket and gave her some bills. She grinned like a
schoolgirl and through her arms around his neck, then
covered his face in kisses and ran as fast as she could toward
the market place. McQueen watched her a minute then
spotted a detachment of British soldiers across the square.
He wondered if it would be enough.

•   •   •

By the time Eddie reached the sea he noticed that the normal
street sounds had been replaced by silence. There were no
children on the street, which was almost deserted.

"Kind of funny, isn't it?" he said in French to one of the
guards. He looked around but could catch no sign of
McQueen or Henry. They were about a mile away from
where the Goose was hidden and he was measuring chances
when there was a loud report of a shot and one of the guards
fell over dead. The scene erupted into chaos. The girls
screamed and tried to run away but bullets were hitting all
around. The guards returned fire but in a few moments they
had all been killed by the fusillade of bullets. The girls tried
to hide, but Eddie knew they couldn't stay in the open and
took them by the arm and they fled down the street.

It was a trap. At the end of the street a horse drawn cart had emerged, and a dozen armed men were waiting for them with heavy rifles. One of them grinned and held up a hand for them to stop. There was no way out. Eddie pressed himself into a doorway and had the girls do the same. They were thirty yards away from the roadblock. Eddie checked his ammunition. He had two spare clips. Not enough to do anything but postpone the inevitable. The leader began advancing toward his quarry.

• • •

A kilometer away, McQueen and Henry were talking and having a cigarette with six soldiers. Someone had just told a very dirty joke and they were all laughing, except McQueen. The soldiers were sitting on a ridiculous looking contraption, part steel-plated cabriolet and part tank. It was the sort of thing only the British army could produce. McQueen stared at it a moment, then turned to the sergeant in charge.

"That's a Beaverette, isn't it?" remarked McQueen. "Made by the Standard Motor Company in Devon. Usually got a Bren," he added, referring to the standard and very underwhelming armament.

"Yes, sir," said the sergeant. "You seem to know your equipment." McQueen had a look at the very small bore cannon in front.

"Sure is an ugly thing, isn't it? What do you use it for? Opening up tins of fish?" McQueen grinned. The sergeant was embarrassed by this.

"Oh, this and that. I'm sure it'll come in very handy. Eventually. We've made some modifications to the gun, you see." The Sergeant patted the muzzle of the forward cannon, which looked like a sawed off stove pipe. "Not very good at distance, but quite nasty close up."

"Is that right? No, I'll bet you couldn't even stop a hold up with one of those," he said with a disarming grin, enjoying it. "I'd be afraid one of the bad guys would kick a hole in the side."

"Oh, I wouldn't say that, sir. You could do quite a bit of damage with that gun if you had a mind to. Providing the target stayed still." Everyone nodded solemnly as McQueen had a closer look at the controls inside the metal box where the driver sat.

"In fact, I'll bet you that just two or three Germans, let's say, could knock this thing over with a 22 caliber pistol."

"Rubbish. Absolute rubbish. How'd you like a little demonstration?"

McQueen smiled and shook his hand. "Exactly what I was thinking. Mind if I drive?"

• • •

As Eddie waited, the gunman approached to within 10 yards and stopped. "Come out, Yank," he said in a bored tone, the English thickly accented with German. "We won't shoot if you come out now with your hands up. Otherwise, it won't go so good for you," and he fired a few shots that ricocheted off the walls and nearly struck one of the girls. Eddie was beginning to lose his patience.

"All right but give me a minute!" he shouted, and from cover fired at the speaker, who fell back. "Get down now," he said to the girls.

As the gunman was walking back to the barricade he was smiling, thinking how he would deal with this arrogant American, when he was distracted by the sound of a high pitched engine. He started to aim his gun but it was too late. The Beaverette, driven by McQueen, rolled into view and stopped. A shout went up as the would be ambushers raised their guns.

The cannon fired a shell which blew apart the cart in a fireball that rose 200 feet into the sky. When the smoke cleared there was nothing left of the attackers except some bloody smudges on the street. None of them lived to see the British soldiers laughing hysterically at the sight of the Beaverette knocked onto its side from the recoil. Henry and the soldiers helped McQueen out of the vehicle as Eddie and the slave girls cautiously peered through the smoke.

"What the hell was that?" said Eddie.

After a round of drinks, which McQueen had been powerless to avoid, they reached the Goose in mid-afternoon light. The plane was fueled and ready for departure. McQueen came out to the three ex-slave girls waiting on the dock, gave them each a few pounds and wished them luck. Two of the girls were too stunned to say anything, but the third girl knew a little English and thanked McQueen.

"I wish we had time to take you home. Where do you live?" he asked.

"We are all from Timbuktu. It is all right. We will be able to find a caravan. I know how to dress as a merchant. Thanks to you. If you are ever in Mali, my name is Outinessa." By the way she said it, McQueen had no doubt that she meant to make his welcome a warm one.

Five minutes later the three girls watched the big plane as it raced across the waves, lifted gracefully into the afternoon breeze and slowly banked toward the west. They did not know their rescuer's destination or that their chances of survival would hang upon a string as delicate as a spider's web. They only knew that they were free, and that the world had changed.

Without any talking, they picked up their few belongings, found a path that led away from the sea and within a minute had vanished into the gathering darkness.

Chapter 10

KHARTOUM SITS at the junction of the Blue and White Nile, and while nominally under British protection there were elements of the Italian army always keeping an eye on the comings and goings of river craft and the occasional seaplane that ventured this far south into Africa.

They landed on the river in the early morning when the water was calm and before the big predators came down to drink and bathe. The city at that time was chiefly devoted to moving agriculture up and down the Nile, and of little interest to European travelers.

There was a small U.S. embassy in Khartoum which served the interests of the few American companies doing business in the Sudan, Abyssinia and the Republic of Central Africa. The staff was comprised of the Ambassador, three aides and a small contingent of U.S. Marines, most of whom were veterans who had seen combat in WWI and for whom this was a temporary assignment of one year. They were under the direct control of the Ambassador, were charged with providing security to the embassy and were equipped with rifles and small arms. In all it was considered a pleasant enough billet for the men who were assigned by Washington to the post, and no wives were allowed.

The ambassador at that time was a man named Kirkendahl, a recent promotion to the diplomatic corps. He had been a prize fighter in his youth, had served with distinction in the first world war, and had founded one of the fledgling airmail carriers with surplus WWI aircraft after the Armistice. He was considered something of a maverick, but in the process of negotiating with Washington over airmail contracts had come to the attention of the Hoover administration, who liked his blunt competence and who needed a capable man for the new mission in Japan. He had served ably in Japan and Peru and when an opening appeared in Africa, Kirkendahl, who loved big game hunting, jumped at it. By chance he was also an amateur scientist, and belonged to several academic research foundations. His hobby was electromagnetism.

He liked Africa. He had now lived here for several years and spoke many of the dialects. It was an easy post, giving him time to pursue his interests while staying out of the crosshairs of official Washington and the shifting sands of diplomacy. Correspondence was slow, by ship, and he enjoyed the illusion of being on his own. He knew that in an emergency he could be reached through Cairo by cable, but as yet no lines had been strung to Khartoum. A man of strict discipline and integrity, the Marines revered him.

Some of this background, which he had learned from Ellison, went through McQueen's head as he and Henry found a taxi at the dock and began the 20 minute ride to the embassy, an ornate sandstone building on the edge of the desert. McQueen always thrilled to the sight of the stars and stripes rippling in the wind, and in the Sudan with it's dry climate and hot sun, the flag seemed to almost glow in the mid day sun.

Inside the richly paneled reception room, McQueen checked his weapons and waited while an aide fetched the Ambassador. In a moment he could hear heavy footsteps on the tile floor and they stood.

"Mr. McQueen," said the Ambassador, "so you work for Clayton Ellison. He's a good man." He said it as if the fact was of some importance.

"That he is," agreed McQueen. Kirkendahl had a dry handshake and seemed to be unaffected by the heat. Introductions were brief. "Let's go to my office," he said. "I understand we have a situation." He put a hand on McQueen's back. "You know, life tends to be pretty dull out here on the Sahara. Smuggling, sheep stealing, that sort of thing. This is the most excitement we've had since the Germans lost their colonies," he said in casual, friendly tone. McQueen was starting to like the man.

They talked for almost a half hour without interruption. McQueen told him about his encounters in Cairo, the German scientists he had seen and the sacking of Banbuku. Throughout the Ambassador listened in silence, only asking a few questions. When McQueen had finished he sat back in his chair and closed his eyes.

"Very interesting. And a little frightening if it's true," he said at last. "Of course, you don't have any real proof, just a lot of supposition and guesswork. And now you want my Marines, is that it?"

"Yes, sir," said McQueen, noting for the first time the shrewdness behind all that charm.

"And what's your interest in all this, Mr. Underwood? I should add that I'm familiar with your work, although I think you may have trouble proving some of your theories about the early Egyptian dynasties."

"My interest is in finding my daughter, sir. If she's gone into the interior with that slave trader, that's where I'm going. As for my theories, I'd advise you to withhold judgment until I publish my papers."

"Fair enough. This thing with you and Ellison, I notice that nobody else in State is in on the plan. Is that right?"

"Yes, sir," said McQueen. "The way he wanted it." The ambassador nodded again.

"If it is true," he began, and now the velvet was gone and the voice has hard and low, "and the Germans are developing some kind of super bomb, we're in a hell of a mess. Under neutrality, we can't confront them officially. Unofficially and off the record, I'd like to see the War department send in a battalion and wipe the Krauts off the face of Africa for what they did in the colonies. That's another story. Here's something else you may find interesting."

Kirkendahl handed McQueen a telegram. "That's to read, not to keep. Ignore all the scientific notation. What it boils down to is this: some of our people in Germany, and there are damned few because if you knew what they do to spies you wouldn't be able to eat for a week, some of them believe that the Germans are on the verge of developing a fission bomb."

"What's that?" asked McQueen.

"OK. There is a small group outside Berlin called the Uranverein, or the uranium club. They've even published scientific papers on their work, until Hitler stopped it. From what I hear, I am very much afraid they are on the verge of discovering nuclear fission. Without going into the science, that would mean they could construct a bomb whose blast would destroy an entire city. To build one you need uranium ore. Lots of it. The biggest source in the world is the Belgian Congo. You've probably seen one aspect of uranium. These." He held up a few green beads. "If the Germans are here in force, it can only mean they're willing to risk exposure to get enough ore to build a bomb. We shouldn't let that happen. Question is, how do we stop them?" The room fell silent.

The meeting had broken up shortly after that. As they were walking toward the Marine barracks, McQueen and Kirkendahl talked quietly. "McQueen, my men are all volunteers. If they want to go, you can have them for six weeks, special detached training assignment."

"It will probably take longer than that, sir," began McQueen before the Ambassador cut him off.

"I know that, but that's all I can do for now. In a year or so we may be at war with Nazi Germany and then the gloves will be off, but until then we have one hand tied behind our back. Dammit." He said the word as if it left a fetid taste in his mouth. "Let's go talk to the men."

Behind the embassy was a small courtyard, and as the Ambassador stepped outside with his guests the Marines came to attention. It was a small contingent made up of veterans and a few young privates who had never known combat, and led by a crusty old top sergeant named Akerson. His sleeve was covered in service stripes and although he filled out the ceremonial blue jacket a little too amply, McQueen knew immediately that he would be a skilled fighter who would not crack under pressure.

"Men, we have a problem," the Ambassador said. "This is Joe McQueen, former U.S. Navy commander, now a pilot on what I'll call 'special duty' for the State Department. There is a contingent of Germans, we don't know exactly what strength, marching into the Congo from a point south of here. We don't know the details yet, but it appears this may be a threat to the peace which we have all fought to sustain since the Armistice. I know it's not what you were sent here for, but right at this moment you may be the only thing standing between us and a catastrophe. I need volunteers for a six week job. You'll be reporting to Mr. McQueen. Some of you may not be coming back," he added truthfully.

A few moments went by, and then one of the veterans straightened up, buttoned his collar and took a step forward. Then another man. Then all of them.

"Thank you, Mr. Ambassador," McQueen said. "You men, how long do you need to report for duty in field pack for sniper and ambush work?" The oldest of the men, Connors, a sergeant, stepped forward.

"Sir, we're ready now." This made McQueen grin. He liked Marines and it showed in his manner.

"OK. In that case, we meet at the docks at six o'clock. Wish we could take all of you, but my plane only has room for three men. The rest will proceed down the Nile by boat, then inland by whatever transport is available. See Mr. Underwood here for the location of the site we're marching on. That's all." The Marines were dismissed by the sergeant and got busy. McQueen turned to Kirkendahl. "Mr. Ambassador, Sergeant Akerson, can I have a minute?"

• • •

A light wind was blowing that afternoon and raising small wavelets on the river as the group assembled on the dock. McQueen reflected that with the extra weight they would need the wind. He finished conferring with Sergeant Akerson. Three young Marines were drawn by lot to fly down with McQueen. The winners instantly had big grins and there was the usual round of boos and curses from the other men, all of it in the best military tradition, McQueen reflected wryly. He had seen the same thing in flight school. Only after a few crashes had the horseplay died down.

Eddie was warming up the engines as the three Marines went aboard with their gear. The river contingent had heavier guns and had even found a bazooka somewhere. All the Marines were in field kit, and each man had an M1 rifle over the shoulder, a medium weight machine gun, and enough ammunition to endure a small siege. Henry stepped up to one Marine as he got aboard and looked him over.

"How much firepower are you carrying, Marine?"

"5000 rounds, sir."

"Good enough. Up you go."

McQueen conferred with Eddie, looked over the remaining men and walked over to the Sergeant. "All right, Sergeant. You know the rendezvous point?"

"Yes, sir. The Arawimi River."

"Right. Eddie's requisitioned a boat and crew. This man will take you to it. For security, there will be no crew, so use your best judgment on navigation."

"We know the Nile, Sir," Akerson added. McQueen pulled out a map and spread it on the dock.

"All right, here's something you haven't seen. According to reports we've been able to get out of Obedieh and Umn Haar, the Germans have left small garrisons in villages throughout this area. Your mission depends on stealth, sergeant. Try to follow the river all the way to the Aradi, then go west to the objective, but get there by the 10th. We'll be on the north side of the river waiting for you. Good luck."

"And to you sir."

A few minutes later the Goose, burdened by an extra 800 pounds of men and cargo, lifted heavily out of the water, aided by the freshening breeze, and turned south. As they gained altitude McQueen looked down and spotted the large dhow and its crew of Marines, tacking upriver. They had never complained, he thought, never asked for more information than they needed, and like the men of the Corps before them did not flinch when sailing into the unknown.

·   ·   ·

The German contingent, now at regiment strength, had been marching for two weeks across the grasslands of the sub-Sahara. They had brought several armored personnel carriers and trucks for hauling the ore back to the sea, and they had met little resistance from the villages. At every opportunity they had pillaged the land for food and livestock, and the rumor of their passing and of their cruelty had gone before them. The soldiers could see it. The land itself seemed to be rising up against them, and several villages had chosen to run for the shelter of the jungle with their foodstocks rather than give them up to the invaders.

Of all of this Colonel Walser was oblivious. His mission had been clearly stated, and he would not let any "local matters" stand in his way. They took what they wanted and gave nothing in return. It was almost 500 miles from the Nile to his objective, and he had been ordered to force march his men. He had never questioned his order before, and he did not do so now. The few scouts and guides they had conscripted argued among themselves as to which direction was best, and many of them ran away in the night.

The lieutenant in direct charge of the men was a man named Wilhelm Borshman, a quiet anti-Nazi who cared about his men and who had fought the idea of a forced march. After much badgering, he had succeeded in getting Walser to reduce the daily march to daylight hours in the interests of conserving their strength.

By the end of the first week, the accumulation of bad planning and arrogance was beginning to exact a terrible price. Because they had mistreated their guides, they were not told which of the wells they drew water from were contaminated. The first signs of vomiting and fever had quickly spread, and after three days most of the enlisted men were sick. They had been forced to bivouac for two more days to let the men recover, much to the impotent fury of the officers, but there was nothing for it but to wait. And to boil water.

They were now in the great Rift Valley, which is a desert divide between Saharan Africa and the green interior, and the scarcity of game meant they had to conserve their stores. Rationing began, and the men complained. So it was no surprise that on the morning of the ninth day they noticed some of their food from the stores truck was missing. There were no animal tracks. They were being robbed.

"I want these thieves found and shot," said Walser, and the watch was doubled at night. Sometimes they caught sight of a pack of hyenas or lions, and then they would hold their fire. At other times a native would be spotted running off with a small sack of flour or a can of beans, and then the night would erupt with the sound of automatic fire. Several natives were killed but the thievery did not stop, and all of this contributed to a general dulling of the force. Several men were reprimanded for drunkenness.

Borshman had taken Walser aside one night after dinner. He could see the men were dull eyed and tired. "*Oberkommandofuhrer,*" he began in deference to the Colonel's rank, "we cannot keep up this pace if you want to have any men left alive by the time we reach the river. I ask permission for a three day rest and to find good water."

"*Nein*, Borshman." was the curt reply. "We have our orders. We will reach our objective on schedule."

"What good will that do if there are no men left to fight? We need to find guides to show us where the water is safe to drink. We cannot keep up this squalid policy of reprisals against the natives."

"Don't tell me my duty, major, " Walser screamed, "or I will have you shot for insubordination." The two men stared at each other. Borshman could see the older man had developed a glint of madness in his eyes. It was not unlike that of the Fuhrer, he thought. He also knew there were several SS men in the regiment, and that as fanatics they would stand with Walser to the end. He bowed his head and withdrew. There would be no rest.

Three weeks later, full of long marches and bad water, 72 men had died of dehydration, fever and animal attacks out of a force of 400, but they had finally reached the tall teak trees of the rainforest. Here there were small streams and the water was good, but they had only their compasses and an old colonial map to guide them, and there was still 100 miles to go. They had to abandon the vehicles.

Because they had no guide, there was no track to follow, and they were forced to cut their way through the jungle. This meant that five men at a time would take turns swinging machetes and cutting through the thick jungle vines. It was brutal work. For a time they tried using flame throwers to blaze a path, but this backfired badly when they were attacked by retreating animals. And so after a week they settled into a brutal regimen of alternating crews of soldiers cutting their way through the jungle.

More men began to die. The Congo has a thousand ways to kill a man, and the Germans were discovering all of them. Poison insects and snakes, big jungle cats, quicksand, and most lethal of all malaria. When a man was wounded he was left with a pistol and two days ration of food. Often as they marched they could hear in the distance behind them the sound of a large animal bellowing, followed by pistol shots. Other times there was no sound of an animal, and then there would be only the one pistol report.

Finally, after another display of cruelty against local villagers, the last native guide vanished one night during the rain. A squad of riflemen tried to track him, but it was impossible.

The jungle had now become a dense nightmare of hanging vines, trackless bogs and rivers. Walser and Borshman had their compasses, but with each passing day it became obvious to more of the officers: they were lost. Forced by the terrain to backtrack frequently, their progress declined to almost nothing.

Even among the disciplined German army, morale now began to crumble with each mile hacked through the increasingly dark and dense jungle. The heat was oppressive and water was strictly rationed. Above them the canopy of trees had closed in, and sunlight rarely reached the ground. The screams of the men who were scouting ahead of them could sometimes be heard when they had surprised a large predator, and one time they had come upon a huge snake with only the legs and boots of a private sticking out.

All of it weighed on the men. At night they built large fires to keep the predators at bay, but this meant they could see the eyes in the distance, watching them. Occasionally they got lucky and shot a big cat, which would divert the attention of the alligators and other carnivores. But most of the time man and beast watched each other and waited.

Slowly, almost inexorably, the food began to run out.

•   •   •

Tarik and his captive had followed the ancient slave trail as far west as Abeshr, deep in the Sahara. He knew every well in that part of the desert, and they were riding young, healthy camels which made the journey easier. They had turned south at Abeshr, and then had come the sandstorms. In the Sahara, which is always hot, storms rise up from the sands at about the same time other regions experience the changing of seasons. There is never any warning. The sky will suddenly show a towering mass of sand and then the traveler will have a few minutes to find shelter or risk death.

After they left Abeshr they had encountered two very severe storms. The first one buried one of the camels alive, and it was only by sheer chance that they found the animal and dug him out before he suffocated. The second storm was worse, and was so severe and lasted for six hours that two of the camels panicked and later disappeared under the sands and were never found. The sand also made finding the wells more difficult and dangerous. They knew that if they failed to find one of the wells that were shown on Tarik's map they would not long survive.

They also knew that in this region of Africa there was no law. Although technically the Sudan stretched as far south as Bel Jebel and west to the French Congo, this was tribal land and the various warlords held sway. Tarik knew he could not fight such forces, and had come equipped with a surprising variety of trade goods, including bourbon, mirrors, canned fruit and the ubiquitous green beads. One or two chance meetings with local Bedouins had convinced Margaret that he at least knew what he was doing with the locals.

She had tried without success to buy or bargain for her freedom, including promises of a handsome reward should he return her to Cairo, but nothing came of it and after a time she had given up asking. He had never tried to press his attentions on her, and so an uneasy truce had formed.

She had to admit that as a scientist and student of human behavior, she found him an interesting man. Tall, rugged, blunt as a rock but restrained by his own curious code of honor, she was to witness many times how his ebullient personality had won over skeptics and potential enemies who found themselves drawn to this darkly charismatic man of the desert. At other times, when good humor had failed, she had seen the fighter within the man, and how he was able to quickly dispatch his enemy almost before the other man knew there was a fight.

And he seemed to have endless stories, stories about ancient battles and kings and queens and how they used or abused their power, which he delighted in telling her at night around the fire, often with slight variations to fit the circumstances. Finally, she had come to regard him as amusing. She couldn't tell if this had been his plan all along, but she felt strangely safe.

At the edge of the great rainforest they reached a trading post maintained by an expatriate Frenchman of dubious character named Serge. It was nothing but a mud house built up over the years, covered in great green leaves and guarded by Serge's several children, each of whom carried a great machete. There was the ritual circling of the two men, the sizing up and the argument over values. To her surprise Tarik had traded the surviving camels - which included a priceless female carrying a calf - for a dugout canoe, about 20 feet long, and gear for fishing. To commemorate the deal, the two men went inside and drank down a small bottle of whisky which Tarik had been keeping for just such a purpose. After half an hour he came out, not drunk but certainly in a good mood.

"Maybe luck is with us. We got the boat."

"Is that all?" she asked.

"What else could we ask for?" he laughed, long and deeply. "He said the Germans are supposed to be many days march from here and they have no boats. We will certainly get there first. I told you, didn't I, that we would do it?" She nodded silently. He could see that she was sad, and wanted her to enter into his mood and would have comforted her, but it was not in his nature to comfort women. He had loved many and fought for many more, and he had many children. But he did not know how to do this thing the English did and it made him feel inadequate for one of the few times in his hard and dangerous life.

"You want to see your father, don't you?"

"I didn't know a slave was permitted to have an opinion," she said at last and returned to the camels to begin the unpacking. She had asked for this life, she reminded herself. She thought of how bored she had been in London, talking to the same people about the same things, and how she had yearned for adventure. Now she had found it.

The next morning they set out from the trading post. The Congo was narrow here, about 100 meters across, and slow moving. To reach the mine they had to go upriver about 20 miles. There was very little breeze but the sky was open above the river and they encountered no one. Tarik was all business now, watching the river and steering the long pirogue. There was a triangular sail, and when the wind was up he would hoist it and they would make good time.

She sat in the front and listened to the sounds of the rainforest around her. In any other circumstances it would have been thrilling, seeing the monkeys and hippos as they came down to the river to bathe or swim, but she could not stop wondering what would happen when they had reached their destination and he had no further use for her.

For a week they toiled upstream, and more than once they were forced to put in to the shore early when Tarik could no longer paddle. Then they would tie up to a tree and eat and stay alert for any large predators that might be near. But all in all Tarik's luck held, she thought ruefully, and their progress though slow was steady.

They reached the Aruwimi River on the fifth day. A small tributary of the Congo, at this time of year it flowed slowly and was clear. She could see the great fish swimming along beside them, and farther down the crocodiles and other big carnivores of the Congo. Here the water moved slowly but very little light reached them and there was no breeze so the sail would not work. If any of this bothered Tarik he never spoke of it, and Margaret sat silently in the bow as they moved through the twisting green canyons. She reasoned that Tarik was right and that the only place to find her father in Africa would be at the mine, and she planned what she would do next.

• • •

And then one morning, as they came around a bend, the jungle gave way to a great open valley and the sun suddenly illuminated them as if a great light had been turned on. Hard against the slow moving river was a rough hewn fortress made of stones, fifty feet high and going back a hundred yards or more. There were several smaller structures and guard houses high up at the corners. No entrance to the fortress was visible. Tarik stood a moment looking at the giant edifice, speechless.

To the left there was a short canal branching off the river running parallel to the main building. At the top of the canal was a small covered storage building where two large dugout pirogues plus several barges were tied up. He could see men unloading cargo from one of the boats and taking it ashore.

"Is that it?" asked Margaret.

"Yes. This wasn't here before," he said. "It was just an open mine, back there, behind those trees." Behind the fortress stood a range of small mountains Margaret estimated at 1,000 feet in height. Ordinarily these would be insignificant because she had seen the great mountains of Switzerland and Wyoming, but after weeks in the flat, oppressive jungle they held the promise of clean air and freedom from the ever-present terror of the creatures that lived near and above the river. Above the fortress was a narrow fissure in a hillside.

Tarik tied up the boat and looked around, his hand never far from the pistol on his hip. Satisfied, he helped her out of the boat.

"Now what?" she asked.

"Stay close." They walked in silence toward the front wall. Up close, it was apparent the stones had been blasted from the mountain and carried down to the river. There were signs of mortar between the stones. As they inspected the wall, Tarik found a door, well disguised and covered in stones. To his surprise the door gave easily as he pushed on it, revealing a grassy upward sloping lawn and a small wooden house at the foot of the hill that stood elevated five feet above the grass. Margaret knew the tribal customs around house building and that this had to be a fairly advanced people. She could see now a thin line of workers ascending out of the mine at the hilltop, carrying heavy looking canvas sacks.

It was a hard climb but 5 minutes later they had reached the guard house., as they called it. The guard was a young tribesman who carried a heavy rifle and spoke no English. It was evidently used as an office. Through the window she could see a desk, filing cabinets and a safe. On the far wall was a powerful looking radio transmitter. Above the house a wire ran almost vertical to a tall tree on top of the hill.

Tarik tried talking with him and after a minute of halting French his Arabic got through and he came back to her.

"He says the boss is up at the mine. And they've been expecting us."

"How?" asked Margaret.

"He didn't say, but it's lucky for us."

"Some lucky. Who is this boss?"

"Olaf, the Dutchman. You can stay here if you like. I won't be long."

"Will there be any food there?"

"Probably."

"Then I'm coming with you," she said, and fell in behind as he started climbing the narrow path that led to the mine.

•　•　•

Just over the crest of the hill was the workshop, which was a long, low building with a roof but no walls that stretched almost 150 meters. Here the raw ore was brought up from the mine and run through crushing machines, then washed and sorted on long tables. In the middle of the building was a large furnace in which the ore was melted down. From this emerged a stream of molten liquid that flowed to a cooling vat.

As they approached the workshop a guard spotted them and lowered his rifle. He proceeded to shout angry instructions at them in a tribal language that Tarik did not know.

"Don't move. We'll wait here," he said. A few more tribesman joined the first and formed a solid knot of angry warriors surrounding them. Throughout Tarik did nothing. Finally, the group began to part and a tall, smiling man pushed his way through. Olaf Steermundt was about 40 and looked as if he had led an exceptionally cruel life. He was a powerfully built man with a nasty scar down his neck and had a neatly trimmed beard which added to the air of the primitive intellectual he had found so useful here in the jungle. His most impressive feature however was his eyes, which were unusually large and betrayed a sheer animal cunning Margaret had never seen before. When he spoke his voice was strangely compelling in its rich baritone with a streak of malice.

"Well, if it isn't my good Tarik! You bastard! A long time," and he let out a sharp laugh. "And how is the slave business?"

"Very well, thank you." They shook hands. Before Tarik could go on Olaf added "And what on earth brings you here to this god-forsaken hole? We don't need any slaves here. These are all freemen, didn't you know? They hate slavers. And who is this beautiful lady with you?"

"Her name is Margaret Underwood."

" American, hmm? Not one of the usual strumpets you generally take up with," he added in an offhanded, curious way that seemed to be part rebuke and part keen perception.

"Mr. whatever your name is, I will gladly pay you handsomely if you can arrange passage to Suakin for me only," she said in an icy voice. Olaf was impressed with her manner and laughed. He held out a rough paw and took her hand in his, never taking his eyes off hers.

"Call me Olaf. Please. I don't suppose she's for sale, is she?" he asked with a wink. Margaret pulled back her hand. "Oh, forgive my bad manners, Miss," he added. "I'm not really what I seem. It's just that we have few women up here anymore and the appearance of one so beautiful as yourself has made me forget what I was doing. Can't get them for love or money, eh Tarik?

"No, not any more," said Tarik, watching Olaf's extravagant interest in Margaret, and she sensed some hint of trouble in their past. "Listen, my friend, we've come to talk business. Important business, and it won't wait."

"You've come on business," she corrected him. "I am a prisoner of this man and I'll make my own terms with Mr. Steermundt, thank you. Is there someplace we can talk?"

Olaf went on looking at Margaret. "Hmmmm. Interesting problem, ain't it?" he said with a chuckle. "How much are you willing to pay?"

"Say two thousand pounds sterling, for safe delivery," she said in her steadiest Englishwoman voice, trying to control the shaking from the suddenly venomous glare of the slaver. "My father is very wealthy." Olaf thought it over and shook his head.

"No, it won't do. 2,000 pounds doesn't mean anything to me," said Olaf, ignoring Tarik's increasing agitation. "Got anything else?" She knew exactly what that meant, but she surprised herself and them by holding her head up high and then very accurately slapping Olaf's face, hard. As she looked at him defiantly, Olaf smiled. Then he laughed.

"Very well. Your pardon, lady. Please make yourself comfortable in my humble home. It's not far from here. Come with me Tarik." Olaf had a brief word with one of the guards, a man who appeared to be the overseer. The two men then walked off, talking and laughing. A guard appeared and pointed Margaret toward the workshop.

The walk took only five minutes. Behind the workshop on a little hill stood Olaf's home. It had once been a church, she saw, and the remains of a steeple were still visible in front. As she stepped inside she was taken by the sense of comfort and taste here in the heart of the jungle. There were rugs on the floor, a comfortable sofa and several chairs, a small piano and in the back a large kitchen and bedrooms. A black woman came out and bowed low.

"I am Hyacinth," she said in broken English. "Please have a seat." On the table were a roast pig and what looked like yams. Hyacinth noted Margaret's interest in the food. "Are you hungry?"

"Oh, yes."

"I'll fix you something. The master already finished his lunch. You can have all you want. " She didn't care anymore about escape or her father or the Germans. All she knew was that here was real food. Hyacinth pulled out a chair for her at the table and for ten minutes she ate in grateful silence, murmuring a thank you when the servant poured what looked like tea. It was one of the finest meals she could remember, and afterwards she sat down on the big sofa and although she knew she should stay vigilant the exhaustion was overwhelming and she was soon fighting the urge to sleep.

A few minutes later Hyacinth came in with a small cotton blanket.

"I saw you closing your eyes and I thought you might want this."

"Thank you," said Margaret, and watched as the servant bent over to close a hamper. The back of her dress was open, exposing part of the skin. On the servant's back were deep scars, as if from a lash or whip. On the far wall was a whip, and a collection of old pistols in a frame. Hyacinth realized the visitor had seen her back and was ashamed.

"Hyacinth, is the master's wife home today?"

Hyacinth looked around, then peered out the windows.

"Oh, he don't have no wife. Sometimes he brings girls up from Kisangani for a few days." As the servant spoke, Margaret started looking for an exit. She could not see the workshop from this room and she could feel the sweat gathering under her arms and her heart beating a little faster. She tried to remain calm talking to the obviously frightened servant.

"Do you make friends with the girls?" she asked. The question seemed to bother Hyacinth. There were two doors facing the workshop, Margaret saw, but they had no doorknob or handles.

"Hyacinth?" she asked.

"No, ma'am, we don't make friends."

"Why not?"

Hyacinth shrugged. "They don't ever come back," she said and knowing she had already said too much went back to the kitchen. Margaret followed her and watched a moment as Hyacinth busied herself with the dishes.

"Where do they go?" There was no reply. Finally, the servant closed the kitchen door and turned toward her and her terrified stare told Margaret what she was afraid to ask. Hyacinth was looking outside. On the hill were perhaps a dozen small makeshift crosses. The servant slowly shook her head. There was no sound in the room as they stood motionless a moment.

"I'd like to go and get my bag," said Margaret, hesitantly. "It's in the boat we came in. You know. I'll only be a minute. Which is the way to the river?"

"Oh, you can't do that. The mister give me hell if you do that," said the servant, nervously. But she had noticed the girl's gaze had gone to a side door off the kitchen, also without a doorknob. The two women shared a long look. Hyacinth was shaking. Then the servant picked up a stack of laundry.

"I have to go upstairs now," she said and left the room. Margaret went to the door and began her search. It took her a full three minutes to find the small key hidden on the shelf next to the door.

• • •

In the office above the workshop where Olaf kept his records and a small radio, Tarik was finishing his story. The din from the crushing machines was loud and he sometimes had to shout. Throughout, Olaf had listened in silence, but as to whether he was interested it was impossible for Tarik to tell, and he began to grow desperate.

"You're sure the Germans are on their way here?" he asked at last.

"Positive. They are well armed my friend, and they will stop at nothing. I have many friends in the British army. They also would want the ore, and would outbid the Germans. If you let me represent you, you will be a very rich man. You can leave the jungle if you want to. I know these men. I can protect you from them. Do we have a deal?"

Olaf thought it over. "And what would your interest be?"

"Oh, a pittance. 20%," said the slave trader. Olaf nodded.

"What about the girl?" Tarik hesitated. He knew Olaf was an unpredictable man, although he always appeared to go out of his way to be gracious.

"Why don't we leave that up to her?" said Tarik. The answer seemed to please the Dutchman.

"And how can you protect me from the Germans?" Now Tarik was rising to the bait, as Olaf knew he would.

"It is a simple thing, my friend, to make the Germans believe the British and the French are near, and that at a word from me they will spoil Berlin's plans and perhaps wipe out the expedition. I am in contact with both British and French elements, not more than two weeks journey from here. The Germans will not risk that kind of exposure. Instead, they will bargain, and the price for your uranium ore will go up." Tarik seemed pleased with his cleverness and lit a cigar. He squinted at Olaf through the blue smoke, waiting for the affirmative response he was sure was coming.

Olaf got to his feet and walked to a heavy metal cabinet. He took out a key ring and unlocked the door. Tarik noticed for the first time that a half dozen of Olaf's men were now in the room, all of them armed. The doors swung open. Olaf spoke a few words and two of his largest men extracted a 50 caliber machine gun, twin barrel, with an ammo belt already inserted.

"You know what this is I expect," he asked a startled Tarik. "Lethal at up to 2,000 yards. Purchased as surplus from the U.S. Navy, courtesy of the Neutrality Act. You see, we've been expecting this day a long time, my good Tarik. I have enough of these and other things to hold off a small army."

"But the Germans have artillery," pointed out Tarik quietly. Olaf nodded, as if expecting this answer.

"Let them. We know the jungle, don't we?" His men all grinned and nodded. "I have nothing to fear from the Germans, Tarik. My scouts have already told me all I need to know about them. They will be here in a few days. We will greet them warmly!" Tarik began to laugh. "Very warmly."

"But the uranium? This is a fortune!" argued Tarik, beginning to sense the trap closing in around him.

"And it will be, I suspect, for years to come. What would I do with a fortune? I can never go back to Europe. I have everything I need here, except for one thing, and you have brought me that. But I must thank you properly for telling the Germans about this place, which you had once swore never to reveal. Or have you forgotten?" Before he could answer, Olaf nodded to his men and instantly Tarik felt the pressure of huge hands on his arms as others took away his pistol and rifle. In moments his hands were tied behind his back and he was led away.

Margaret was out of the house and hurrying up the path when the guards led a struggling Tarik towards a large pit. She didn't hear him plead for his life, or see the look of horror as they reached the edge and he looked down and could see the cobras on the floor of the pit, quietly asleep. Nor did she hear his scream of terror as the guards pushed him in. Olaf stepped to the pit and looked down.

"I'm going to retire for the day. I'm not to be disturbed."

"Yes, boss," the overseer said quickly. The men were happy. Olaf might be gone for several days. There would be a rare day of rest.

• • •

Fifty yards from the house, the path ended just outside the fortress walls, where the clearing ended. Margaret was breathing heavily and looked back. There was no pursuit. She looked at the food she had taken from the kitchen. A good sized ham, enough for several days if she was careful, some bread, a bit of strong twine and a bottle of whisky all wrapped in a tablecloth. There was also a very large butcher knife, recently sharpened. She had also taken one of the old pistols off the wall but didn't know if it was loaded. It was not much, but she was determined to take her chances in the jungle, alone, before she would die in that house.

She stopped and put the food down. The earth by the path was wet from the morning rain, and she quickly smeared her clothes and skin with the black mud until her white shirt and khaki pants were reduced to a gray, mottled blur. She found a stick and with the twine fashioned a crude spear. her heart began to slow down. She had learned much from her father about survival in the wild but had never had occasion to put it to the test.

With a last look back, she turned and started up the path, looking for higher ground where she could watch the river. And wait.

Chapter 11

AFTER A REFUELING STOP they landed the next morning at the ghost town of Banbuku. The Marines had proved to be as stoic as McQueen had expected, and spent most of their time checking their gear, which suited him fine. If anything the city appeared to be more deserted than before. They were on high alert as the Goose taxied to the ruined dock, which had been stripped of everything that could be sold.

"All right. We're here to find petrol. Anyway we can. You three men will be our recon. Concentrate your search along the river bank warehouses. Eddie and I will search in town. Henry, you're staying here with the plane. Shoot at anything that approaches if it's not us.

"Gladly, but don't leave me here too long. I get lonely."

"We'll try," answered McQueen, and the Marines quickly moved down the dock and started working their way along the shore. The fires had at last gone out and McQueen could see they had been well trained, with two men covering each door as the third man went inside. It was a tactic designed to minimize the possibility of surprise.

The three young Marines - Anderson, Snyder and Wilson, all of them from the Midwest - walked quietly on the gravel at the water's edge and spoke only in low whispers. Apart from the wind there was no sound. They passed a warehouse that was partly reduced to rubble and showed signs of recent habitation. The hulks of two burned out restaurants were next, and after a quick look inside they moved on. It was not until they stumbled upon a small brick building partly hidden under the ruins of what must have been a two story hotel that they realized they were not alone. As one of the Marines was about to enter the building he caught sight of something in the distance, like the sun reflecting off of glass. Had he seen any combat he would have recognized the sniper scope, realized that his life expectancy could be measured in milliseconds and dropped to the ground. As it was the sound of the rifle shot and the impact on the Marine's chest were almost simultaneous.

Immediately the other two opened up with short bursts from their Thompsons, and moments later the German sniper fell out of the tree top where he had been living for the past weeks and landed face down in a pool of water. The man who had been hit, Wilson, was face down in the dirt. They turned him over. Whether by chance or design the bullet had struck the steel plated cigarette case he had bought in Istanbul the previous year and glanced off, passing through the skin under his armpit and bleeding heavily. With Snyder covering, Anderson put his wounded comrade over his shoulder and carried him back to the Goose.

In the center of town, McQueen and Eddie had just found a few cans of petrol buried underneath a wooden floor in the home of the former British official in charge of colonial justice for the region. Of the man and his family there was no sign. McQueen and Eddie quickly ripped up the boards and took two five gallon cans each. It was a slow process getting back to the Goose, but they made it and with the help of the two Marines were able to find enough petrol cans under the rubble to get the Goose to 90% capacity.

The onward trip into the Congo was much more difficult. Because of the time of year, the water levels in the southern Sahara rivers such as the Etwonda was too low to risk a landing, so they had detoured south to the Uganda basin. Even so, the water levels were low and there were several submerged trees that had they hit the Goose would have meant the end of their mission. Petrol was plentiful because of the proximity of the British garrisons, and they spent the night in Wadelai on the Nile as guests of the British commander. The small garrison was housed in what had once been a disreputable hotel, and the liquor supply had somehow remained intact.

The fire was growing low in the fireplace by the time the brandy was brought out, and by eight o'clock that night confidences were being shredded left and right. The local commander was a by-the-book captain named Davies, whose chief complaint was being stationed so far from Gibraltar, where he thought there was an excellent chance of promotion. Two of his officers shared the same general opinion, although most thought the Germans were only bluffing in the Rhineland and Austria. Henry tried to raise the issue of English fecklessness in dealing with the Soviets and was roundly condemned. Even Eddie, who normally enjoyed British company, could find little to like in this group. When McQueen tried to raise the subject of a German force marching toward the Congo and the need for coordinated action, the commander had pointed out that it was French territory and a French problem and that His Majesty's Government would in no case get involved.

The three young Marines cared for none of this talk, and concentrated on drinking as much whisky as they could and on correcting a couple of English officers who opined that the British soldier was the toughest in the world. The Marines challenged the Brits to an arm wrestling contest and won, dead drunk.

Listening quietly that night and greatly amused by the brash Americans was a French trader named Leconte, who was returning to his river outpost from Darfur and had heard disquieting rumors about a force of men moving through the region. The British commander excused himself and went to bed, followed by his men. Leconte and McQueen stayed up late talking.

"It's no use trying to motivate the Brits just now," he pointed out. "Pacifists to the core. Same thing with our people. They keep hoping Hitler will get what he wants from someone else and go home."

"What do the French have in this area?" asked McQueen casually. The trader thought a moment.

"All I know is the Foreign Legion has a fort about a hundred miles north of the Congo, place called Fort Bamiku. The only thing they love more than women is a good fight. Almost doesn't matter who wins. Most of 'em are crazy, but good soldiers."

"Sounds like my kind of people," McQueen said. He thought this over for a while and they talked into the night about the qualities of a good fighting man and some of the stories of the Foreign Legion McQueen had heard but had never believed. Leconte assured him they were true.

They talked about the Congo, and the great tributaries that flowed into it, and possible landing sites. McQueen knew that this was the riskiest part of the venture so far. If he was unable to find a decent stretch of water they would be forced into a crash landing, and there were precious few flat grasslands in that part of what many still called the Kongo.

"Have you got parachutes aboard?" asked Leconte.

"A few," said McQueen. But without supplies or ammo, a parachute escape would mean certain death.

In the morning as McQueen and company were getting ready to go, he had a final word with the trader. "You headed back toward Bamiku anytime soon?" he asked.

"In a few days. The army is trying out a new two engine Sparrow and I'm supplying replacement parts. They've invited me to go for a look at the back country." By this time the British commander was back, getting ready for breakfast and noticed the two men talking quietly in the corner. They shook hands and McQueen hurried outside to where Eddie was waiting impatiently for him.

"Wind's changing, Joe. What was all that about?" McQueen gave him one of his trademark grins, which Eddie knew usually meant trouble. Or that he had done something extremely clever.

"Is this going to raise my life insurance rates?"

"Maybe. Little bit of strategic thinking. Always pays to study Clauswitz, you know," and they walked quickly to the

Goose talking about the outlook for river or lake landings along the way.

• • •

The Marines under Akerson had sailed their dhow as far up river as Bel Jebel, where they encountered rapids and could go no further. The heat was excessive here, not like the dry heat of Khartoum, but they were toughened by the trip and well armed. Discipline was excellent.

They were in lion and elephant country now as they secured the boat and prepared to head west toward the rendezvous point. Camels were useless in the grassy terrain and they had searched for two days for horses without success when one of the Marines met a Belgian trader who said he had an old Hispano Suiza truck for sale. The tires were flat but the engine was sound, and after the usual haggling a price was agreed to and the tires were replaced with pneumatic tires that would afford greater durability if less comfort. The Marines cared nothing for comfort.

On the third day after reaching Bel Jebel, therefore, they started out with a month worth of rations and ample first aid supplies offloaded from the dhow. Akerson had insisted on one 50 caliber gun, and though it weighed 120 pounds it was deemed worth the trouble.

The truck carried them for several days, through the British protectorate lands, the Nilotes tribal lands and finally to the edge of the map: the Congo. They were within 100 miles of their destination, but the truck could go no further. They found a village where the elders said they would guard the truck until their return, and in gratitude for a bag full of chocolate, silks and toys even loaned them the services of a *khartugeliman*, which is Niltoes for guide. He would see them as far as the upper reaches of the Arawimi, from where they could float down the river to their destination if they could build a raft.

Akerson thanked their hosts and gave the chief a small pistol and after the men had spread the load among the 10 men they started off on foot. The men took turns carrying the precious radio, which the Ambassador had insisted they take. The chief watched them go, and after they were a hundred yards away they disappeared into the jungle and were seen no more.

• • •

McQueen had been flying for three hours due west when the first signs of trouble in the left engine cropped up. He had been listening carefully, and now he could hear the engine missing. The oil pressure gauge was falling ever so slightly, and he motioned for Eddie to look. In the back, the Marines were asleep.

"What does it look like?" shouted McQueen.

"Probably a clogged pump. It's the sand. We'll have to set her down pretty soon."

"I was thinking the same thing. Where are we?" Eddie brought out the map and they fixed their position as just coming up on the Nyassa range, a stretch of mountains that ran north and south.

"Here," said Eddie. "That's all flat tableland."

The landing at the small village of Malindi was rougher than expected. Flooding had left deep ruts in the valley floor and the Goose hit one hidden gully and almost went nose over. But at last they were on the ground and Eddie got to work on the faulty oil pump.

"You men find us a good take-off strip, into the wind," said McQueen and the young Marines began searching the area. The village was a mile away and so far no one had approached them. McQueen was beginning to think his luck was holding when a tall tribesman wearing the feathers of a chief appeared with a half dozen men with spears. McQueen went out to meet the men.

"Stay with the plane," he said to Henry.

"No you don't. I'm coming," said the older man

The nearest thing to a universal language in sub-Saharan Africa is Bantu, which is the mother tongue of Zulu, Kongo and dozens of other dialects. After ritual pleasantries, which included gifts for the chief, the men began to talk.

McQueen explained where he was going and the demeanor of the tribesmen instantly became hostile. They were being warned, the chief said.

"Much death in the Congo. White men bring," said the chief.

"What death?" asked Henry.

"Burning sickness." He motioned for one of his men to come forward. The man held out his arm. It appeared to have been covered in boils. It meant nothing to McQueen or Henry.

"Have you heard of a white woman near this place? Maybe a prisoner," asked Henry. He showed the chief a picture. The chief nodded. But despite repeated efforts by Henry no other news could they get from the tribesmen, who wanted only to keep their distance from the white men who might bring the burning sickness.

By the time McQueen got back Eddie had repaired the engine and the Marines had found a stretch of takeoff dirt. Eddie had tried to raise Akerson's men on the radio with no success.

"OK," he said. "Let's get out of here." They climbed into the Goose and taxied to the windward side of the strip and five minutes later were only a dot in the afternoon sky.

• • •

Walser had not slept in three days. The effects of malnutrition and constant threat from the animals plus the need to maintain iron fisted discipline had sapped his energies and he was beginning to hallucinate more in the daytime. But his will was strong and he had vowed before the men that he would never give up. It was a question of honor.

There were only 49 men left alive now. Since the food ran out they had tried to catch small game, and although this sometimes worked it was not enough, and for the last three days they had taken to eating the flesh of the men who had died or been mauled badly by the jungle cats that prowled the jungle and seemed to be following them.

That day they had stopped the march early. The men were exhausted from cutting their way through the jungle, which seemed to grow thicker with every mile. Walser maintained scouts both in front of and behind the main body, and that morning Borshman had decided he would defy Walser and led a small detachment ahead to find the scouts, who had not been heard of for hours. 200 yards up the hill, near a huge ficus tree, they found a bloody trail. It led to another tree where the only thing left of the scout were his shoes and part of a hand.

"Major," breathed one of the soldiers, "you have to do something. He's going to get us all killed."

"Ya, this is madness," added a second soldier. They stared silently at Borshman, who wiped the sweat off his brow and scanned the area. In a nearby tree was a giant rock python, at least 22 feet long, Borshman thought. He studied the giant reptile a moment, wondering why it was so thick around the middle. Then with a sickening wrench in his stomach he saw the scouts feet sticking out of the python's mouth.

He watched for a moment, then turned back to the two waiting men, their uniforms in rags, covered with sweat and dirt and open sores. He could not help but admire the incredible courage of these men, and realized that they had come to the end of the expedition.

"How far are we from the nearest river?" he asked.

"Several day's march, Herr Major."

"Very good. I will speak to the Colonel tonight. We will find another route to our objective. Get word to the rear scouts to return to base."

The scene at "dinner" had been grim beyond words. Eating human flesh, even cooked, carries disease risk. The raw flesh of the fallen was contaminated with parasites, unknown to the others, and a severe form of jaundice was setting in. The men stared all night at Borshman, quiet eyes in the darkness. Borshman could feel his heart pounding at what he knew was coming. He checked his pistol again.

After the fires had been put out, he approached Walser's tent. Walser was waiting for him with a rifle. There were 10 loyal SS men with him. "I have heard that you are the leader of a mutiny, Borshman. We have gathered all the weapons. Do you know what the penalty is?"

"You're mad, Walser. As mad as Hitler. Give up this insanity now before it's too late!" Borshman moved to signal some of his men.

Outside, the starving men heard three gunshots and a single, choked off scream. Walser emerged from the tent and walked over to the men.

"There has been a mutiny. It is over now. Heil Hitler."

In the morning, as they were leaving, the soldiers looked up at Borshman's body, hanging upside down from a tree. It would not be long, they thought.

• • •

In Lisbon, the news that McQueen had discovered a secret German plan to march into the Congo in search of uranium had hit Ellison like a bomb. If it was true, he thought, it vindicated what he had been discussing privately with Group 301 since Hitler came to power. At the same time, it meant the Western powers faced the threat of an early knockout punch from which they could not recover. Suddenly, Portugal looked like a very small refuge indeed.

He was reminded of this the next day when the German ambassador made an unexpected call at the embassy. Ellison had found the man, Von Joost, to be urbane and pleasant, but underneath the smiling facade was a shrewd operator.

"We have heard that there is an American force operating in the south Nile region," Van Joost began. "As you know this is a violation of our unofficial neutrality agreements and naturally we would like some explanation," he said with a smile. Ellison thought it over. It was always best to give the Germans the impression of candor and so he decided to be honest.

"Mr. Ambassador, what can you tell me about your own force that has been active in Banbuku and was last seen marching into the interior," asked Ellison.

"I know nothing about that."

"It appears we are both in the dark," agreed Ellison. "I also have a report from our embassy in Cairo that several German scientists have been seen, some of them I believe hiring and outfitting dhows for traveling upriver. Odd isn't it?"

"Oh, rumors, Mr. Ellison. Many Germans appreciate Egypt as a place for vacation. I imagine the men you refer to were there for leisure. But about this force of Americans..." and now the voice was hard, as he brought up an accusing finger. "We want to know what mischief they are making near our former colonies, the ones the allies stole from us!" Although he had not raised his voice, the impression of the overbearing Teutonic swagger was unmistakable. For a moment there was silence in the room.

"Mr. Ambassador," began Ellison calmly, "I must consult Washington before I say any more, but surely Germany has nothing to fear from a handful of U.S. Marines out on maneuvers?" Von Joost felt the jab and regained his composure. Ellison had a point, he knew, that could not be brushed aside.

"I too will consult my superiors. But I can assure you that if German interests are threatened, Germany will respond without hesitation."

After Von Joost had left, Ellison had exchanged cables with Kirkendahl that morning and the picture was becoming clear. Ever since Hahn and Meitner had discovered fission that February, there had been quiet rumblings throughout the diplomatic corps that Berlin would take some kind of action. McQueen's report of running into a German physicist in Cairo, combined with Von Joosts touchiness and the news from Khartoum left little doubt. The Germans meant to take advantage of the weak Belgian government in the Congo and seize the supply of uranium at its source. The world's leading producers in 1939 were Czechoslovakia, Congo and

Canada, with the first two being by far the largest. Thus, if Berlin was able to seize and hold this strategic asset she would have an insurmountable lead in the coming race to develop an atomic bomb. Kirkendahl wanted to tell State the whole story, including the Marines in the field in hopes of forcing Washington to take a stand. Ellison was more cautious.

The two men had met at a conference earlier that year in London, and over dinner at the Savoy they had drifted into the theoretical possibilities brought on by Enrico Fermi's discoveries. It had been a grim meeting, because most of the important work was being done by German scientists - chiefly Hahn, Meitner and Strassman.

"Head in the sand, that what it is, dammit!" had said Kirkendahl to the table, and one or two had nodded in assent, including Ellison. The other ambassadors and staff had urged caution. They knew about the strategic value of the Congo deposits, but the idea that Berlin would be bold enough to sneak a force through British mandate lands in Africa seemed preposterous, given the area and the antipathy of the tribesmen to European colonialists of any stripe.

And yet Ellison also knew that the Germans were capable of breathtaking leaps of audacity under Hitler. By sending McQueen into the Congo as an unofficial U.S. emissary, he knew he was skirting dangerously close to the Neutrality Act and could potentially embarrass the Administration.

It was time to inform the White House.

The next morning Ellison was on the Pan Am clipper and after a brief layover in the Azores was sitting two days later in the waiting room of Cordell Hull, looking at the framed pictures of Washington at Valley Forge and trying to decide how not to put his foot in his mouth. He knew that Hull's main interests were the expansion of international trade and that although he was a fierce defender of American interests, his concern for the fate of Hitler's non-American victims was much less certain.

The meeting had been what he expected, icy and brief. There was an American freight pilot named McQueen, he was following a small force of German soldiers into the Congo and it might be part of a larger plan cooked up in Berlin. Ellison had no other firm information to lay before the Secretary and distracted by other matters, Hull wanted nothing to do with Africa. If an American pilot was getting mixed up with the German army that was his business, not that of the U.S. State Department. Ellison realized with relief that Hull could not have heard of Group 301, and tried to raise the issue of uranium but was quickly cut off. He decided not to mention the Marines or their training exercise.

That night at his hotel on New York Avenue there was a quiet knock on the door. The smiling man outside might have been a university professor, in his houndstooth coat and the beard going to grey. Ellison recognized him as Admiral J.W. Harmon and a founder of Group 301. The two men shook hands warmly.

"Well Clayton, I see you survived State. That calls for a drink if anything does. Looks like you need one," the admiral said in his friendly, deep baritone. "Anyway, no good talking here. Too many ears." Harmon had a car outside and in 20 minutes they were relaxing in a quiet pub in Georgetown. In a corner booth near the fire, Harmon had listened as Ellison talked. An extremely shrewd and intelligent man behind the friendly mask, the Admiral was notoriously blunt and difficult to read. But as the Assistant Chief of Naval Operations, he was in a position to get things done, which in Ellison's mind now outweighed all other concerns.

"You've got your neck way out on this one."

"I know that, sir. I'm prepared for the consequences."

Harmon thought this over. "This man McQueen," said Harmon slowly. "What happens when he runs into the Germans? How do you keep a lid on this thing? We're not at war with Germany."

"Let's just say that he's a resourceful man, admiral. I imagine he'll think of something." Harmon let out a snort of laughter.

"All right, what do you need from me?" Ellison smiled. He brought out his daily planner, which had a small map of the world, and pointed to a spot on the west African coast, just south of Nyanga in French Equatorial Africa.

"Do you have any ships available for blockade duty, here?" he asked.

"What are we talking about blockading?"

"German freighters. Maybe a sub or two." Harmon studied the map.

"Interesting problem. I'll need some time. We could put a couple of PBYs in there, maybe based in Portuguese West. I'll look into it. But Clayton," he said "If this thing blows up, it's the end of a few damn fine careers."

"Then let's be sure it doesn't," added Ellison.

•   •   •

None of the German soldiers who had died in the jungle with Walser would have recognized the small American force of Marines moving through the savanna toward the high plateau where the rivers began, even if they had gotten close enough to see them. Unlike their German counterparts, by the time they reached the rainforest the Marines didn't even look like soldiers, nor like Americans. They were covered from head to foot in camoflage outfits devised by Akerson that were so thick and covered in leaves and branches that from 100 feet away they were virtually invisible. To conserve energy in the heat they traveled in short bursts of 5 miles and then rested. To increase their chances for survival they threw away all of their military rations and had the guide teach them how to live off the land, which water they could drink and how to know when they were being stalked by one of the larger predators. They never fired a single shot. By the time they reached the headwaters of the Arawili each man had lost 15 pounds, but they moved through the land of elephants and big apes without a sound. Going down the rapids was going to be the easy part.

•   •   •

The origins of the Aruwimi River are high in the Blue Mountains, a range of snow-capped peaks along the border with Uganda and overlooking Lake Albert. The river flows and twists almost 2000 miles from this source to the Atlantic, and is one of the most dangerous in Africa, its watershed almost entirely comprised of dense forest. This is the home of the great mountain gorillas.

McQueen had been flying for three hours when one of the Marines, Anderson, came forward. "We've been listening for a signal from Khartoum and Wilson picked up something that sounds like Germans talking in the clear. He knows a little German, and they're talking about reinforcements. Just thought you'd want to know."

"Thanks," said McQueen. "Let me know if you hear any other good news." As the Marine took his place Eddie spotted through an opening in the clouds what looked like open water and pointed.

"What does that look like?" he yelled to McQueen as they banked sharply for a better view. Eddie motioned for McQueen to drop down and got his binoculars out. As the plane descended through layers of cloud he could see there were no visible sand bars or trees in the water. But landing, Eddie knew could still involve considerable risk. McQueen was skilled at doing what they called in the Navy a hard splashdown, meaning that the flyer almost pancaked the plane in when the landing area was too small for a normal approach. But no pilot could compensate for insufficient length on take off. Without at least 500 yards of open river, the Goose would be stranded. The only hope then would be to float the plane down river to a better spot, if there were no rapids and one could be found. Or in an extreme case the plane could be partially disassembled and taken overland.

All of these scenarios went through Eddie's mind as he studied the river, estimating distances and wind direction. He took out a map and tried to identify their position. He knew it was going to mean taking a chance. He also knew that in another two hours the plane would be short on fuel. Back in Lisbon, he was developing a special estimating telescope for just this purpose, but it was still on the workbench.

He shook his head at McQueen. "I don't like it, Joe, don't like it a damn bit! There's not a breath of wind on that water and I can't see more than 300 yards or so for take off. On top of that, it looks like the ceiling is maybe 500 feet, so if we came out of this wrong, we may never find it again. Why don't we track back to that valley where we saw the lake on the Uele. We could put her down there and wait it out." McQueen looked up from the map. In the distance a storm was moving in, the leading clouds black and full of moisture. He looked at his fuel gauge, at the dwindling hole in the clouds below him and motioned for Eddie to come over.

"Tell the Marines to get braced for a hard landing." The two men looked each other a moment. Eddie nodded and went back to the passengers.

"You men get ready for a pancake. That's what we call it. Get your vests on. If we land OK, get ready to throw out the anchors, fore and aft. If the plane starts to take on water, kick out that window and swim for shore - and don't forget to help the professor here" added Eddie with a grin. The

Marines grinned right back and looked at Henry, who had his eyes closed as he concentrated on keeping his stomach under control. Eddie patted him on the back.

"We'll be OK, doc. You're flying with the best damn pilot in the Navy," said Eddie.

"Navy be damned! Does this thing have a bathroom?" was all Henry would say.

"Happy landings," said Eddie and returned to the co-pilot seat.

McQueen had been busy adjusting the flaps and the propeller pitch for maximum torque. With his passengers braced, he nosed the Goose over and they began the long decent from 8,000 feet through the thick clouds. As the engines reached their maximum RPM the noise was deafening but he was in a hurry. For the next 6,000 feet of drop they had to fight to keep sight of the landing zone through the clouds. Around and around they went, circling the narrow opening in the clouds like a piece of wood around a drain. At 3,000 feet the clouds suddenly closed in and they flew blindly down until, just above 600 feet, they reached the bottom and there in front of them was the river.

What Eddie and McQueen saw was not reassuring. There were multiple twists in the river's course, and very tall trees guarded every approach.

"Can you see anyplace that looks good?" asked McQueen. Eddie shook his head.

"The trees are too high. I couldn't see 'em from up top." McQueen made two low level passes at the river as rain started to pelt the windshield, but they could find no suitable landing path.

"We got no choice. I'm heading back to the Uele," shouted McQueen. As the words left his mouth, Eddie pointed at something off to the left.

"Over there!" shouted Eddie, and McQueen banked violently to avoid a flight of migrating Nile flamingos rising from the river. But the motion of the plane had revealed a deep opening in the trees that had been invisible before. Eddie tapped McQueen's arm and pointed. "Look Joe! Through there!"

They came around again as the rain suddenly intensified, skimming the tree tops. When they reached the gap, McQueen dropped the nose and throttled back the engines as they slipped through the opening and suddenly the water rushed up to reach them and there was a tremendous splash as the Goose hit the water, bounced once and then came to a stop 15 feet from the opposite bank. McQueen kicked hard right rudder and the plane swung easily away from the overhanging trees.

"Get the anchor out!" shouted McQueen, and a few minutes later the plane was moored a few feet from the shore. The rain continued to intensify and they could see little of what was happening at the shoreline. Once Henry thought he saw a hippo with her baby come down to the water and slip in, but otherwise they might was well have been inside a waterfall.

"We'll wait it out here," said McQueen. "Eddie, check on Henry."

Eight hours later the rain finally stopped, and the Marines found enough loose foliage at the shore to anchor the plane to the bank. The camoflage took a while longer but at last it was done. They did a good job, and from anywhere above or across the river the plane could not be seen. Only from the near bank could one see that the mass of green leaves and branches was an airplane. Henry, who had assisted the Marines, had to admit that McQueen's choice of green paint now made a lot of sense.

Daybreak came, and with it a brief break in the weather. McQueen got out his sextant and as the Marines checked their gear and Henry busied himself with observing the flora and fauna, was able to determine their position.

"Here," he showed Eddie on the map, "is where we were supposed to land. This is where we did land, 10 miles upriver. The other Marine detachment is probably there by now, and possibly our German friends. That means we don't have the luxury of traveling by night and sleeping by day. We'll have to rig the raft and get downriver as fast as we can. Any objections?" He looked around. The Marines were ready and wanted no pep talks. McQueen was worried about Henry. He didn't look well and had been eating poorly for days.

"You gonna be all right, Henry? If not, this is the time to tell me." In answer, Henry took out his flask and took a small sip of whisky.

"Merely a touch of air sickness my friend, brought on by your virtuoso flying. I'm fine. What can I carry?" he asked. McQueen looked around for something and found a small jug of water. "That's it?" an incredulous Henry asked.

"We need you healthy to translate. Still remember your dialects?"

"Most of them, although if I'd known where we were going when I left London I would have brought my reference books. Still, I suppose it can't be helped," he added, and picked up the jug.

The Marines, in makeshift camoflage from head to toe, had finished preparing the raft. There was enough food for four days rations, no more. The rest of the space was given over to ammunition belts, light machine guns and various ordnance which fascinated Henry. As before, Eddie was left behind with the Goose.

"Check this thing, Eddie," McQueen shouted as they were about to push off. There was a small hand-cranked radio in his pack, and after a quick test confirmed it was working the men pushed off and began paddling down river. Despite repeated attempts, McQueen could not raise Akerson on the radio, or the Cairo Embassy.

• • •

Fifty miles off the coast of Senegal, the rain squalls that had clung to the African coast for days were starting to lift. The small German fleet inched its way south, taking pains to avoid the British patrols that regularly moved between Cape Town and Gibraltar. The fleet consisted of two submarines running submerged and a disguised 10,000 ton freighter, the *Socotra*, flying a Greek flag. If boarded, the captain of the freighter could show that he was carrying a cargo of rice, bound for Madagascar. If the boarders looked closely, they would discover nothing more sinister than a few dozen crates of rice. The captain even spoke passable Greek. He could explain, in Greek and broken English, the camoflage painting as a precaution taken to warn off pirates.

What they would never find were the sealed orders from the Reich marine commandant which were hand delivered to the captain while she was at anchor in Cairo, instructing her to wait off the coast of Portuguese West just south of the point where the Congo empties into the South Atlantic. He would be contacted on the 11th by a special code known only to three people in the German navy. The orders also specified that if attacked en route he was to scuttle the ship. If attacked or boarded after picking up his unspecified cargo in the roadstead he was to prevent by all means the search and seizure of the ship, sinking her by dynamite in the hold if necessary. The orders did not mention the two quiet spoken, bookish Germans who had come aboard. They had kept to themselves below decks during the voyage and were always dressed as coal stokers. The captain had not asked their purpose, but once he had overheard them talking about someone named Fermi. Being a loyal German he had ignored it. He knew from what the commandant had told him that if any of the crew learned anything about the true nature of the returning cargo they were to be shot and dumped overboard. He didn't ask what would happen to his men once they delivered their cargo in Bremen.

As the *Socotra* plowed through the long Atlantic swells coming up from the Antarctic the captain stood on the bridge and thought again about his orders as he watched a British packet destroyer passing 5,000 yards to starboard. It was getting dark and the freighter was running without lights and with camoflage there was a chance they would not be spotted.

Like everyone in Germany he knew that war was coming, and he knew that whatever came he would do his duty. Germany must never give in to encirclement by her enemies, he told himself. He watched the British destroyer a few minutes longer. The ruse was holding and it lifted his spirits. He could smell the evening meal being prepared. Hot sausages and potatoes, he guessed. Maybe they would get away with it. He signaled to his 2nd officer to take the wheel and started down for dinner. But in spite of the good luck and his duty and the smell of the sausages frying on the stove, in spite of everything, he reflected that if he ever arrived home safely to his wife and children it would be a miracle - or the English were asleep.

Chapter 12

THE LATE AUTUMN HEAT hung heavily as McQueen and his party silently paddled down the slow moving river. It was hot, exhausting work, and McQueen took turns with the marines paddling and steering the heavy raft, keeping it clear of snags and the occasional curious alligators that populated this part of the Aruwimi. The only one who seemed unaffected by the heat and insects was Henry, who had found the sight of several potentially new species of tree snake fascinating.

They traveled without incident for two days, although the drenching rains more than once forced them to stop and bail. Once McQueen had one of the marines run a wire to the top of a tree and they were able to contact Eddie using a code McQueen had improvised before leaving, but otherwise they were now beyond the help of civilization. The most dangerous times were at night, when they anchored briefly at the shore. Twice they had to break silence and shoot large cats that came too close. As they got closer to their destination the marines fitted silencers to the rifles.

By the end of the third day there were occasional sightings of natives collecting food, and a few shots were heard in the distance. The occasional trader could also be seen passing near the river, leading a pack of donkeys laden with boxes. As they came around a bend one of the marines thought he could hear the sound of machinery in the distance.

Darkness was beginning to creep up from the jungle as they came around the final bend, drifting silently with the current. From under this canopy of vines McQueen was the first to see the walls of the fortress rising from the river. There were fires burning in clay pots on stanchions above the walls but no sign of life. In the distance, the open gash of the mine could be seen, yellow light and steam spilling out of it like a scene from Hades. There was a distant throbbing sound.

"What do you think?" said McQueen to Snyder. The young marine, his face blacked out, blinked at him and nodded toward a tower on their right. It took a moment for McQueen's eyes to adjust to the light, but yes, there it was. Three figures with rifles, high on the tower, watching. Snyder kept on watching.

"They haven't spotted us," he said quietly.

"Let's keep it that way. Bring us closer to the shore," nodded McQueen. Using their blackened oar as a rudder, the raft drifted slowly to the right shore under a tree and went aground on the mud. For several minutes nobody moved, waiting to see if they'd been discovered. Two guards came down to the shore, a few yards away, and smoked cigarettes as they talked. Henry leaned forward to listen.

"They're speaking Panga," he whispered to McQueen. "Something about bodies. Where to dispose of bodies. They're talking like there's an epidemic going on." Henry looked at McQueen. "Should we wait for the others?"

McQueen had been asking himself the same question. "They know we're coming. Just not when. If she's in there she's as good as dead as soon as the guards spot Akerson and his men," he said in a rough whisper. "This has to be done quiet." He looked at the marines. "I need one man to come with me. Which one of you is best with a knife?" Wilson came forward and held up a hand. Silently, a 10" blade appeared from out of a black handle. "You'll do," said McQueen. "The rest of you stay with Henry. If we're not back by midnight it means we're dead. In that case, take the C4 and try to get to the mine and blow it up. And keep Henry safe. He speaks the language and might be able to talk his way out of trouble."

"Me?" said the startled Underwood.

"It's all Bantu country from here on. They don't love the English but they hate Belgians, so don't use any high school

French or you're liable to end up with your head on a stick. If we don't come back, get to the river and take it down to the French garrison at Mbandaka. Radio for Eddie. You'll be OK."

"What are you going to do?" asked Anderson, the youngest.

"We're in the freight business, my friend. One delivery," he said as he picked up a small canvas bag of explosives, "and one pickup. Stay out of sight and wait for the signal," he added, holding up a well-used flare gun. "Red flare means blow the front gate and wait for us. White flare means we didn't make it and good luck." McQueen and the two marines shook hands. "Let's get a move on," he said to Wilson.

Five minutes later two darkened figures slipped into the inky water and swam silently ashore, holding their equipment over their heads. Near the shore McQueen thought he felt something big move against his leg and held his breath for a minute waiting to be pulled under. But the creature passed them by, perhaps looking for bigger prey. Henry watched his friend for a few minutes until he could see him no more and settled in for the long night.

•   •   •

Off the coast of Cameroun, the lookout on the HMS Cargill had been on duty for several hours and he was tired. The steady roll of the Atlantic sometimes had a mesmerizing effect on young seamen, he knew, but there it was again, sticking out of the water. He rubbed his eyes and looked again to be sure, then whistled into his intercom.

"Bridge, lookout. Periscope 30 degrees off the starboard bow." The officer on duty brought his binoculars up. It took only a moment to sight the periscope and he knew that there were no British subs in these waters. He reached out and pressed the alarm button.

"Signal general quarters!" yelled the officer. At once the ship came to life as the muted sound of the alarm went off below decks and men ran to their battle stations. The officer was trained to remain calm in such circumstances and picked up the phone that connected him to the fire control station directly below where he was standing. "Periscope sighted, 6000 yards, starboard," he said clearly. "Alert the captain." Two minutes later the captain was on the bridge.

"Andrews, have they spotted us yet?" The Captain took his powerful set of binoculars and studied the sea until he could see, in the fading light, the periscope. What he didn't see was that behind it was a radio antenna.

"I don't know sir. It seems to be holding course 045 relative, not closing."

"Very well," he replied. The Cargill was patrolling the African coast alone, looking for Italian smugglers moving oil to Milano. Normally it was a routine and somewhat boring business involving nothing more than search and interdiction. Although German freighters were occasionally active in these waters, there had never been any hostile activity. But a submarine was different.

"Radio fleet headquarters. Periscope sighted. Give our position. Shadowing. Await instructions." The radioman finished writing and went around the bulkhead to the radio station, got out his code book and began translating the words into five-letter groups.

7000 yards away and 120 feet below the surface, the U-188 glided on battery power toward the rendezvous point, still some 900 miles away. When the submarine had developed temporary engine trouble that required stopping for 8 hours while repairs were made, the faster freighter had gone on ahead, hiding in a squall and effectively invisible from the pre-radar British fleet. With it had gone the U-251. Now trying to catch up to the squadron, the Kapitan of the U-188 had nothing on his mind except bed when the radioman came to his cabin.

"British destroyer sighted, Kapitan. Heading 190 degrees, speed 18 knots. We have intercepted a radio transmission." The *Kapitan* knew that they had been spotted, and he knew the thoroughness of the British. They would not rest until they had destroyed his boat.

The Kapitan brushed past the radioman and almost ran to the conning tower. He took over the periscope from his first officer and had a look. "Come left to 050 degrees," he said sharply. "Load number one torpedo tube. Down periscope." Instantly the submarine began swinging into position.

Four minutes later the captain of the Cargill was still looking for the periscope when one of the searchlights picked up the wake of a torpedo. "Full speed ahead, hard right!" the captain shouted. But it was too late. Traveling at 53 mph, the torpedo, one of the new German magnetic models, detonated directly under the keel of the ship, well astern of the engine room, instantly opening a 30 foot hole right under the main magazine. It was pure luck. As the German Kapitan watched, the Cargill seemed to evaporate in a ball of flame that reached 500 feet into the sky. Moments later the wind revealed that the ship had split in two, and as the fireball dissipated the broken ship began its long, slow plunge to the sea bed, 8,000 feet below.

In Gibraltar, the radioman at Fleet Headquarters received half of the coded message. When nothing else came through, he radioed for a repeat transmission. After another minute had passed, he pressed a red button on his console that summoned the watch commander.

The two figures in camoflage moved slowly through the trees, keeping well away from the fortress walls and the sentries. Both men carried machetes and when necessary cut down brush, but for the most part their movement was silent and unseen. They were covered from head to foot in grass and small branches. McQueen thought it was overkill but Wilson had assured him that it was the only way to remain unseen and besides, this was how the Marines did things. McQueen had reluctantly agreed, and after a large black leopard had passed 10 feet from their hiding place without noticing them he had to admit he had been wrong.

After half an hour of climbing they reached a low hill and climbed a tree from where they could look down on the fortress and get a good look at the mine. There was a constant stream of workers going into the mine unencumbered, and an equal number of men coming out, carrying heavy looking wooden boxes.

It was the crudest form of human slavery, realized McQueen. The boxes were taken to the huge workshop, where the crushing machines and processing equipment did their work. They had built what looked like a narrow gauge funicular rail line from the workshop to the river. The processed ore was loaded into huge wooden crates, waiting for transport to the river, where, McQueen guessed, pirogues or rafts would take the cargo, perhaps disguised as mullet or grain, down to the sea. With the appropriate payoffs it would be no problem to get it aboard a freighter. McQueen found himself full of admiration at the sheer audacity of the whole scheme.

As McQueen was explaining to Wilson in whispered tones what was going on, he was aware of something moving near them on the ground. It might have been a large animal but he could take no chances. They climbed down and had a look. There was nothing.

"Must be seeing things," he said to Wilson. "Let's get uphill and see if we can fall in behind this lot. If we can't find her in 20 minutes, we'll set the charges and try to get out."

They were starting to move toward a line of trees and had gone perhaps 20 yards when a raspy, half-choked voice behind them said "Hands up." McQueen spun around.

Three weeks alone in the jungle had left their mark on the wild eyed, mud encrusted female who pointed a rifle at them from 10 yards away. McQueen started to move his hand toward his pistol but McQueen froze when he heard the bolt slide into position.

The standoff continued for a few moments. "All right. Who are you and what do you want?" said McQueen finally. He could only suppose it must be someone from one of the villages. There was no answer. He asked again in Bantu, but still nothing as the rifle held steady on them. Then he began to notice details: grey-blue eyes, the slightly upturned nose, a whisp of honey blonde hair. He realized with a start that he had found her.

"Margaret?" he said quietly. He pushed aside the camoflage covering his face, and wiped off the mud with water from his canteen. "It's me, honey. Joe. Joe McQueen."

As if through a shroud, the pains and terrors of three weeks in the jungle began to recede. She lowered the rifle. For a long moment there was no change, then he realized she was crying. He took a step forward and held her in his arms. The sudden feeling of warmth and safety, even the raw animal smell of him, was overwhelming and she thought she had never felt such relief before. Unable to speak, she looked up at his eyes which were smiling. "Are you all right?" he said. She nodded, and with the flood of emotions came the knowledge that she must look like a wreck. Impressing even Wilson, she made an effort to clean herself up but it was useless and finally gave up. Then she slapped him, once, hard on the face.

"What's that for?"

"That's for letting me get captured by that son of a bitch slave trader, you, you ... Oh, and some soldier of fortune you turned out to be! I've been hiding for weeks in that cave, stealing food at night from the guards. I'd given up hope.

Oh, damn!" She was getting emotional again, which made her even more angry. Wilson began looking around, getting wary of being out in the open.

"Joe," he began.

"Yeah I know. What are you doing here?" asked McQueen as she took an offered canteen from Wilson and drank deeply, revealing several nasty scrapes on her neck and face. His question could wait. Slowly, the terror of the night, much like the terror of every night, began to subside and she could think without fear.

"Follow me," she said. A few yards away was the camoflaged entrance to a small cave. As they went in Wilson had a last look around and put back the bushes that concealed the hiding place.

Inside was a cave about 30 feet deep, consisting of rock walls and the roots of the large banyan trees that grew everywhere. There were a few boxes, a rough bed made of grass and a few cans of food. As she took off her coat McQueen realized she was at least 20 pounds lighter than the last time he saw her.

It took her 20 minutes to tell what she knew about the fortress and Steermundt. Much of it was a jumble of disconnected words and people, but when she described how the ore was dug from the mine, transported to the workshop and how they made the green glass that was used as currency in the Congo, McQueen appreciated the precision of her thinking and marveled at the details she had collected.

"It's all in this note book," she said, handing it to him with a grin. "I figured if I didn't survive somebody might need it." There were numerous traders, she explained, coming and going at all hours of the day, and Steermundt had amassed a fortune by trading goods for gold. A German trader had stumbled onto the fortress a year ago, and that had given Olaf the idea of refining the uranium powder against the day when the outside world would pay a high price.

"How do you know all this?" asked McQueen, full of admiration for her courage.

"My friend helped me. Her name is Hyacinth, the house maid. That's where a lot of this food came from. Whatever happens, we have to help her escape. But you haven't said why you're here."

"I've got your father with me, down at the river. We came to get you out," he said. McQueen thought for a few moments. He turned to Wilson. "We have to find this guy Steermundt before the Germans do," he said. "Give me the C4. You get her back to the raft. See that Anderson looks at those bruises. Might be infected. You know what else to do." He compared his watch to Wilsons, then turned to Margaret. "Where does the Dutchman hang out?"

"I've only seen him at the workshop, but he's always surrounded by guards. I think it's where he keeps the gold." McQueen nodded.

Henry had started to itch. The camoflage paint and greenery he was wearing made him invisible but at a price. "They've been gone a long time," he remarked to Snyder, but the marine was busy with the silencer on his rifle and didn't answer. Henry went back to scratching and was still at it when he saw the movement coming down the bank. He tapped the two marines, instantly alert. Wilson had worked out a signal, and as he got close made a winding motion with his left arm. The two marines relaxed and went to help them. Upon seeing her father, Margaret smiled.

"Hi, Dad. Funny meeting you here." Henry rushed toward her.

"Margaret!" he cried. As they embraced, Anderson started looking at her wounds and she noticed Snyder opening a burlap bag and taking out what looked like a long tube.

"What's that?" she asked.

McQueen was nearly at the workshop. After burying the C4 explosive and some of his ammunition he had decided to reconnoiter and had crawled on his belly the last 50 yards, very slowly. He looked at his watch. He had been kidded by Eddie for spending so much money on a Swiss watch, but it had its uses, he reflected, such as precise timing. The second hand showed 10 seconds left. He looked up at the workshop window. The tall Dutchman was now plain to see. Four seconds. Three. Two.

Suddenly, there was a deafening explosion from the direction of the river, and a big ball of yellow/orange flame billowed up into the sky. Immediately the workshop began emptying out of workers and guards, running towards the river. An alarm began to sound. He could hear the Dutchman shouting instructions, and the louder sound of an African dialect being repeated. On the watchtower nearest the river, a guard was pointing at something upriver. McQueen took out his binoculars and adjusted for distance.

It happened too fast for him to react. One moment he was looking at the river, the next he was surrounded by six heavily armed native guards. On instinct, he lunged at the man nearest him and was close to wresting his rifle away when something hit him on the back of the head and darkness rushed up to meet him.

•　•　•

The remnants of the German expeditionary force, filthy, ragged shadows blending into the foliage, moved slowly through the killing jungle, no longer hopeful of victory but merely to survive another day. What had started as 400 soldiers and officers was now reduced to Walser and 37 men, all of them little more than walking skeletons. Lack of vitamin C eventually results in jaundice, and the eyes of the soldiers were all a pale yellow now. The last of the food was long gone and they subsisted on the few jungle berries and the occasional carcass of a large rodent not fully consumed by the jungle. Most of the men were too weak to chase down game with a knife. Sensing their proximity to the river, Walser had forbidden any use of rifles for killing game. Even water was scarce, only sporadically found after a rain, then quickly collected into canteens.

The men no longer sang songs or talked as they walked. They had learned that noise attracted predators, and for the last few weeks the nights had been punctuated by screams as, despite every precaution, one of the soldiers was dragged off into the forest. To combat the terror the men had begun sleeping in tight formations and in circling the camp with fires which discouraged many of the smaller cats and snakes.

And then suddenly, the forest began to thin. Walser was in the lead and was the first to see the incredible sight. A river, quite wide and flowing steadily in the right direction. He shouted at his men "Water! You see! We've done it men!" and ran forward to the shore.

Over the next half hour the rest of the men toiled up the hill and put down their weapons, grateful for the opportunity to cleanse their bodies of the stench and parasites that had plagued them for the last 30 miles. One of the men had even thought to bring a bar of soap, and for a moment discipline went out the window as the naked men washed and scrubbed away at their skin, and at the ragged remnants of their uniforms, most of which was cut off now at the knees.

Under the hot tropical sun, they sat on the river bank, feeling 80% human again. One of the men had rigged a crude net and had managed to snare a few of the big river catfish, and Walser had unexpectedly relaxed one of his iron rules and allowed the men to build a small cook fire. The fish was excellent and the combined effect of the food and fresh water had a fiercely galvanizing effect on the resolve and will of the survivors. They had come through hell, and nothing now could frighten them. Walser said nothing, but he had not risen to the rank of Colonel without being a shrewd judge of men, and he knew that despite the terrible price they had paid, the men who had not died or deserted would be difficult to kill. The martial pride that is the birthright of every German rose in him, and he even caught a couple of the men grinning at him.

"Yes, we did it, men! You did it, and all of Germany will be proud of you when they hear of this exploit. I will recommend every man who returns to Germany for an Iron Cross. I mean it. Yes. I am proud of you." There was silence in the camp. And then a tremendous shout went up, and could be heard far down the river.

An hour later, the scout returned from his reconnoiter. He was a calm young man from Stuttgart, and the only man who was fluent in Bantu. "It is one kilometer down the river, Herr Reichsfuhrer. An encampment, perhaps 500 meters square, guarded by many natives. But no artillery. I told the guard I wished to see the owner but he became very hostile."

"And what about this man Steermundt?" asked Walser.

"I could find no trace of him, sir."

"Very well," he said, and turned to his young lieutenant, now second in command. "We leave immediately! I will clean out this nest of vipers." The lieutenant saluted and began shouting orders.

Chapter 13

WHEN HE AWOKE, McQueen found himself in utter darkness. He felt the back of his head and could feel no warm blood on his fingers, and sat up. He was hungry and his body ached from the clubbing he had endured. His eyes began to adjust to the light and soon he could see there were two other men in the room, which was in fact a very large pit. He got to his feet.

The walls were of stone but gave no handhold. Around the floor were a few scraps of food, some bones of small animals and a water cask. There was one wooden chair. The other two men sat on the ground, immobile as statues, staring at something. As they did not appear to pose any immediate threat he allowed himself a more careful examination of the surroundings. Above him, perhaps 35 feet away, was an overcast sky. It was afternoon. There was no noise, except for the very distant hum of machinery.

And on the opposite side of the pit was a wall with three doors.

Keeping an eye on the two men, who had still not moved, he examined the doors. The first was made of heavy timbers and was recessed into the wall. Behind it he could hear no sound. The second was made of steel and on the other side he could hear what sounded like distant but heavy breathing. The third door was a translucent, greenish glass through which he could see the distorted images of shapes moving back and forth. There was no sound, but a terrible stench arose from the edges of the door. McQueen knew it as the smell of rotting flesh.

As he turned away from the third door, he saw that one of the men had gotten to his feet. The man was Caucasian and tall, about 6 feet 3 inches, perhaps 40 years old at the most, very thin and had a long beard and blonde hair. But what arrested his attention was the eyes, which looked like burning black coals in a lake of white snow. The man began to stagger toward McQueen.

"Who are you?" asked the frail looking man. He had a British accent.

"My name is McQueen. Why are you here?"

"I knew of a man named McQueen. He was a sea captain or a pilot. I think. Based in Lisbon. Our chaps hired him for something."

"The same." The man walked up to McQueen and looked at his face. Satisfied, he became animated and went to the first door and listened. In a moment he was back. He lowered his voice to a whisper.

"They often listen at the door. There is no mercy here. My name is Glenville. I'm a British officer. I've been here for... I don't know. Four weeks I suppose. It's a miracle I'm alive. I've had no food for days. Too weak." McQueen helped him to the chair. "What are you doing here?"

McQueen gave him a highly edited version involving the rescue of a woman and the guarding of a certain military asset in the vicinity. Immediately Glenville's eyes lighted up and he almost laughed.

"You're trying to prevent the Nazis from getting the stuff, right?" His voice was almost giddy with excitement. McQueen nodded. "Jolly good! Damn good! If we ever get out of this wretched place alive you must tell me the whole bloody story. He's mad you know, mad as a hatter."

"Who?"

"Who else? Olaf, at least that what he calls himself. Olaf Steermundt. His real name is Deibner. That name mean anything to you? No? His brother is one of the founders of the uranium club in Berlin. They knew about this place in the early 20s. All this business about being Dutch was just a ruse to deflect suspicion and to jolly the locals into building this place so far in the jungle no one would ever find it. But he made one mistake. He decided to go into business for himself, but he didn't have the technical know-how to refine the stuff into the powder that the scientists want. So he found a man in London named Mandel, sort of a crackpot scientist, and bribed him to come to Leopoldville for a talk. Showered the man with money - and he was getting all he needed from Berlin. Then after the twit showed him how to do it, even helped him procure the damned machines, it all went wrong. Those are his bones over there, in the corner.

"What about the green beads?"

"Just a cover. It helped him spread his net out a thousand miles in every direction. I was trying to bring him out when they caught me. They're good, these Bantu. Born trackers. Almost invisible till they're right on your back. So here I am," he ended bitterly.

"How do we get out of here, that's all I want to know."

"See those doors. The food is that way. When I got here there were three other men, all European traders that had crossed Deibner. One by one they tried to make it to freedom through those doors. The first one, a Frenchman from Montpellier went through the wooden door. Before it slammed shut I saw two 20 foot cobras closing on the man. The screaming, well it didn't stop for a long time. The middle door, the iron one, that used to be OK. They kept a tiger behind that one, and after he'd eat one of the guys he'd be too full for a few days and you could dash in and steal some of his food - if you can call it that. That's how I kept alive. Then he nearly got me." Glenville showed him his leg, where the deep gash of claw marks was partly healed.

"What about the third door?" asked McQueen. Glenville began to cough, terrible wracking coughs. He laid down on the floor. McQueen wanted to talk more, but Glenville's eyes were closed, his breathing a dry rattle. From the sound of it, McQueen guessed he was dying.

The other man, who had remained motionless throughout the interrogation, now turned his head to McQueen and the two men stared at each other. It was Tarik, severely emaciated but alive, and he recognized McQueen at once. The Algerian slaver grinned savagely at the irony and got slowly to his feet.

"Well, my old friend Joe McQueen. Come to die with us, is that it? Very funny! Who are you rescuing today?" he laughed in a hoarse whisper. McQueen started toward him, his fist raised, but stopped short.

"I wouldn't do that," said Tarik. " There's only one way out of here, and it's not through those doors. Looks like you need me again, Yank." He walked over to have a look at the American. "But I can guess. You're here for the girl."

"No. But you wouldn't care about that. Show me the way out and you can live." Tarik laughed again. "Not so fast. What are you doing here, McQueen?"

"Why?"

"Information has value. You help me, I help you."

McQueen didn't have to think long. "No deal," he said as his fist slammed into Tarik's jaw, sending him to the ground. McQueen went to the first door to listen. As he was about to push on it there was the sound of a tremendous clamor above ground. He looked up and could see men running along the rim of the pit. Somewhere in the underground labyrinth, the sound of a heavy iron door closing got Glenville to his feet.

"Get ready," he said.

"I say let's make a break."

"Too late. They're here."

The first door opened and from out of the darkness strode Olaf with three armed guards. He was wearing a lab coat and took his time looking over the three prisoners. In his hand was a hunk of what might have been roast pig wrapped in paper. "Hello, scum," he finally said. "Getting enough to eat!" His harsh laugh punctuated the air as he looked at the meager scraps on the floor. "I see that my pets have been generous. That's good. The two of you better be ready to talk because they're getting hungry in there," he said with a gesture to the doors. "And so this is the great Joe McQueen. We've heard a lot about you, sticking your nose into other people's business. You're a long way from Lisbon."

"That's right." Olaf could see that McQueen would not flinch easily and turned his attention to Tarik and Glenville.

"You were going to tell me about the British, and he was going to tell me about this American coming down here to spy on me. But here he is."

"So what?" asked Tarik.

Olaf smiled. "Exactly. Looks like we don't need you any more, does it?" He turned to his guards. "Door three." The two larger guards picked Tarik up bodily and began carrying him toward the glass door.

"No! I'll talk! I'll talk!" he screamed. Although he put up a stiff fight it was no contest. The third guard opened the door and they threw him into the darkness and the door closed with a metallic click.

"Now where were we?" began Olaf calmly. McQueen and Glenville didn't answer. They were all watching the third door. A dim light came on in the distance, and they could see the outline of Tarik's body against the glass, clawing at the hinges as he screamed to be rescued. For a moment all was quiet, Tarik's head whipping back and forth looking for his adversary. Then without warning the jaws of an enormous reptile opened up from above him and with a muffled grunt closed over Tarik's head and lifted him off the ground. The legs kicked for a moment against the glass and then the creature lifted him up to swallow.

"Good thing he didn't talk sooner or I'd have had to feed him one of my workers. They only eat every three weeks but they like a big meal," Olaf grinned through bad teeth, and handed the meat to Glenville. Surprised, the emaciated Englishman immediately began to devour the burnt hunk. "So, Mr. Glenville, what do we talk about today? Are you ready to tell me about your contacts in London?" Glenville, who had been through this routine with Olaf a few times already, knew that he would never leave the river fortress alive, but over the past few minutes a plan had begun to take root in his mind and he forced himself to concentrate on not betraying it. For several moments he ate in silence.

His strength returning, he turned to his captor. "I don't mind dying, Deibner."

"Who?"

"Yes, I know who you are, and so do many others in London. You'll never get that uranium to the Germans. Or to the Soviets or the French for that matter."

"You know about that, huh?" said Olaf, impressed. "I wouldn't have thought you Brits had the guts."

"Not everybody is in the appeasement game, friend." Olaf smiled again. He sat down and lit a cigar.

"You're behind the game, Glenville. You would not believe me if I told you who my most important customer is. You'd never guess. But you'll both be dead in a few minutes, so what does it matter?" Olaf opened his tunic and took out a cable. "This is from my friends at the Japanese charge d'affairs in Cape Town, offering me five million dollars in gold for my first shipment. It's already on the way. Surprised?"

"Frankly, yes," said Glenville. "What about your German customers?"

"They'll wait. We've figured out how to process the ore into U-235."

"Uranium hexaflouride."

"That's right. The world will be coming to me, and I can charge anything I want because my customers will be the winners. Too bad you won't be around to see it." He was about to turn to his guards when the dying Englishman sprung his trap. The long metal spike had been carefully removed from the chair, hidden in Glenville's tattered shirt. As Olaf turned, Glenville withdrew the spike, it's point honed to a sharp edge on the stone floor, and sprang upon Olaf's back, holding the point to his neck. Olaf tried to shake him off but his assailant had a strength born of desperation and hung on.

"Drop your guns or I plunge this into his throat!" shouted Glenville. The first guard hesitated. "Get out of here!" shouted Glenville to McQueen. "You have to tell them!"

As Olaf tried to free himself, there was a tremendous explosion that shook the walls. The distraction was enough. Olaf threw off his attacker, took out his pistol and was about to shoot him when a second explosion, much bigger, rocked the pit and threw everyone to the ground. Smoke began pouring into the pit.

"What was that!" screamed Olaf. A guard came running in.

"Boss! The Germans! They here! Big guns. Kill many! Come quick!"

Glenville heard this and started to laugh. "Now what, Deibner? You're about to be the richest dead man in Africa." Despite his pain, Glenville laughed.

"You knew about this?"

"No. But it was inevitable, wasn't it? What are you going to tell them? How are you going to save your neck? Only one way. You need us now, don't you?" There was a moment's doubt, then Olaf turned to his men.

"Tie their hands and bring them" he said quietly, and they quickly bound and dragged Glenville through the door as other guards shoved McQueen forward.

From the high front wall, the scene below was now almost complete. The Germans stood along the shore, looking like dead men. The portable mortar was in place, and at Walser's order another round was lobbed into the fortress. There was a sickening boom and from the smoke a few bodies could be seen flying into the air.

Olaf arrived with his retinue and surveyed the damage. He quickly ordered Glenville moved to the front of the barricade and they put a hat on him similar to that worn by Olaf. The two human predators eyed each other a moment, each hoping to capture the other alive. "Who are you?" shouted Olaf.

Walser stood proudly in the center and waited until Olaf appeared on the parapet at the northwest tower. "My name is Colonel Walser, and I am sent here by Berlin to collect our merchandise that you have promised. Hand it over to us at once and you may live."

"To us? You have 25 men. We have four thousand. Lay down your weapons," thundered Olaf.

Walser motioned for another mortar round to be loaded. "You are a thief and a traitor to the Fatherland, Deibner, and I give you 5 minutes or I will blow up your puny walls with you in it. No more!" Walser ordered his men to take cover.

In answer, Olaf smiled. Walser could not see this but McQueen did and he was curious. "You see these Nazis," he began. "No manners. I hate Nazis. However, one must be prepared. I knew that the river would be our most vulnerable point. And now they've walked into my trap." Olaf turned to his chief lieutenant. "Is everything ready?"

"Yes, sir."

"Well what are you waiting for? Let's make our guests welcome." The lieutenant grinned his gap-toothed smile and held up the red flag. Walser saw this as he was preparing the plastic explosive charge which would demolish the wall.

"Herr Colonel, what is that?" said one of the soldiers. Flowing silently down the slope toward the river was what looked like a sea of black ooze, on a front a hundred yards wide. There was no way around it. One of the men ran forward.

"Oil!" he shouted. Walser motioned for his men to fall back, but the sea of black kept coming, faster now and thicker.

"Back to the river!" shouted Walser. "No shooting!" But several of the men had begun to stumble as the black tide covered first their shoes, then their legs. Others had reached the water and were waiting for orders.

From the parapet, Olaf watched the unfolding scene calmly, scientifically, as one would watch a chess match at the Savoy in London. As if on cue another skirmish began, as Olaf's men began firing on the soldiers trying to get to the river. Operating from the cover of the trees, most of their shots were off the mark, but occasionally a bullet would hit home, and then with a scream and a spray of blood the German would go down, clutching his stomach or his leg.

The oil covered almost all his men now, and Walser realized the jaws of the trap were closing. He brought over two of his men. "Take the explosives and work your way to the wall.

From his vantage point, McQueen could see the two soldiers running toward the wall, carrying a large sack. Olaf was busy giving instructions to his men and at first it meant nothing to him. Then he saw it. A native soldier ran wildly toward the Germans and lobbed a flaming bottle toward their position. He was quickly shot, but the bottle burst into flames and within seconds half of the German soldiers were engulfed in flames, screaming wildly as they burned to death. Olaf saw this and fired off several rounds in a spasm of joy.

"Yes!" he shouted. The remaining soldiers retreated to the safety of the water. In the distraction, the two German sprinters had made it within 50 yards of the wall. Olaf looked down at the new peril.

"Shoot those two!" Olaf screamed, and the guards opened fire on the two soldiers, who were using the trees as cover. They ran again. In a few moments they would reach the wall. The rifle fire increased, but the two Germans, perhaps preferring a quick death to more months in the jungle, defied the odds and kept closing.

Walser also saw this and decided to take a chance. "The rooftop!" he yelled, and those of his men who could stand concentrated their fire on Olaf and company. They were, unfortunately, excellent marksmen. The first to die was a guard, felled by a spray of machine gun fire that ripped into his chest as he tried to signal for more rifle support. Two more of Olaf's men fell trying to flee. In a rage, Olaf turned his rifle on the remaining three guards.

"The next man that tries to run gets a bullet in the back!" he shouted, and turned back to the battle.

The dust was dancing with bullet strikes as the two German soldiers gathered themselves for the final sprint. They had devised a simple plan. They would split up the plastic explosive into two packages, and run a circular route to the same point, hoping to confuse the defenders. A momentary lull in the firing came, the senior man shook hands with his #2 and they broke cover. Instantly, the air was full of the soft kiss of bullets passing near their heads. The tree cover was thinning as they emerged into the clear for the final 20 yards. The junior man was faster, and would have arrived first but for the bullet that tore open his shoulder. His companion was luckier. As rifle fire concentrated on the fallen soldier, he made it to the shelter of the wall and unslung the package. Sheltered by the overhanging wall and trees, he was now immune to snipers.

From the river, Walser shouted for his men to stop firing. There was a sudden silence. "Last chance!" he shouted to Olaf. But the parapet was empty. Seeing his peril, Olaf and his party were in the process of retreating when suddenly the world seemed to end.

McQueen was thrown to the ground by the force of the biggest explosion he had ever felt, and looked up in time to see a 75 foot wide hole blasted in the front wall where they had been standing a minute before. Through the smoke there were huge chunks of rock flying straight up into the sky and then raining down. Several of them fell on the guards, one of them a large brute who had been chained to Glenville. More explosions followed and the rocks fell like shrapnel, flying at all angles. It was time to go.

As McQueen got to his feet he could see Olaf running for his workshop. From the river, Walser had just reached the breech in the wall and was machine gunning down the few natives who had not already fled. Modern weaponry, thought McQueen ruefully as he turned to run. There was another blast 30 yards away. The large rock that hit him square on the leg didn't break the bone, but it was enough to send him to the ground, where his head hit a boulder with a sickening thud and he blacked out.

• • •

A hundred yards upriver, Anderson and Snyder also heard the deafening explosion as they waited with Henry and Margaret. They had seen no flares, and the debate had become heated about whether to go look for McQueen when Snyder suddenly grinned and pointed at something at the water's edge.

Akerson and his marines had finally arrived, two days late but a far cry from the ceremonial embassy force they had once been. Every man was now a survivor. Anderson and Snyder wasted no time in joining their comrades. "Report, Marine," said Akerson, and Snyder gave a brief description of the situation. The sound of battle was louder now, the explosions nearer.

"German mortars, Sarge," said Anderson.

"They got plastic, too," added Snyder. "McQueen and Wilson are in the fort."

"Right," said Akerson. He approached Henry and Margaret and held out a hand. "Good to see you, Mr. Underwood. I'm glad to find you alive, Miss. I'll ask you to stay here." He turned to the men. "Let's move out." Henry wanted to discuss it, but there was something about the self assured manner of Akerson that precluded discussion. There would be time later for such things. With no further words, the small force began pushing through the jungle toward the sound of battle.

Chapter 14

WHEN MCQUEEN got to his feet most of the battle had moved up toward the workshop, where a small contingent of native soldiers were still fighting. There was a strong smell of burning flesh in the air and he was nearly sick. His head was on fire and he couldn't stop the dizziness. With an effort, he picked up his automatic rifle and started moving off the battle field.

At the back of the compound was a buried labyrinth where Olaf and the scientists had conducted experiments on workers in the early days of the operation. There was only one way down and it was off limits to all personnel. The walls were lined with heavy concrete and steel reinforcing bars. Only a direct hit by a very large bomb could break through.

After the outer wall had fallen Olaf had run to the workshop and given instructions to the most loyal of his men, promising them a fortune if they repelled the soldiers. Seizing the moment, he ran to the underground storehouse. The padlock finally yielded to the key and he sprinted to the far end of the corridor, past the make shift operating rooms and rusting medical equipment imported from Berlin years ago. In here the sound of battle was muffled, but he knew that his life expectancy was now measured in minutes as he threw open the vault door and started loading a hand truck with the sacks of gold coins and small bars, still with the embossed mark of the Swiss bank from where they originated.

He could only carry out a fraction of the treasure, but it would be enough. Enough to buy native help, to get the cargo to the waiting Japanese ship, then to recruit an army and return in triumph to his kingdom. This time he would be more careful with the Nazis.

In ten minutes he had finished. He hauled the gold to the stairs, well away from the entrance, then took out a heavy hand grenade and wedging it in the door, pulled the pin. Ten seconds later the powerful blast collapsed the stone walls around the entrance. With any luck the secret would be safe. He knew what he must do. There was a small recessed path used to move pushcarts full of merchandise out of sight. Getting the gold aboard would be no problem. Then all he had to do was wait for the diversion to take effect. He thanked his stars that he had prepared so carefully against this day. It was almost going to be too easy, he thought, as he walked into the bush and disappeared.

•   •   •

Walser had now rounded up 50 guards and interrogated a dozen in his brutally simple fashion. "Where is Olaf?" he demanded of the first man. When the terrified native confessed ignorance the guard shot him and they moved to the next man. After half a dozen of these encounters, the remaining survivors began to cooperate. The next man didn't even wait to be questioned, but merely pointed toward the secret labyrinth.

•   •   •

The pain in McQueen's leg was now severe. The rock had torn through the skin of his leg and although he had stopped the bleeding it was impossible to do more than hobble on his good leg. All around him small arm fire kept up a steady drumbeat, but he was too tired to discover who was involved. He remembered where he had hidden his machine gun and the precious few bricks of C4 explosive, and that he had a job to do. But even if the Germans didn't recognize him he knew he would probably be shot unless he could get to shelter and bind up his body. To his left there was a gaping hole in the fortress wall. He saw, through the drifting smoke and stench, the little shipping dock on the canal that Olaf used for his river trade. It was unguarded.

It took him nearly 10 minutes to walk and crawl to the canal, but after several near misses he finally dragged himself and his gear to the edge of the water and collapsed near the largest barge, a rough wooden skiff about 50 feet long.

When the fighting had died down to sporadic sniping, he decided to take a look. He struggled to his feet. Near the ruins of the fortress, there was absolutely no sign of natives, either workers or guards. The field appeared to be deserted except for a curious sight. In the flat ground nearest the river a force of some 20 men was slowly moving uphill. He wiped the sweat out of his eyes and looked again. It was the American marine detachment, and they had found something.

•   •   •

Wilson and Akerson crawled on their bellies toward the labyrinth. They had improvised camoflage on their uniforms and helmets and had not been spotted.

"Who's at the crest of the hill?" asked Akerson.

"Germans."

"You sure?"

"I'm sure. I recognize the bastards from the jungle. The one on the left has a swastika tattoo on his neck."

"How close did you get?"

"Maybe 10 feet. He walked right under me." Akerson motioned for his men to come up.

"OK. Set up a mortar."

• • •

Walser stood at the sight of the former entrance to the storage bunker, now a pile of rubble. "What am I supposed to do with this?" he asked the trembling native. "You're sure there was gold in there?" The native nodded. "What happened to the ore? The yellow powder?" The native talked to the man next to him.

"This man say, he worked for the Boss. All powder gone to the boats."

Walser suppressed his rage. "Show me." They had climbed up the steps to the ground floor in the small hut whose purpose it was to conceal the entrance when the first mortar shell landed just outside, knocking down the wall and killing three soldiers. "Take cover!" screamed Walser as two more mortars came in, killing another two soldiers. Walser managed to wedge himself under two of the dead bodies when the next mortar came in right on target, and killed the last of the German soldiers. They had come through 1,500 miles of jungle, snakes, malaria and hostile natives only to die in a storage hut.

Ten minutes later, as McQueen was bracing himself against a piling the first Marine approached him.

"Who are you?" he challenged.

"The name is McQueen, friend."

"Oh, Mr. McQueen, sir. Good to find you alive. Guess we can relax now, huh?"

"Not quite. There are two men we have to find. Get your NCO over here fast."

For an hour the marines searched for signs of Olaf or Walser, to no avail, as a corpsman bandaged up McQueen. The sun had reached its zenith and the men needed a rest. They had tried to round up some of the natives to bury the bodies, but almost all of them had run for the hills. Wilson and Akerson came over.

"No sign of either man." McQueen nodded. He looked at the small pile of munitions the marines had brought.

"You got enough fire power in there to seal that mine?" he asked, pointing to the narrow gash in the hillside that was partly concealed by trees and brush.

"More than enough." Akerson sent a marine to scout and an hour later, from a safe distance, the Marine ordinance expert detonated 25 pounds of C4 at a depth of 100 feet below the surface. The explosion knocked everyone to the ground, but when the smoke was cleared the top of the hill was gone and the entrance was buried in 50 feet of rock.

"What now" asked Akerson.

"I need to radio someone. Can one of your men string a wire to the top of that tree?" The job was done faster than McQueen could have expected, and the sight of Wilson up in the tree, almost falling several times, was the first time laughter any of the men had known in weeks.

• • •

Fifty miles upriver, the days of forced inactivity had caught up to him. Tired of canned beans, Eddie had rigged a fishing pole and had just caught a fish when the radio started buzzing and snapping. It was a big fish and the fight moved him downriver another 20 yards. After a few moments the radio died and the light went out.

• • •

As McQueen tried to make contact with the Goose, another pair of eyes was watching him from the depths of the jungle. With all attention on the radio, and staying low, Olaf pushed the wheeled cart down the path toward the canal. In a few minutes the gold was aboard. All he had to do now was get back to the foreman's shack and activate the charges. He could almost taste the Saki now and allowed himself a moment to wonder what the world would be like should Japan prevail over her enemies.

Olaf reached the shack without incident. Inside, under a false floor plate, was a single lever. He thought of all the work and engineering that had gone into this, how he done the work himself rather than risk his secret being known. His enemies thought they had won! In a few bitter moments they would learn their mistake.

As he raised the floor plate he noticed a faint shadow moving to his right, but ignored it. Then some instinct made him turn around. Just in time, thought Walser, as he plunged the 10" knife directly into Olaf's chest and simultaneously clamped a gloved hand over his mouth to muffle the scream. Olaf struggled for a moment, then his heart stopped and he slumped to the floor, dead. If he had been alive, Olaf would have remarked that this creature who had ended his life hardly looked human, covered as he was in human blood and mud, his arms scraped and bruised. Curiously, the one thing that was clean on Walser's uniform was the SS swastika emblem around his neck.

Wasting no time, Walser wiped the blood off his knife on Olaf's shirt and closed the floor plate. He opened his tunic and took another drink of the brandy he had been saving for the triumphal entry of his men into the mine. They were all dead now, he reflected bitterly. But it was not in vain. They would be avenged. He had stayed hidden while the battle had raged, then had seen Olaf pick out one of the small barges and put a sack inside. Being in the shadow of the bigger vessels, he had hardly noticed it before. After the traitor had left, he had inspected the barge and found that in the small hold there were dozens of wooden boxes marked "U-235." There was also a shortwave radio on board. He had almost shouted for joy at the sight, then quickly went back the way he had come and waited, knowing that Olaf would return.

Now it was done. All he had to do was wait. Wait until it was safe, until the Americans were distracted elsewhere. Then he would make his escape. It was all within his grasp now. He wondered how the Fuhrer would reward him.

• • •

An hour later, the Marines had found Olaf's body and were scouring the area to find his killer. "Come on, Eddie," McQueen said into the radio, still trying to reach his co-pilot and silently cursing a blue streak. He looked up in time to see one of the marines coming into view leading Margaret and Henry into camp.

"Over here!" he shouted, and walked forward to Henry holding out a hand. The two men shook hands warmly. Looking at Margaret, ill fed and exhausted, McQueen thought he had never seen a more determined, beautiful woman. She had somehow managed to keep a hairbrush, and before they sat down took a moment to brush her short auburn hair and wipe the dirt off her face. As she sat down McQueen could see the sheer exhaustion on her face.

"Well, McQueen, good to see you alive," said Henry as they shook hands. "I hope you have some food because we're starved."

"I think we can find something," said McQueen, and one of the Marines was dispatched to put together a lunch.

"Of course, I suppose you know I can never thank you enough for finding my daughter." He blew his nose and looked around the battle scene. "So this was it, the great man's hideout. They told me something about what happened here. What a pity. I suppose he was mad after all."

"It wasn't madness that killed him, Henry, it was greed. I wish I knew how many people he was trying to sell the stuff to, but it's buried back there now, along with maybe 10 tons of gold. Make an interesting dig for an archaeologist like you someday, in about a thousand years."

He turned to Margaret, and his voice was at once respectful and calming. "We're going to get you out of here as fast as we can. I know this has been rough, and as soon as I raise Eddie we'll fly you out. It's a little tight but I think we can manage a take off. Are you well enough to travel?"

She nodded silently, but managed a smile. "Thank you. Is there someplace I can get cleaned up?" McQueen motioned for Akerson to come over.

"Sergeant, can you knock together a shower for this lady?"

"Can do, sir," he replied. Two of the marines rigged a field shower, and half an hour later a freshly scrubbed Margaret sat down with the marines to a lunch of k-rations and fish.

"How soon can we leave?" she asked after eating the last bite on her place.

"I hope tomorrow, if we can reach the plane today. But you'll be safe here with the Marines." He added with a grin, "Although, by the looks of it, you can probably take care of yourself."

The rest of the day was taken over by packing their gear, checking on ammunition and searching for any signs of the uranium. But except for a few green beads there was almost nothing. They had finished interrogating the few Germans who surrendered, and it was apparent that their commanding officer had escaped.

After burial duty, Henry made his own inspection of the site and Margaret slept in her tent. At sundown McQueen finally reached Eddie, who reported that the radio had become corroded by the extreme humidity and that he had taken it apart and cleaned off the components. A pick up was arranged for early morning and Eddie settled in for one more night sleeping in the Goose and hoping that nothing larger than him would come calling in the night.

. . .

It was two hours after sunset on the hot and windless night when McQueen and the Marines finally finished talking about their plans for getting back to civilization. There was a long debate about going east versus west, and the security situation, and in the end it was decided that the marines would return under Akerson the way they had come, and the rest of the party would make for the French outpost at Brazzaville where McQueen knew they could refuel. Everyone was exhausted, and after a last look around they turned in. McQueen busied himself with writing a report for Ellison, asked Akerson about the search to find the German colonel, then turned off the lights.

Later that night, something moving down the river caught the eye of the sentry, who thought it was a log. He was the youngest marine and had fought bravely during the skirmish with the German soldiers and now he was tired. Taking no chances, he walked down to the water and saw a dead tree floating down the current. Satisfied, he returned to his post near the campfire and lit a cigarette, a priceless luxury that he had found in a storage shed. A full carton of American cigarettes! He sat down and started thinking about how much he could get from the other guys for a pack.

From the edge of the canal, the smallish man in the water watched the forgoing and remembered to keep silent. He was hungry and dehydrated from the whisky, but his chance had come. By putting his shoulder into the barge, which he had untied from the dock, he found that by pushing with all his strength he could move the heavy craft slowly toward the river. With a final shove it was free of the dock and moving on its own. He climbed aboard, and immediately flattened himself on the deck not far from the wheel.

He knew it was a risk. Without the engine, he couldn't make headway to steer, and if the barge hit a snag he could be stuck, or worse, capsized. But with its shallow draft the barge merely floated into the river, picked up the current and began moving downstream.

It was another nerve wracking mile before Walser risked starting the diesel engine. Thankfully it was a newer model and after warming up the plugs the engine coughed once and began to turn over quietly. The moon on the water showed that the river was wide and navigable for at least another half mile. He would pull in to shore and try to contact the freighter for instructions. With the sudden realization that he had won, Walser laughed out loud.

• • •

Off the coast of Point Noire, near where the Congo empties into the Gulf of Guinea, the *Socotra* had now been waiting for three weeks, dodging and evading the British picket destroyers that occasionally steamed through, escorting merchantmen from Cape Town. Bad weather had been their greatest ally. It only by sheer luck they had not yet been spotted, the captain knew, as he peered out at the South Atlantic from the bridge.

The crew had grown surly with the incessant exposure to enemy fire, but the officers were a disciplined group and so far morale was holding. Even so, the captain had thought it wise to consult with his peers and had summoned the captains of his two escort submarines to discuss strategy. The physical meeting was unusual on the high seas, but risking a radio intercept was out of the question.

However, little had come of the meeting. The men agreed that fuel would soon become a problem and that in all probability the field force must have failed, but their instructions were clear. They were to wait, regardless of cost, and no one wanted to challenge the order, which came from the highest level in the Reichsmarine.

At 19:20 hours that night, as the chief radioman was about to go off duty, he suddenly heard a faint signal. It's origin was from the east, and as the Morse code began coming in, he was startled upright as he realized that the top secret

Operation 125 code was coming in, giving the appropriate longitude and latitude of the engagement. He reached out and pressed a button that went directly to the captain's cabin as he began to write down the five letter code groups.

The radioman was just finishing as the Captain hurried in, followed by his executive officer. The radioman signaled to the sender the "all received" acknowledgement, and the key went silent. The two senior men in the room watched in silence as Mueller decoded the message. It was a complicated code based on the date and position of the ship, and each letter required careful calculation. After 10 minutes the work was done and the radioman was dismissed. The captain read it and handed it to his XO. "Bring us in close to shore and have a work party prepare the equipment in hold #1," said the Captain.

•   •   •

The sun in the Congo comes up to the sound of the monkeys and birds howling for their breakfast. McQueen rolled over in his bunk and sat up. It was still grey outside, but there was something wrong. A Marine was standing outside.

"Mr. McQueen, do you have a minute?" he said. McQueen got to his feet and pulled on his boots, strapping on the Colt 45 pistol he always carried and without which he felt naked.

"What is it?"

The marine pointed to the sky. The Goose was circling, looking for a place to land. "Aircraft sighted, sir. Thought you'd want to know."

"Thanks," said McQueen, and walked to the river. The smell of fresh coffee was in the air and a marine was pointing to an animal carcass floating down the river just as the Goose touched down, skipped lightly over the obstruction and came to a stop. After so much death and jungle, it was a welcome sight and the men broke into a spontaneous cheer as Eddie taxied up to the wharf.

"Hey Joe! Miss me?" he asked as McQueen helped tie up the plane. Henry and Margaret had come to the wharf and there were handshakes all around. "What's the plan?" asked Eddie.

"Brazzaville," said McQueen. "We're back in the freight business."

"Halleleuhah," added Eddie. "It's about time." It took an hour to pack the Goose and by that time the Marines were ready to march. McQueen took Akerson aside.

"As soon as I get my passengers back I can give you air support once you reach the Etwonda," said McQueen. Akerson shook his head.

"That's all right, sir, just a walk in the park for my men. Well, take it easy." The two men shook hands and

McQueen was about to go when Akerson put a hand on his shoulder.

"Say, wasn't there another boat there last night?" McQueen walked down the wharf and tried to remember.

"You sure?"

"Oh, it was there all right. Got it right here in the report. 'Found five small craft near the battle scene. Only four here now." Like the clever man who has overlooked the obvious, McQueen remembered the small wooden barge that lay almost invisible next to the larger boat. Yes, that's how it must have been, he thought, kicking himself for not setting a watch on the vessels in the canal.

"He's on the river, probably with the uranium ore. He could be half way to Leopoldville by now," said McQueen, trying to think.

"You want us to wait here?"

"No, I'll handle it. Got any C4 left?" They talked to the quartermaster. There was exactly one brick left, plus a detonator.

"What are you gonna do with that?" asked Akerson. McQueen took the explosive in its canvas sack and put it over his shoulder.

"I'll have to think of something. Can you take a couple of civilians with you?" he asked.

"Sure. Who you got in mind?" McQueen ran to the Goose, where Henry and Margaret were already aboard.

"Change of plan. Looks like the German commander is on the river with the ore. I can't let him get through. You and Margaret will be going back with the Marines. You'll be OK. Wait for me in Khartoum and we'll try to pick you up." McQueen started to removed their small pieces of luggage when Margaret thrust out a hand.

"What are you going to do?" asked Margaret.

"Try to spoil their party. "

"I don't care if it kills me, but I am not going back into that jungle on foot. And may I remind you that this is my charter and I'll call the shots." Both of them looked at Henry, who smiled and tried to look inconspicuous.

"I think she has a point, Joe," said Henry. McQueen was not happy about it. There was a long, tense moment. "Besides, you've got my treasure chest on board. I can't leave it."

In a light rain, the Goose lifted off at 8:15 that morning, banked sharply over the river and setting the flaps at 10 began to follow the mighty Congo as it flowed southwest to the sea.

•   •   •

The *Socotra* was laying three miles of the West African coast and the wind had freshened to a steady 20 knots coming out of the south. Again the captain scanned the horizon with his binoculars, then picked up the intercom.

"Any sign of smoke on the horizon?" he asked. In the crow's nest, the lookout checked again.

"No, sir." The captain gave orders for the freighter to turn into the wind. A light chop was stirring up the surface, but they would have to risk it. He watched as the fore deck of the freighter opened up like a clam shell, exposing a 75 foot long catapult that rose on hydraulic lifts until it was free of the hold. On the catapult sat a modified Blohm and Voss HA139. The 4-engine seaplane had room for six men and had machine gun turrets installed in the nose and waist. The pilot spoke briefly with his escort, all armed heavily, and got aboard. Five minutes later, in a stiff breeze, the steam powered mechanism fired off with a loud report and the 5,000 lb airplane, aided by rocket thrusters, was launched over the bow. The captain watched as it climbed almost vertically into the sky and vanished in the clouds. Already the catapult was descending into the hold and in a few minutes the freighter would once again look like the battered tramp steamer she had once been.

· · ·

Walser was 30 miles down the river, motoring steadily and keeping an eye out for anything hostile when he heard the engines coming from the west. The barge was gliding along under a canopy of trees, and he eased it out into the middle of the river for a better view. At first there was no sign, but then he adjusted the binoculars and there it was, the four engine plane. He saw the flashing signal light and responded with a makeshift flare he had constructed from left over materials found on the barge. The plane wagged its wings and started to descend.

•   •   •

The Goose was cruising at 9,000 feet when Eddie pointed to something below. McQueen leaned over and caught sight of the German seaplane as it slipped through the clouds. "Looks like he knows something we don't," said Eddie through the intercom. McQueen nodded.

"Try to get Lisbon on the sideband, plain language. Ask for Ellison." Eddie adjusted the radio and began to call out as McQueen put the plane into a shallow bank to hold position. McQueen could hear static on the line, and then the distant voice he knew well, the embassy's radio operator, a man named Muntz, from Wisconsin.

"Lisbon Export," said the voice. This was code for the American embassy.

"Priority for the managing director," said Eddie. "This is Red Tango," the code name established for McQueen when calling on urgent business. There was a few moments of dead air. Then the voice returned.

"Go ahead, Red Tango. I have the director now."

"This is the director. Who is calling?"

McQueen took the radio. "This is Hawkins, African airways. We have a new competitor moving in and would like permission to deliver our counter offer in person. Over." There was a brief pause.

"Any chance of a friendly merger?" said the quiet voice.

"Negative," said McQueen.

"All right, but try not to upset the Queen. Lisbon out." So! McQueen motioned for Henry to come forward. The scientist, whose natural curiosity and love of flying had distracted him for the last hour, made his way to the cockpit and knelt. Eddie put headphones on him.

"All right," began McQueen. "this is where we earn our pay, Henry. They haven't spotted us yet so we still have time. I can put you and Margaret down on the river near a trading post that the Belgians used to run if it's still there and you can take your chances till we get back to you, if we make it in once piece. Otherwise, you're in for the full ride." Henry listened carefully, walked back to Margaret and they talked for a few moments. McQueen looked back and caught a glimpse of Margaret grinning at him.

McQueen motioned to his co-pilot. "Eddie, that plane doesn't have the range to get this far inland from German territory. Try the British emergency channel on 1530 and send a coded message alerting all vessels to be on the lookout for hostile German surface craft off Gabon and Portuguese West. Or submarines."

"We're not starting a war, are we?"

"I promise to be good."

Eddie got out his British code book and turned the radio to the frequency that was reserved for emergencies and acts of war. He began tapping out the message.

When Henry returned he was shaking his head. "Well, it's like this. She's not afraid, but I'd like to live a little longer, so we'll take your offer."

"Strap yourselves in."

•   •   •

The German seaplane, commanded by the Luftwaffe's most skilled naval pilot, touched down a quarter mile behind Walser without difficulty and taxied under two engines to the waiting barge. Within moments the crew had opened the forward hatch in the nose and were ready with a line. Walser had dropped anchor and as the first rope snaked across to him he caught it and made fast the line.

The soldiers were on the barge unloading their heavy machine guns when one of them heard the sound of Lycoming engines and pointed. The pilot took out his binoculars and watched for a moment as the plane approached their position from the east at about 3,000 feet.

"British spy plane. How about a little target practice, just to keep him away," he said calmly.

•   •   •

In the cockpit, McQueen was scanning the river for a landing spot when the first bullets whizzed past the window, a hundred feet away, followed by tracer rounds. He banked sharply but the bullets began closing. Below they could see the barge and the big 4 engine plane moored to it. There were flashes of light coming from three points on the deck. McQueen knew that any moment they would find the mark.

There was a cloud bank below them, and he aimed for it, blindly. Clouds in Africa can be nightmares. Moments later as they entered the undulating white void they encountered their first serious turbulence. The plane was tossed back and forth like a paper toy. Henry almost flew out off the bench.

"Looks like we've lost the element of surprise," said McQueen into the headset. "Bring up the satchel." Eddie did as he was told as McQueen lowered to full flaps and put the plane into a shallow dive. Immediately the plane slowed down to just above stalling speed. Eddie looked at McQueen as if he was expecting some word, but there was only grim determination on the chiseled face.

Down they dropped through the clouds, circling to 2,000 feet, then 1,000 feet, hugging the shreds of cloud and bouncing violently. Eddie noticed that McQueen had attached a detonator to the explosive and was adjusting the timer.

"Just one chance, that's all I want. Keep us in the clouds as long as you can," he said. Turning to Henry and Margaret, he shouted "Get on the deck and stay there!"

With Eddie at the controls, they began circling through the white nothingness above the African jungle.

•   •   •

On the barge, the soldiers scanned the sky for the intruder, but it had vanished in the clouds.

"No sign, Herr Major," said one of the men.

"Very good. He's had enough. Secure the guns." The loading resumed. Soldiers were hurrying to load the boxes of ore onto the seaplane as the pilot supervised the work. Walser came over carrying a gold bar. For the first time he noticed the SS badge on the pilot's tunic. "How many of these can we take?" he asked.

"None."

"Not even one, for the Fuehrer?" asked an incredulous Walser.

"Not one. My orders are to carry out as much of the ore as possible, and you are to continue down the river. Alone." Walser was dumbstruck.

"But... that's impossible. I have sacrificed everything for this. I must be allowed to complete my mission. It's a miracle I'm still alive." The pilot casually took hold of his pistol.

"My orders are specific, Colonel. You have failed. The mine is destroyed and the man Deibner is dead. You will have to answer for this failure. Return to your barge, please."

Walser returned to the barge and watched in silence as the boxes were carried to the waiting plane, his boxes, his legacy. So, he was to return to Germany in disgrace, providing he survived the trip. His career was over. Knowing the Fuhrer, a firing squad would be at the end of the journey.

As he pondered this fact, absolutely sure in his conclusion, he knew there was only one thing to do. Yes, that was it. He could still be the hero. He would re-open the mine after the Americans were gone. They would welcome his ingenuity, his resourcefulness. Yes, that was it. If only this fool of an SS pilot didn't get in the way.

Casually, moving very slowly, he stood behind the heavy caliber machine gun and watched the loading. He waited until all the men were on the plane, then released the safety and pulled back the firing clutch.

From the air, the river appeared to shimmer like a jewel in the sunlight as the Goose began its slow return, flying now at 75 feet above the treetops. With Eddie at the controls, McQueen was standing in the doorway, the satchel of explosives in his hand. "Steady," he said. "I think I see something."

On board the HA139, the loading was almost complete. The pilot called his second in command over. "Ready to cast off. When the lines are out, shoot that idiot and come aboard."

"Zu Befeul!" said the soldier, and turned toward the door. For an instant he froze, looking out the window at the sight of Walser, standing behind the machine gun, aiming at him. He had a moment to wonder what the man was doing, and then there was a flash of light and the first bullets crashed into the plane. The soldier was cut down, but before the startled pilot could respond the bullets pierced the fuel tank and a yellow orange ball of flames erupted and quickly engulfed the plane.

Walser watched calmly as the seaplane sank into the Amazon. One blackened body floated to the surface. The crocodiles, scared off by the explosion, would soon be back he knew, leaving not a trace.

He was already thinking of the story he would invent for the Abwehr when he looked up at an astonishing sight.

The Goose was hopping the trees, less than a mile from the river when the fireball rose into the air. As they reached the water, McQueen set the timer for 8 seconds and waited. They cleared the last trees and there was the river, and just ahead of them the smoking remains of the seaplane.

"A little to the left!" shouted McQueen. As Eddie banked over, the barge was dead center in front of them at 200 yards. McQueen leaned out the window, pressed the red button on the timer and launched the package. As if in a trance, Walser watched the black canvas bag wafting down to him, saw it hit the deck of the barge and lodge against the bulkhead almost under his feet. If it occurred to him to jump overboard it came too late, as the 32 oz of C4 high explosive detonated, taking with it Germany's only hope for an atomic bomb.

As the Goose climbed, McQueen felt the tremendous explosion and looked back. They circled once, and as the smoke cleared there was absolutely nothing left of the barge, its contents or the man who might have delivered victory.

• • •

A week later in Lisbon, Ambassador Ellison closed his file and walked to the window. He watched McQueen and Margaret strolling to his old Land Rover and drive off. It looked like they were laughing at something. Ellison smiled. There would be questions to answer in Washington, he knew, and the German ambassador was downstairs and threatening a formal protest, but all of that could wait. Even the troubling development about Japan trying to acquire a bomb would wait. He poured himself a stiff whisky and took a drink.

They had been lucky this time.

About the Author

Rod Barkley is an essayist, playwright and filmmaker. His first book, *Evening in Atlantis,* was published in 2011. He lives with his wife and family in Glendora, California.

www.ingramcontent.com/pod-product-compliance
Lightning Source LLC
Chambersburg PA
CBHW020822180626
46814CB00001B/69